TO A
NATIVE SHORE

BOOKS BY VALERIE ANAND

Bridges Over Time *series*

The Proud Villeins
The Ruthless Yeomen
Women of Ashdon
The Faithful Lovers
The Cherished Wives
The Dowerless Sisters

To A Native Shore
Crown of Roses
West of Sunset

TO A
NATIVE SHORE

a novel of India

Valerie Anand

SPEAKING VOLUMES, LLC
NAPLES, FLORIDA
2017

To A Native Shore

ISBN 978-1-62815-409-2

For Neena and Cicely

Like those Nicean barks of yore
That gently, o'er a perfumed sea,
The weary way-worn wanderer bore
To his own native shore.

EDGAR ALLAN POE, *"Helen"*

Contents

Acknowledgements

The author would like to acknowledge the help given by
Heal's Fabrics Ltd. of Tottenham Court Road, London, and
Mr. S. R. Richards, Regional Controllers, H. M. Coastguard,
Swansea Search & Rescue Region, for the preparation of
the background of this novel. The information which they so
willingly provided was of the greatest value.

V. A.

Avtar Singh's Family _____

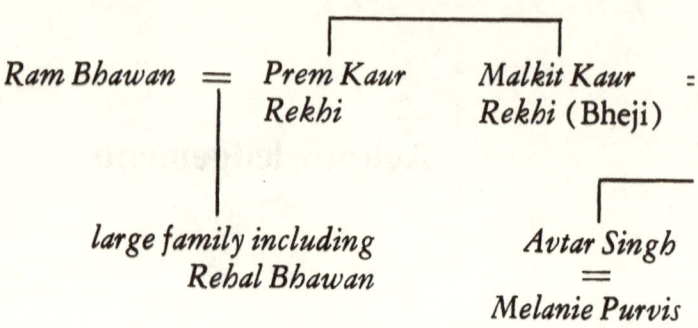

Ram Bhawan $=$ Prem Kaur   Malkit Kaur   =
         Rekhi   Rekhi (Bheji)

large family including   Avtar Singh
Rehal Bhawan $=$
               Melanie Purvis

Melanie Purvis's Family _____

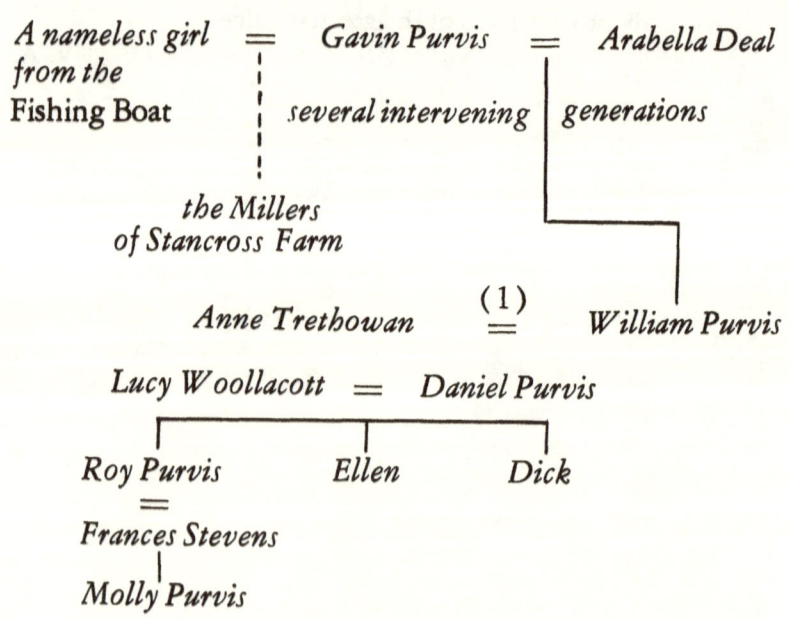

A nameless girl $=$ Gavin Purvis $=$ Arabella Deal
from the
Fishing Boat   several intervening   generations

the Millers
of Stancross Farm

Anne Trethowan $\overset{(1)}{=}$ William Purvis

Lucy Woollacott $=$ Daniel Purvis

Roy Purvis   Ellen   Dick
$=$
Frances Stevens

Molly Purvis

Narinder Singh   Asha Kaur = Jatinder Singh Arora
                   (Bhabi)

Arwinder Kaur   Surinder Singh   Ranjit Singh = Balwant
      =   Arora   Kaur
Saranjit Singh

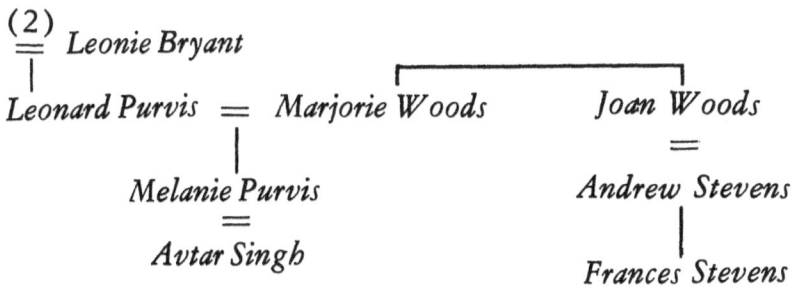

(2)
 = Leonie Bryant
Leonard Purvis = Marjorie Woods   Joan Woods
                                             =
       Melanie Purvis   Andrew Stevens
            =
       Avtar Singh   Frances Stevens

Prologue: Asha

The lattice work of the window broke up the moonlight into little discs and droplets. It threw a traceried pattern of black and white upon the floor and across the broad divan. The colours of the carpet were blanched or shadowed out of existence; the crimson and gold were drained from the discarded marriage sari heaped at the foot of the divan. And to the girl crouched on the floor by the window, gazing out into the cloisonné moonlight, that was significant.

The colour had gone out of the world along with hope.

Perhaps it was always like this. No, that couldn't be true. It was not so between her parents, or her mother would not welcome her father home so gladly when he returned from an absence. It was not so with her young aunt whose marriage they had all attended only two years ago. Her aunt had cried on her wedding day because she was leaving home and was afraid of the stranger to whom she was going. But three days later, when Asha saw her again, she was so happy that she could not speak the most commonplace sentence without bubbling into laughter. No. For them, it had not been like this.

There was movement in the hot darkness behind her. She did not want to turn round. The rustle and creak as her husband's body stirred on the divan made her shrink still further away from it, and as she did so, the marriage bangles chinked on her arm. She glanced down at them. They were gold, but in this light they might have been made of steel. How very appropriate.

"Asha," said the whisper from behind her, "leave the window. Come back here."

She went, reluctantly, because there was nothing else to do. She was his property now. "We shall see you at home sometimes when you come to visit us," her father had said. "But never if you quarrel with your husband. You will not be welcome then." He had not qualified that in the least degree. He had not said: "If you quarrel with your husband without due cause." If she fled in the morning and ran home to her parents, their door would be shut in her face.

Could she be exaggerating, making too much of the revelations of this night? At barely seventeen, how much did she know of what was normal and what was not? She had known this man for only a few hours. But during those hours . . .

Taking her place beside him again, slowly, unwillingly, enduring once more the touch of hands from which she instinctively shrank as from the touch of a reptile, she thought of the abasing things he had asked—no, ordered—her to do and knew that she had not exaggerated.

But she was his wife now and that was irrevocable. She could make no new beginning now. This was the will of God for her. To live with this man. To sleep with him. To give him a son.

A son. Yes. Her mother had told her that. So had her mother-in-law. All men wanted sons and a wife's business was to provide them. But once the son was in the world . . . even just one male child . . . then perhaps she might . . . might . . .

As yet she could hardly imagine even a negative rebellion, a policy of simply saying no. Beyond it she could not go at all. But as she yielded once more to this man's travestied notions of the process which would beget the son, and obeyed his whispered instructions (why, oh why did he never speak aloud?), there was a curious sensation under her heart as though she had conceived something already, not a child but a hard hot lump of feeling, its nature unfamiliar to her.

Asha did not recognise it then; she did not fully recognise it ever.

It was anger. It was hate.

Part One

CHANDIGARH

The Half-Perceived Design

It was too hot to work.

Melanie Avtarsingh rubbed a hand over her damp face, leaving a thin smear of aquamarine paint behind, and sighed. Sheets of abandoned cartridge paper lay in front of her on the Benares brass coffee table. They were covered with smudged and hesitant outlines in pencil or crayon. An attempt to work directly in paint had proved no better. The idea which had blazed in her like a fluorescent revelation during the hot Indian night had faded. She would never, she thought, capture it now.

She glanced enviously across the sitting room at Surinder. Her young brother-in-law was also working there, of necessity, because it was the coolest room in the house. Surinder was studying for an exam, and his engineering textbooks were spread out all over the room's one sizeable table. He even brought his books to meals, these days, and would sit raptly perusing them while his right hand occasionally groped across the cloth in search of another piece of toast or a banana. No one objected. Surinder's future was vested in those massive technical tomes.

Quietly, fearing to disturb him, Melanie began to clean her brushes.

The whole house was quiet. Avtar, her husband, had long since gone to his morning surgery, after a breakfast time at which he was almost as preoccupied as Surinder. He had an unusual case of diabetes and a measles-with-complications among his patients at present and Avtar with a medical problem on his hands was Avtar in another world. From the hall came a faint swish-swish as the maidservant, Leela, plied her broom, and from somewhere overhead there came a murmur of low voices: Melanie's mother-in-law, Bheji, and her sister-in-law, Arwinder, upstairs, probably deep in the arrangements for Arwinder's imminent wedding.

There were no other sounds. And, she thought once more as she put her painting equipment away, it was so *hot*.

Melanie looked at the whirring fan overhead, wishing that the air it moved could be ten, or even five, degrees cooler. Her scalp was prickling under her knot of dark hair. She rubbed runny paint from her fingers with a rag. In these temperatures paint went thin and pens leaked; liquid make-up ran like water. The one thing that frequently failed to run *was* the water. The taps had been dry again that morning. Melanie, standing in the bathroom of brown-speckled stone, had had to make do with a ration of washing water dipped from the tin bath which served as the back-up supply when the mains supply was cut. The rains had been poor and the cuts, even in the second half of August when normally matters improved, were still heavy. Lack of hydroelectric power in the hills was causing power cuts as well. In England, one took water and electricity for granted. Here, they were precious as rubies. And after three years, Melanie was still not used to it.

When the cooler weather did eventually come, she told herself as she slid spoiled sheets of paper stealthily together, she would be able to occupy herself with her designing again. The heat was undoubtedly the trouble. That and—let her be honest—lack of incentive. Surinder—sitting with his young shoulders hunched above his books, his topknot of long hair, not yet incarcerated in its daytime turban, spilling loose ends unregarded, his whole attention on his task—Surinder had incentive. People demanded results of him and he felt impelled to deliver. In the days when she had been a fabric and wallpaper designer at Hallowens in Oxford Street, London, results had been demanded of her too. Hallowens had been a good company to work for, full of colour and enthusiasm, and she had been almost happy enough there to be reconciled to the fact that Hallowens was in London, and not in the beloved west of England which was her home. But it had expected much of its employees. There, she too had delivered, regardless of heatwaves, snowfalls, fog, rain, or colds in the head. She allowed herself another small, undisturbing sigh, and was not sorry to be interrupted by Arwinder.

❧

Interruption was perhaps too unceremonious a word to be applied to Arwinder. She appeared noiselessly at the open door, dressed plainly in an old blue tunic and trousers, and wearing no make-up, for this was the traditional bridal Lent. Until the wedding, Arwinder would pay little attention to her appearance, the better to startle the beholders when the marriage day arrived. In the case of Arwinder, however, the tradition was being hopelessly undermined by the fact that her natural good looks were such that no amount of neglect could conceal them. Arwinder—Arwin for short—had the fragile bone structure, the grace of movement, and the dark liquid eyes of a fawn. Dressed in an old potato sack and a pair of muddy boots, she would still have been stunning.

She said softly, with a conspiratorial and understanding glance from Melanie to Surinder: "Mummy and I are going for shopping today instead of tomorrow. The Patels will come tomorrow; we got a letter just now. So we must get my marriage sari today. It's exciting, isn't it?" Arwin produced the triangular smile with which she had been beguiling her family since she was old enough to smile at all. "A week and a half to go and already the house is filling up. Will you come into Chandigarh with us? Or . . ." Her eyes fell on Melanie's work and her voice became contrite. "Perhaps you are busy?"

"No, I'm not," Melanie assured her. "Not at all. This was only just to pass the time. I was thinking perhaps I should go and help Leela, as a matter of fact."

Arwin smiled again. Between the two of them, it was an old joke, a sisterly ritual. "Leela doesn't need any help, you egalitarian Britisher. Her husband is rickshaw-wala only; she needs her job. If you do it for her, she will be very angry. You will come?"

"Yes. Just give me ten minutes to get ready."

"Take twenty," said Arwin, amused. "We have all day."

༄

Melanie went upstairs, cleaned face and fingers, and deposited her designing implements in the bottom of the cupboard whence they had come, and which they shared with a suitcase full of such legal documents as passports, house deeds, insurance papers, vaccination certificates, a number of books, and some discarded sandals and out-of-favour headscarves. She removed the old cotton dress which she wore in the house and twined herself into a pink and cream sari. When her husband had been in England, where he had spent two years gaining extra medical experience, he had given up wearing the turban on the grounds that he liked to blend with his surroundings. Now that she was living with him in India, Melanie felt much the same. She was slightly taller and heavier than most Indian women but her hair was dark and by now she was permanently suntanned. At a distance she passed for Indian. Only at close quarters could people see the Western bone structure, the golden brown eyes with their unquestionably European setting, and what Avtar called "that eternally Occidental expression." Melanie's face held nothing of the curiously consenting, accepting expression which was a hallmark of so many Indian women. Her grandfather, who had spent his life studying human behaviour professionally, had once told her that eyes as markedly front-facing as hers were characteristic of hunting creatures such as cats and owls and foxes. "You'll always hunt down the things you want from life," he said. "You'll never be content with what life sends you unasked." Only, thought Melanie as she applied lipstick, in this climate it was much too warm to go hunting. Even for a brand-new idea in design.

Her mother-in-law, too used to the heat to notice it, was waiting for her at the foot of the stairs. "If we'd thought of it before," said Bheji in her brisk, cheerful voice as she shepherded them out through the front garden to the grass-edged road beyond and waved imperiously at a passing motor rickshaw, "Avtar could have given us a lift to the shops. Or else left the car for you to drive, Melanie. You must miss your driving. I am always telling Arwin she should learn it too. Perhaps Saranjit will teach her when they are married. Now, I think we can all squeeze into this." She advanced on the rickshaw driver and began an animated argument with him. He was insisting, as they usually did, that his three-wheeler was only permitted to take two passengers, but in a tone of voice which suggested that he was open to persuasion. Bheji's right hand gestured energetically in the air, reinforcing a spate of Punjabi. The driver shook his head. Bheji refuted him with another volley of words (no Indian, male or female, ever felt called upon to accept or consent to the initial terms proposed by the vendor of any goods or services). The driver nodded at last and Bheji waved them forward. They climbed in, fitting themselves into place with difficulty. Arwin might be built like a gazelle and Melanie might be no more than average European size, but Bheji's fine Eastern bones had long since vanished under comfortable layers of golden flesh. The operative word was *squeeze.*

"We shall not buy just the one sari," Bheji pronounced, fishing a businesslike shopping list out of her handbag and twitching the end of her crisp white cotton sari with its scattered pattern of pale green leaves out from under Melanie's feet. "We have not yet enough for your trousseau, Arwin, and Melanie must have new things too. Saranjit Singh's family are well off and we must do them credit. We will call at the tailor on the way home and also the caterer and the jeweller . . ."

"I *love* shopping," said Arwinder, contentedly.

In the shopping precinct, the white buildings and the

broad pavements with their thin drift of sand sparkled under a sun which made Melanie's eyes ache. They paid off the rickshaw and Bheji led them purposefully across a patio, past some hopeful beggars whom she brushed aside as though they were importunate mosquitoes, and then, at last, into the welcome shade of a cloisterlike arcade. "Your favourite shop, Melanie," said her mother-in-law, pointing at a doorway a few yards ahead. "We will start there. It is the same one that I brought you to for your own first saris, and it is always cool inside. This constant heat has been affecting you, I think. You have been too quiet lately. We shall sit down and choose saris, and then we shall go and have coffee and ices—"

"Oh, bother," said Arwinder.

She was not referring to the prospect of coffee and ices. Two ladies were approaching from the other end of the arcade. One was middle-aged and the other was young, but both wore widow's white. The elder was guiding her companion along for all the world like a trawler Melanie had once witnessed from her grandfather's house on the north Somerset coast, escorting a too-venturesome yacht to harbour during a gale. It was a most unlikely simile to enter one's head in this sun-saturated place, but for a moment the memory of that small maritime drama hung before Melanie's eyes and blotted out the white arcade arches and the blaze of light beyond. She shook herself to clear her head and realised why Arwinder had said *bother*.

Afterwards, she thought: Yes, that was when the change of direction began. The day I tried to pass the time by putting a design on paper and couldn't see where the pattern was leading. The day Bheji and Aunt Asha had that odd dispute about Arwin's sari, and we couldn't see where that was leading, either. That was the beginning.

9

Arwin was saying anxiously: "Mummy, I feel so awkward. I don't like to be buying my marriage sari when Balwant is there."

Melanie said: "Can't we dodge into the shop quickly and pretend we haven't seen them?"

Bheji, frowning them both to silence as the two parties drew close, raised her voice and said clearly: "Asha, *Bhabi,* but how nice!"

~

Soon, in October, it would be exactly three years since Melanie had walked down the steps of a British Airways VC10 into the blanket-warm air of Delhi Airport, setting foot in India for the first time, coming to live there as Dr. Avtar Singh's British wife.

That day would also be the third anniversary of her first meeting with Avtar's family. The event, to say the least of it, had not been an unqualified success.

"We shall stay in Delhi for a week or so before we go on to Chandigarh," Avtar had told her before they left England. "You should do some sightseeing, and from Delhi we can go to the Red Fort and to Agra where the Taj Mahal is. We shall stay with some cousins—not very close—they are friends as much as relatives. They are very westernised and you will feel at home. But when we first arrive, we shall go to Aunt Asha's flat because everyone will be coming to Delhi to meet us who can, and her flat is so big."

She knew why they weren't actually going to stay with Asha. Asha had been unwilling to extend that much of a welcome to her nephew Avtar and his foreign wife. Aunt Asha had written to Avtar while they were still in England, and though Melanie had not seen the letters, she had a good idea what kind of letters they were. "She thinks I'm getting too Western in my attitudes. The way I act doesn't befit a well-brought-up Sikh boy," he had said once, reading one of these epistles at breakfast. He grinned as he said it, and folded the letter up, clearly not at all distressed. It was Melanie who was distressed, as for the first time Avtar's distant family swung into focus as people with whom, presently, she must live; as people she would have to please; as people whose opinions would matter both to Avtar and to her.

As a result, when they stood ringing the bell on Aunt Asha's doorstep while a group of small children on a balcony overhead gazed large-eyed at Melanie's English summer dress, and the smell of unfamiliar cooking spices wafted out of nearby windows, she was bilious with dread and already, less than twenty-four hours out from Heathrow, hideously homesick.

She could remember it still: the uprooted, flotsam nature of that fear; the sense of being suddenly transported to a strange country, into the midst of a strange language, where people would judge her according to criteria she had not been reared to meet. "Aunt Asha will be all right when she's used to you, and the rest of them I promise will like you very much," Avtar had said, but Melanie was afraid to believe it. She clutched his arm tightly as the front door opened.

Aunt Asha, forestalling her maidservant, came to the door herself. She stood on the threshold, a dumpy little woman dressed in white, palms pressed politely together in a formal greeting. She spoke, in Punjabi, and her pouched eyes with the half-circles of dark pigment under the lower lids examined Melanie over the tips of the joined fingers. Melanie's mouth, already dry, became shrivelled.

They were taken to a sitting room crowded with divans

and small tables and people: relations, friends, neighbours. There were introductions. She was urged towards a short, sturdy, grey-haired woman whose face had a marked resemblance to Avtar's and was told that this was his mother, whose name was Malkit Kaur, but whom she should address as Bheji. Bheji, to whom Melanie would be grateful for the rest of her life, promptly embraced her and said in English: "Well! My new daughter!" Melanie, her panic receding a little, returned the embrace and was passed on to Arwinder. Her artist's eye was enthralled at once by Arwin's filigree gracefulness and her fright soothed still further by Arwin's friendly smile. Gaining confidence, she let herself be introduced to several more people and arrived in due course at a pale girl with enormous brown eyes who, Arwin said, was Balwant, daughter-in-law to Aunt Asha. Left with Balwant for a moment and finding that she spoke good English, Melanie began to talk to her. But in the midst of the conversation, Balwant's expression grew anxious and her eyes wandered from Melanie to something behind her. Melanie turned round. Aunt Asha and Avtar were arguing.

Since the argument was in their own tongue, she could not follow it. But it clearly concerned herself. Aunt Asha threw a comment at Bheji, who answered in a mild, peacemaking tone but let her eyes rest briefly on Melanie. Asha then addressed a young woman—a neighbour, Melanie thought—who was nursing a small child on her lap. The young woman also glanced involuntarily towards Melanie. Their eyes met. The girl dropped her gaze to her child and said impulsively, speaking to Aunt Asha but using English: "I think that is so sad." After that, Melanie needed no translation. Avtar, she knew, had warned his family that no children could be expected from this marriage, that a kidney complaint in Melanie's own childhood had removed that possibility forever, and that he, personally, did not mind. But Aunt Asha had undoubtedly just made an adverse comment on this state of affairs. Stomach clenching as fear and home-sickness surged back, all her unsteady self-confidence gone and everything that Avtar had told her about either his family in particular or India in general gone as well, clean out of her memory, she turned back to Balwant and said the first thing she could think of. Which, unfortunately, was: "Is your husband here?" Whereupon Balwant's big eyes filled with tears which proceeded to overflow down her gentle face, while Melanie watched aghast.

Someone must have intervened at that point. She had dim recollections of Avtar at her side, saying somewhat im-patiently: "Balwant is a widow. Didn't I tell you what the white sari meant?" The girl with the baby came and told her more. ". . . only married a year, such a pity, she hardly even got to know him. He was away studying so long and then the week after he came home he was killed in a traffic acci-dent while he was riding his scooter. Traffic is so terrible in Delhi. It was just last January. Dreadful for her and for his mother . . . he was the only son . . ."

Hearty, cheerful talk broke out. She found herself, shaking with nerves and embarrassment, seated on a sofa between Bheji and Arwin, being offered tea and biscuits. It was the first time she had tasted cardomum-scented tea. She recalled making some social comment on its fragrance and hearing her voice go trembly in the middle of it. "Now, forget it all," said Bheji comfortingly, as if the disaster just behind them were of no importance (*Dear* Bheji, thought Melanie in retrospect). "You will get accustomed to all our ways in time. You must try these spiced biscuits and if you like them I will show you how to make them. You must teach me English cooking too."

A deep-end introduction to a new family in a new world, and it had left its traces. She had encountered Aunt Asha and Balwant at family gatherings a good many times since then—oftener during the last year, since they had moved from Delhi to Chandigarh—and managed to exchange small talk without mishap and in Punjabi at that. She spoke the language now. And three years was three years; Melanie had made a place for herself in the family, and her childlessness was no longer a matter for comment, while Balwant, to all appearances, had also made the adjustment to her widowed state. Nevertheless, Balwant was not the person either Melanie or Arwinder would have willingly invited on an expedition to buy someone else's marriage clothes, and Aunt Asha was still not a person Melanie would have willingly invited anywhere.

～

From Melanie's point of view, the encounter had an additional nuisance value. It would distract her mind from the concentrated enjoyment of her favourite shop. Which was a pity.

It was a beautiful shop, cool from the breeze of three huge ceiling fans, aromatic from the sandalwood tapers burning by the door, and vivid as a rainbow from the shelves of cottons and silks which lined the walls. No one who had ever worked with fabrics in any capacity could fail to be excited by this place. And no one accustomed to shopping in Western cities could fail to like it either, Melanie thought as the four of them settled into the customers' chairs facing the broad divans where the salesmen sat, cross-legged and djinnlike, ready to snap their fingers and conjure their merchandise out of the shelves for closer viewing. In the West, in London, even in the luxurious surroundings of Hallowens retail store, customers were not encouraged to sit down. Hallowens did in fact have a few chairs scattered about, but the staff regarded anyone who used them very much as traffic wardens regarded illegally parked vehicles. Hallowens prided themselves on service to customers, but the concept of infinite leisure was peculiar to the East.

A rapid conference was already in progress between Bheji and the nearest salesman, while Aunt Asha, leaning intently forward, threw in a word from time to time. The salesman's thin brown fingers clicked. A teenage assistant swarmed sailor-fashion up a run of shelves and on the divan below it began to rain saris. A pile of silk, shining in every kind of gold-embellished scarlet and crimson and cerise, grew before their eyes. Bheji pulled a heavily embroidered length towards her. "They keep good choice here," she remarked. "But *this* is not the quality we want." She pushed the silk away and pulled another gleaming fold out of the pile. She turned civilly to Aunt Asha. "Bhabi, what do you think of this?"

Comments, candid and untroubled by any consideration for the salesman's feelings—sari salesmen never looked as if they wanted to murder their customers but Melanie often wondered why not—began to fly.

"That silk is much too thin, Malkit."

"And this has poor embroidery. All these threads are loose."

"Mummy, this is a very pretty coral colour."

"No, *no*, it is too plain, Arwin. Now there is this stuff with red and gold threads interwoven; this is not bad quality. Or no, this is better. The embroidery is reasonable."

"That embroidery is superb!" Melanie murmured to Balwant, who was next to her. "It probably costs the earth."

She spoke to bring Balwant into the conversation and

was gratified to receive a tranquil, smiling answer. "But one expects a marriage sari to cost the earth, Mrs. Avtarsingh," Balwant said. "Only we shouldn't say so too loudly, or the salesman will put up his price."

Melanie laughed. Turning to listen to the discussion on her other side, she found that Aunt Asha and Bheji were now disagreeing, although Aunt Asha, no doubt also afraid that the vendor would raise his price if given the least encouragement, was putting her case in an emphatic undertone. "This must be the one, this red and gold woven material. Arwin is my brother's daughter and she should have what is the best. This is fine quality."

"It's too heavy. I've known a girl faint in a sari too heavy. It will be hot and what if we have a power cut and no fans during the ceremony? Also, the gold tone does not suit Arwin's complexion." Bheji was not using an undertone, since none of these observations was likely to affect the price adversely.

"That is just the strip lights in here," Aunt Asha insisted. "Arwin, hold this against you. Walk to the door where the daylight is."

Arwinder walked obediently. "Heavy material will hang well," said the salesman, accurately identifying Aunt Asha as an ally and addressing her directly. "It swings and catches the light. You can see, in the sunshine through the door."

"Too expensive," said Bheji firmly.

"When it is my brother's daughter, nothing is too expensive. Malkit, if there is money difficulty . . ."

"There is no money difficulty," said Bheji crossly, probably more on account of Asha's persistence than real disapproval of the sari or its cost. "My husband was against immoderate spending on marriage. When he was in the hospital those last weeks, he said to me—"

"Yes, yes." Asha waved a plump hand in the air. "People say this and that but when it comes to the point they do differently. I have heard you say, myself, that Saranjit's family will expect things to be done well." This was a well-aimed shaft, and Bheji's visibly increased annoyance acknowledged it. Asha took the sari from Arwinder as the latter came back, and put it on the divan with a proprietary pat. "I shall give this as gift to Arwin myself, whether there is money difficulty or not. There, Malkit, you cannot say no to that." Bheji was obviously longing to say no and regain command of the situation, but was unable to squeeze the word past Aunt Asha. "What is the price?" said Asha to the salesman.

There was a swift and expert haggling session between Asha and the salesman while Bheji sat by, silently fuming. Balwant stared at the floor and Arwinder, looking embarrassed, fingered a length of cheap and tinselly material as if seriously considering it as a purchase. Acrimonious agreement on the price of the red and gold sari was reached and the assistant began to pack it tenderly into a cardboard box. Bheji cleared her throat.

"We must all have new saris for the wedding," she remarked. "You must allow me to make gifts to you and Balwant also, Bhabi. You will want white or ivory colour, of course, but I think Balwant must have a pastel shade for a festive day. She is too young to wear white always."

This was war.

"We feel," said Aunt Asha, disconcerted, "that it is better she keeps to white."

"I'm sure," said Bheji, "that your brother, my husband, would agree with me. He told me not to wear white for him always and, as you see, I did not do so." She shook out the front pleats of her discreet green leaves. "There is a pale blue

I see up there which is just the thing. Bhabi, it would give me such pleasure, and Balwant too, I know."

"Balwant?" demanded Aunt Asha. The tone was half hectoring, half questioning. Balwant said shyly: "It is so kind of Aunt Malkit, Bheji." Melanie jumped a little; she had heard Balwant call her mother-in-law by the name that meant *dear mother* before but could never get used to it. "It is such a pretty blue," said Balwant, her eyes on the shelving and her expression indisputably wistful.

"You have so often said what a good daughter-in-law Balwant is to you," said Melanie's Bheji, with a delightful, vengeful smile and a militant gleam in her eye. "You cannot refuse me, Bhabi, surely?"

᷎

"Well, really!" said Arwinder, seated beside Melanie in a cycle rickshaw. Bheji followed in another, accompanied by the large number of parcels they had accumulated in the course of a lengthy expedition. "Imagine Mummy insisting on a blue sari for Balwant, and all because she was cross about not being allowed to choose mine. I would never have believed it."

"It had its funny side," Melanie said.

"Oh, yes, I know. And of course, Aunt Asha did not mean to irritate Mummy. It is just her way. She meant to be kind. I hope she won't be cross with Balwant. It is a pity she is so traditional. Really, it will be nice for Balwant to wear something different. She looked pleased."

"Yes." Melanie watched the straining calves of the rickshaw proprietor as they moved noiselessly up an incline. Once, in her early days in India, she had offered to get out and walk at this point, but found that it offended her rickshawman. "I'm glad I'm not Balwant," she said. "You

18

say Asha is kind, but she wasn't kind about me when I first came. You should remember. You were there."

Arwinder sighed. "I think she doesn't realise when she hurts people. Her marriage was unhappy, you know. She was married when she was only seventeen and her husband turned out to be a very unpleasant young man. It was not her parents' fault. I'm afraid that when the match was being discussed, his parents concealed his faults from hers. She was quite wretched for a long time, and people are nicer if their lives are happy. She would have been better with more children, with grandchildren, perhaps, but she had just the one son and he is dead. So she makes a fuss instead of her brother's child, and upsets Mummy."

"Surinder doesn't like her," Melanie remarked.

"No, I know." Arwinder giggled suddenly. "Whenever she comes to see us, he scoops up all his books and goes to work on the roof, no matter how hot it is. We shall see him do that later. She is coming for tea; I heard Mummy ask her. They patched their disagreement up while we were having our ice creams. Now it's funny, but Avtar can get on with Aunt Asha, have you noticed? Even though they have argued many times."

"Yes, they have," said Melanie with feeling.

"Oh, not just about you. Don't be silly," said Arwinder. "There is a bit of a rebel in Avtar. He cut his hair and put away his turban long before he met you. He wrote home about it, so that we wouldn't be taken by surprise when eventually he came back. Aunt Asha was so angry! No Sikh man should ever do such a thing, she said. She wrote to him many times while he was in England, saying what she felt, and getting crosser than ever when she got back answers that proved he'd taken no notice. She told us all about it! But when he actually came home, he made it right with her

19

somehow, after only a little argument or two. He understands her better than we do, I think. Perhaps because he's a doctor and has to be good at understanding people. Will he be home yet, do you think?"

"No," said Melanie. Suddenly, she had begun to feel tired. The sense of aridity which had afflicted her as she struggled with her paints had returned. The wrangle in the sari shop had left her with a sense of distaste too, and now she was physically uncomfortable as the dust blew up from the rickshaw wheels and clung grittily to her skin. "He was to be at the hospital this afternoon till surgery started again," she said, "and he has calls to make after that. I think he'll be home quite late."

A Mild Case of Schizophrenia

At the house they paid off the rickshaws and Bheji, setting down her packages on the low wall, fished in the postbox by the gate to see if any more mail had come. With an understanding smile she handed Melanie an airmail envelope with a familiar sharp-pointed handwriting on it. Melanie forgot that she was tired, hot, and dusty, and had seen hardly anything of Avtar for days, and raced in to read it in privacy. She sat in the basket chair by Avtar's bed and ripped the letter open. Her grandfather wrote once a month at least, but his letters always seemed too few. "They have an effect on you like insulin in a diabetic," Avtar had once remarked, somewhat disapprovingly.

"My dear Melanie," Gran had written. "How are you? I see from the papers that the rains have been poor where you are, so it must be very hot. It was the same when I travelled in India before the war. I was glad to get home and smell the sea mist from the Atlantic again.

"You'll be pleased to know that that book of mine, *The Organic Computer*, has gone into its tenth impression. This is very satisfactory as it means I can pass my old age in comfort here at Gavin's Cliff and still keep the roof in repair. In fact, I've just had the coal fires removed and electric ones installed. I can afford it and I'm past the age for shovelling coal, especially from an outside bunker in the rain.

"But I must say that the greatest pleasure I get from the success of the *Computer* is the way I have now confounded the impertinent reviewers of the first edition. I recall one of them saying that I put him in mind of a bulldozer on a drunken spree, attempting to demolish all coherent social structures. Such nonsense. As you know, the book merely says that societies should be ready to modify themselves in accordance with circumstances; that is the nature of evolution. Of course, it was fifteen years ago and people were more narrow-minded then. How old were you at the time of the original edition, Melanie? You were still living in Ambersford at the time. You must have been about eleven.

"Life goes on here as it always did. Your Uncle Daniel, or half-uncle, I should say, has leased a new meadow along the Amberscombe Road, just over the Devon border. His business is prospering. Either your Aunt Lucy is the brains behind it all or else he gets it from his mother. He certainly didn't get all this equine acumen from me. Not that the acumen is perfect. He isn't riding at the moment because his right arm is in plaster. On his own admission he 'fell in love with' a little roan mare at a sale and the first time he took her out on the road she shied at a tractor and tossed him into the hedge where he unfortunately met a tree stump. Your cousins are well and little Molly is growing fast. Frances has lately added a Siamese cat to the household and she has also done a lot of decorating inside the house (pointless in conjunction with a Siamese cat, I would have said, but that's her affair). She has an obvious flair for decor, rather like yours for designing. Blood will tell. I hope you haven't stopped designing altogether. I don't want to see you going to waste.

"I'm still wrangling with Ivor Winnaford over the origins of the names Ambersford and Amberscombe. He—and a small but vociferous clique of our fellow Western Counties Antiquarians—insist that the Amber element refers to the colour of the River Darr. Complete and utter nonsense. Amber is a corruption of the French word ombre, meaning shadow. It's to do with the shadow that Ravensridge casts over the Darr Valley of an evening. I've actually found a Norman French source to confirm it. But Ivor, whose mental processes frequently remind me of Hampton Court Maze, still goes on blathering about peat colouration in the water. . . ."

～

To spend a morning choosing saris in the company of Aunt Asha and Balwant, and then come home to a letter from Professor William Purvis of Gavin's Cliff was enough to bring on a sharp attack of schizophrenia. Chandigarh and Gavin's Cliff, Aunt Asha and William Purvis were two different worlds and two different species. It was hardly possible that one person, one Melanie, could inhabit and communicate with both.

On the shelf by her own bed was a copy of Gran's con-

23

troversial best-seller, *The Organic Computer*. She looked towards it, seeing her grandfather's incorrigible, opinionated image in her mind's eye, pipe clenched in teeth, eyes sparkling with a wicked joy in living. That book was the product of forty years of research, travelling the world as a professional anthropologist, studying and analysing one society and culture after another. At the end of it all, he had sat down and written up his conclusions, and the result had made him a great deal of money and as many enemies as even Gran knew what to do with.

Gran's contentious thesis was that all ideologies, all cultures—whether religious or political—were programs, analagous to computer programs, which were imposed on the young by their elders in order to regulate their conduct. In the effort to make a thorough impression, said Gran, the teachers or parents were apt to present their programs as eternal truths, not susceptible to change even when circumstances altered and disaster lay clearly visible ahead unless change was accepted. It was essential, declared Gran, that people should recognise the programming process for what it was, and be prepared to rewrite their own programs when required. The book was entertaining and stylish, backed by horridly convincing arguments, and quite remorseless. By the time Professor William Purvis had finished, scarcely one major system of political or religious thought remained which had not had a heavily armoured vehicle driven clean through the middle of it, and there was scarcely a single prophet or philosopher who had kept his stature; they had all been reduced to mere human proportions by, as another reviewer (an admiring one this time) had put it: "Well-aimed cutlass slashes at their clay ankles."

A large number of their adherents were understandably

furious and several governments of the more doctrinaire sort indignantly banned his book from their countries. Which was excellent publicity, Gran always said, and did his sales as a whole no end of good. He had done exceedingly well out of it all.

That, Melanie recalled, was one of the things that his old friend Ivor Winnaford had thrown at him during their frequent quarrels on the subject. She sat holding Gran's letter in her fingers and gazing towards the bookshelves, but not now aware of either. She was seeing Gran and Ivor: Gran explosive and skinny, Ivor large and calm with his round pink face made only fractionally pinker by conflict, hurling their arguments back and forth across the parlour in Gavin's Cliff. Behind them was the bay window with its view of the sea, and by the door stood the grandfather clock, ticking steadily in its slow deep voice. Gran was in his favourite feet-apart stance on the woolly sheepskin rug by the fireplace; Ivor was seated massively in the armchair under the picture which he himself had painted. By profession, Ivor was a professor of history, teaching at a west country university. But in his spare time he was a more than competent artist. He had given *Light and Water* to Gran as a present one Christmas. It showed the nearby rocky headland of Heverton Point, reflected in a calm sea which in turn cast luminous dapples on the arch of a cave. Despite the libellous remarks in Gran's letter, Ivor was one of the few people who could ever stand up to William Purvis in debate. "People *need* their cultures, their religions, and their customs," he had said in the course of one particularly fierce passage of arms. "Destroy those and you can destroy a whole nation. And there *you* sit, William, destroying away and making a fortune out of it!" "Not a fortune," said Gran. "The taxes are too high. And I'm not destroying anything, don't talk rubbish. I approve of people sticking to their customs as long as the customs don't harm them. I even go to church in Ambersford at Christmas, so as to keep in touch with the cultural roots of my own society. . . ."

"That's hypocrisy," said Ivor.

"No, it isn't. I told the vicar why I went and warned him I might heckle him, and all he said was that if I made a nuisance of myself, he had a county champion all-in wrestler in the congregation so I wouldn't be a nuisance for long, but that if I behaved he'd be more delighted to see me than any regular member of his flock, and then added something cryptic about the road to Damascus. I am not destructive, Ivor. But adapting to circumstances is the heart of evolution. The creature that can't adapt at the right time dies. Look at the dinosaur."

"No one," said Ivor, "knows what happened to the dinosaur. Find another example!"

The counterpoint of the old argument played itself over in Melanie's head. As if she had been teleported there, she saw the detail of the parlour at Gavin's Cliff, and then as though she were a ghost, haunting it, she drifted through the walls and saw it from outside. She saw a grey stone house on a cliff perch above the Bristol Channel, with pines on the soaring gradient behind it and a path of trodden red earth leading from it, under the trees, going down to the town and the harbour below. Lightly, as one did in dreams, she rose on the west wind and saw the land of her origin from above, as the hovering kestrel did, and the gull. She saw the strong and rocky cliffs which fringed it and the rivers, brown with peat, which threaded through every valley and swelled to estuaries wherever the cliff wall broke. Sea and river and bog, water as an element, were living presences here, having to be taken into account whenever you built a house or bought a field. The sea, which in Chandigarh was a factor altogether missing, in Melanie's home dominated whole lives and had been known to take them.

Drifting inland now in her imagination, she saw hills comfortable as vast fat cushions, their coombes shaped like the dents of giant fingers, covered in a summer patchwork of corn gold and pasture green, with here and there the deep green pile of woodland. To the west rose the bare dark heights of Exmoor, purple when the heather was out, smoky brown at other times, or black when the sky was stormy. In the valleys were the towns and villages. One was Ambersford village where she was born. She saw old terraced cottages of pink stone forming the main street, giving it a haphazard charm because every roof had a different height and pitch from its neighbour. In front of the houses were cobblestoned strips. The cobbles could twist ankles like telephone cable and people mostly walked in the road, but the National Trust had slapped a Preservation Order on them and that was the end of the matter.

She had not seen England since she left it with Avtar, a few months after their marriage. She had wanted to visit it but Avtar's reaction to the mere suggestion was so unpleasant that she had never made the suggestion again. It was the worst quarrel they had ever had, and the wounds might never entirely heal.

Not that she had been living in Ambersford, or at Gavin's Cliff, when they met. She had left the west country, physically, at the age of fourteen.

There was nothing especially new to Melanie in the sensation of being divided between two worlds. She always had been, ever since that drowsy August afternoon when she and her cousin Frances, riding two of Uncle Daniel's ponies, descended the zigzag path off the side of Ravensridge in search of tea at Melanie's house, expecting to find there nothing more than that.

The day the world ended.

The Day the World Ended

Melanie thought of it as the day the world ended because for her it had been just that: the passing away forever of her childish certainty that life would go on always just as it was, in the world which she had known since she was a baby.

That world consisted mainly of Ambersford village, near the border between Devon and Somerset, at the edge of Exmoor. Here she lived with her father in a house appropriately known as Roadend, because it was the last house in the village and the last habitation along the road until you got to Amberscombe at the head of the valley. Roadend was an old house, because the village was old. The shell of Roadend had stood for five and a half centuries and its walls, inside and out, were more than three feet thick. Melanie's father had once tried to make a serving hatch between the kitchen and the dining room but gave up after he drove a three-foot-six iron rod into the wall to measure the thickness precisely—and lost it. Roadend was a picturesque house with huge black ceiling beams which had once been ships' timbers, and a massive oaken front door. Tourists frequently photographed it. But to Melanie it was normal and as a house should be. She could remember living in no other kind.

Her Uncle Daniel—strictly speaking her half-uncle since he was the product of Gran's first marriage while her father was the result of the second—lived with his family in another old house up behind the church, close under the hill called Ravensridge. He dealt in hunters and children's ponies and he too was in the centre circle of Melanie's world. She could scarcely conceive of a life in which she did not ride one of Uncle Daniel's ponies at least once a week and sometimes much oftener.

At its outer edges, Melanie's fourteen-year-old world took in many square miles of forest and moorland, of which she had an intimate knowledge acquired from the backs of the ponies. There were also other people and habitations. In one direction, for instance, lay Amberscombe village, with Exmoor surging into the sky beyond it like a vast heathery wave. In the other direction was the local seaside town of Heverton, with its beach and its harbour and High Street where her father was branch manager of a department store. And beyond the harbour, beyond Heverton Point, was Gavin's Cliff where Gran lived when he was at home.

At fourteen, Melanie was beginning to distinguish between the inner and outer circles of her life, and knew that Gran and Gavin's Cliff, although they were on the other side of Heverton, belonged to the inner one. Gran and the Cliff were important influences in her life, although she had only just started to recognise it.

Within this world of hers there were, so to speak, various countries and tribes. The farmers and tradesmen of Ambersford and Amberscombe formed one group; the fishermen in the cottages by Heverton Harbour formed another. The professional and business community amounted to a third. All of them were concerned to a greater or lesser extent with a fourth type of industry: the tourist trade. Ambersford and Amberscombe were beautiful and ancient. Ambersford possessed a ruined castle, and both villages boasted fine fifteenth-century churches with famous rood screens. Heverton had an exceptionally good beach. By coachload and carload, the tourists poured in from May to September. Half the households of the district let rooms in summer; the tills in the Heverton shops rang merrily with the sales of swimsuits and suntops or, alternatively (since the weather of the west country was uncertain), raincoats, umbrellas, and fishermen's knit sweaters. The trade was seasonal and separate from the real life of the area, yet went far towards financing it.

Melanie's family had links with all these subdivisions. It had links too with a wider world, for Gavin's Cliff was often invaded by Gran's intellectual friends, of whom Ivor Winnaford was one. There was also a branch of the family in London. Every summer, Melanie's cousin Frances came to stay for two weeks and every winter after Christmas, Melanie made a return visit. She hated the return visits but tried not to show it in case the adults, with their peculiar scale of values, allowed this to interfere with Frances's visits to Ambersford. She and Frances liked each other, and enjoyed their summer fortnights.

On that August day they had taken the ponies to the top of Ravensridge and galloped its three-mile length. Frances rode at home and could acquit herself well though not quite with Melanie's élan. Having cleared their systems of the yearning for speed, they rode idly back until they were again above the village, and began the slow descent of the steep zigzag paths down. Despite the drowsy warmth of the day, Melanie remembered, it had been clear, which was a sign of rain to come. The Bristol Channel looked as if it were no more than a broad river which you could cross with a run and a leap to land without undue effort in Wales, and across the valley they could see what the tourists who dotted the mound where the ruined castle stood, were wearing. "It's going to be a bad day tomorrow," Melanie said, and had no thought of omens as she said it.

It was five by the church clock when they reached the stables. Roy, Uncle Daniel's sixteen-year-old son, was rubbing down a horse tied to one of the loosebox doors. He grinned at them as they clattered in. He had, even in those days, a separate grin for each of them. For Melanie, his first cousin and someone he saw nearly every day, it was a fraternal one. For the visitor Frances, who came rarely, who belonged to the other side of Melanie's family and was no blood relation to him, and who in addition had curly hair and was much prettier than Melanie, it was appreciative. It was certainly Frances's presence which induced him to say kindly that he would offsaddle the ponies for them, as it was very hot and they must be wanting their tea. Never had Roy offered to unsaddle a pony for Melanie on her own. Frances knew it, and gave him a sweetly flirtatious smile as she handed her reins over. And Melanie remembered how, without a trace of premonition, she had teased Fran lightly about it as they made their way back to Roadend. The front door of

Roadend was open, and they went straight in. Loud, angry voices were coming from the sitting room on the left. They forgot Roy and paused in the hallway, looking at each other.

"It might be the Show committee," said Melanie doubtfully. "But . . ."

"No," Frances agreed, pulling off her hard hat and running a hand through her damp brown hair. "That sounds like family. What on earth—?"

The sitting room door was not quite closed. One voice suddenly emerged from the others, raised to get itself an exclusive hearing. "I'm surprised at you, Leonard, really surprised. You seem to know nothing at all about your own daughter. Why won't you leave her at the Cliff with me? I'll look after her. *And* see she meets young men when the time comes if that's what you're in such a stew about! For God's sake why can't you at least ask the child what *she* wants?"

"That's Gran. I didn't know he was here," said Melanie, puzzled.

Her father's voice came, close to the door. "She isn't old enough to know what she wants. It may just be that I know more about my daughter than you do. She's growing up and it's time she saw more of the world than this one corner of Somerset. It's also time she thought of something else besides horses. She needs wider horizons and . . ."

"Are you suggesting that I'm parochial, you cheeky pup?" bawled Gran, sixty-eight years putting a mere thirty-eight in its place. "I'm a professor of anthropology and I've been round the world twice. Are you implying that *I'll* narrow her horizons?"

"Yes," said Melanie's father.

There was a placatory mumble which Melanie recognised as her Uncle Daniel. He was saying something on the

33

lines of *let's sit down and talk all this out quietly*. It was ignored. "In London," said Melanie's father clearly, "there'll be theatres and dances—"

"Discos!" said Gran in disgust.

"—and concerts and the ballet. And travelling abroad is easier with Heathrow on the doorstep. Later on there'll be jobs to choose from and, yes, plenty of young men to choose from too. There aren't any young fellows here. They all go away to work in the towns as soon as they leave school and you know it. As it is, she may not find it easy to marry; there's this business of not being able to have children . . ."

His voice faded. Uncle Daniel came in, audibly this time. ". . . difficult when a child has no mother. A tragedy, Marjorie dying so young . . . quite true that Melanie shows an artistic talent and ought to have the best opportunities. I'm sure Leonard is doing the best he can."

Gran growled something indistinct but certainly disparaging about Leonard's notions of the best. Her father said: "We'll have a good standard of living with this London managership of mine. She'll soon adapt and—"

"You'll break the child's heart!" said Gran melodramatically.

"I hope you won't encourage *her* to think that," said Leonard Purvis. "There's one thing that never seems to occur to you—and if I hurt your feelings I'm sorry—but does it never strike you that she might be better off with just one father instead of two?"

That was followed by silence, and its staggered quality penetrated even through the door to the two startled eavesdroppers in the hall. Frances suddenly awoke to the fact that eavesdropping was in fact what they were doing. She went pink and moved to the stairs. Melanie knew that she ought

34

to follow but her feet appeared to be stuck to the carpet. Beyond the terrible sitting room door, the silence broke again. Gran and Leonard Purvis were both shouting at once. Uncle Daniel was saying: "Now, now, we mustn't get overheated," in the rumbling west country accent against which Gran had fought a losing battle throughout the whole of Daniel's boyhood (it didn't occur in either Gran or Leonard), but once again he was being ignored. Leonard Purvis's voice gained the ascendant. ". . . she spends as much time with you as she does with me; you tell her what she should think and how she should behave more often than I do. Poor child doesn't know where she is between the two of us. Well, that's all over. We're going to London!"

Too suddenly to give Melanie any chance of retreat, the door was flung wide and Gran shot out of it. He stopped dead at the sight of her. At the top of the stairs, Frances made a muffled sound and fled into her room. Melanie, white-faced and wide-eyed, stood helplessly where she was. Gran, switching instantly from rapid and irate movements to calm, slow ones, took pipe and tobacco out of his ginger tweed pocket and began methodically to fill the bowl. "You're back, then. So you heard. I'm sorry. We didn't want you upset, Melanie."

"Melanie, is that you?" her father shouted. "Come in here!"

She went in, slowly. Gran followed. Inside, Uncle Daniel was sitting in an easy chair with a miserable expression on his square, wind-browned face, staring at the polished brown riding boots stretched before him on the hearthrug. Her father stood leaning his shoulders on a bookcase near the door, as if he needed the support. He was a tall man with thinning dark hair and a narrow-boned face.

Except for the golden brown colour of his eyes, a characteristic he shared with his father and his half-brother, he was nothing like either of them. "Melanie, were you listening?"

"Yes, I heard . . . some of it. I couldn't help it."

"We were shouting our heads off," said Gran pugnaciously. "They could probably hear us in Edinburgh. And if I'd been Melanie, considering what it was we were shouting about, *I'd* have damn well listened. The child's a human being, not a ruddy angel off a tombstone. And you're a human being too, Leonard. Don't come those stainless marble airs with me. I'm your father, let me remind you!"

"I didn't say I was blaming her," said Leonard Purvis. It was impossible to tell whether this was an afterthought, for the purpose of deflating his father, or the truth. "I only wanted to know how much she had heard. I meant to explain it to her today in full anyway. Melanie, I have been offered and have accepted a post as assistant manager, with the prospect of becoming manager, of Hallowens in the West End of London. I've bought a flat in Croydon, to the south of London. It's a pleasant district and there's an excellent school. This house has been sold. I didn't tell you before because there is always a risk that arrangements of this kind may fall through. But it's settled now. It will be a wonderful chance for you, at your age, to be near London. You can visit Gran in the holidays if you want to, of course."

The world was reeling. London? She had been there. When she visited Frances. She detested it. She could not then have said why. At fourteen one was not articulate enough for that. Only as an adult did she come to understand that the buildings were too close, the skylines of roof ridge and office block like a fist in the eye—when the eye was adjusted to the width of the Darr Valley or the Bristol Channel. And only as an adult did she slowly realise that

36

London lacked certain underlying rhythms which for her were important. It was a loss to Melanie, to be conscious of the seasons only as a change in temperature, with the shift from bare trees to green leaves and back again through the blaze of autumn passing almost unseen. It was a loss to her to be unconscious of the times of ploughing and harvest, to be bereft of the great social occasions of her home, like the Ambersford Show or the first meet of the hunting season.

Even then—even now—she admitted to herself that she still did not quite know why the loss was so great. She knew only that it was so.

At fourteen, she could express none of this at all. Clinging to one familiar concept as though it were a lifebelt, she said: "Will we be here for the Show? I've entered Badger in the jumping."

There was a flash of impatience in her father's face. "You can come for the Show next year if you really want to by then. But this year I'm afraid not. We're moving the weekend after next. You won't miss it much, you'll see."

He didn't understand. Gran did, but Gran had fired off all his ammunition and was now as helpless as Melanie herself. Uncle Daniel, still staring at his boots, probably understood as well but he was easygoing and would not fight for her more than he had already. He did mutter something about: "Worse things than growing up yur. I grew up yur," but for the third time he was ignored. Her father's mind was made up, with the best of intentions. He loved her but he didn't know her. He was a thousand miles away from her, petrifyingly out of touch.

In the end she adjusted very well, or so everyone said. Her accent faded. She did well at her new school and better still at art college. She made friends and joined the design team at Hallowens Fabrics and Furnishings, the production company which was a sister to Hallowens Retail Furnishing and shared the same building. She was a success. She had experienced a little natural homesickness at first, everyone agreed, as was only to be expected, and then she showed what a good sensible girl she was. "Just as her mother, Marjorie, used to be."

Melanie could barely remember her mother and had little sense of kinship with her mother's family. Even Frances felt more like a friend than a relation. Melanie knew herself to be a Purvis all the way through. "Sensible, hell," she said disgustedly, sitting in the basket chair by Avtar's bed in Chandigarh.

She had never adjusted, not under the surface, not even though she had tried her best to do so. Nor had she ever, although once more she had tried, been able to forget her father's crucial, obtuse failure to understand.

She had lived with him in Croydon and together they had made visits to Somerset to see Gran and Uncle Daniel. They had gone there together for the wedding of Frances and Roy, for it was Frances in the end who went back to Ambersford to live, and not Melanie. After the move to Croydon, Leonard Purvis lived another eight years, until a heart weakness, striking early, brought about his death.

But it always seemed to Melanie that that warm August day in Ambersford was the day on which she lost her father, and he was finally replaced by Gran.

Recollections in the Dark

Downstairs there was a minor commotion. Doors banged and voices surged upwards. "Melanie!" Arwinder called. "Are you there? Our guests are arriving for tea. My fiancé is here already, with his parents. Are you coming down?"

Melanie folded up the letter and told herself that it was absurd, this bereft feeling. India was her home now. During her first year, once the initial shock of homesickness had passed, she had written euphoric letters to Gran and Frances and her friend Jane Hanworth in London, praising her in-laws and their close, protective family circle. (She had made gentle fun of Asha. After all, there was only one Asha.) And what had changed? she asked herself. Nothing. She

39

loved Avtar and more than loved his family. Her own mother had been dead since Melanie was five, and she had no brothers or sisters. Avtar had obligingly presented her with his, and it was a gift she valued. She changed her creased sari for a fresh one, combed her hair, and went to join the cheerful babble below.

On the way down she met Surinder coming up, books under his arm and eyes fixed on the stone stairs which led to the roof. After that she was not surprised to find Aunt Asha among the guests in the sitting room, fanning a shiny face with a magazine while Balwant poured tea for her. Saranjit, Arwinder's betrothed, was helping Bheji to dispense biscuits and sweetmeats, and his parents were ensconced in adjacent armchairs, with the brass coffee table between them to hold their tea things. They were a handsome, if slightly over-powering pair, their strong, good-humoured faces very alike. They had a sly trick of accentuating the resemblance. Ajeet Singh's precision-tied turban matched the blue flower print of his wife's sari exactly and they both had the same kind of tortoiseshell spectacle frames. Saranjit himself was non-descript at first sight, but the eyes behind the spectacles which he too wore were kindly and intelligent, and the jaw be-hind his beard was well defined. Arwin will be happy, Melanie thought. And then, with a troublesome return of that bereaved feeling: But we shall miss her.

Arwinder herself was presiding over jugs of lime juice and lemonade, and had two of her girlfriends for company. As Melanie finished greeting the rest of the guests, they beckoned to her.

"We are talking of the ladies' Sangeet party, Melanie. Two days before the marriage, we think, on the Thursday, because everyone can manage that."

"Mine was two days before," said Balbir, who was the

elder of the two and had been married just after Melanie came to India. She was accompanied by a tiny, thumb-sucking daughter, who sat perched on a stool, black pigtails sticking out at right angles, and stared at Melanie solemnly.

"We thought we'd use the big room upstairs, Mummy's and mine, because it opens on to the little kitchen roof and we can push all the furniture out there out of the way," Arwinder said. "And Nirmal here has suggested that you might have ideas for decorating the room. Do you think you could?"

"You need have the ideas only, Melanie," said Bheji, joining them. "Some lime juice for Mr. Ajeetsingh, please. We shall make the boys do all the work. My sister Prem's family will be here soon and she has all those teenage boys, and Surinder can help. And, of course, there will be Rehal."

"Rehal?" said the unmarried Nirmal involuntarily, and then plunged her face into her glass of lemonade in confusion as Arwinder, Balbir, and Bheji all broke into laughter. "Well, well, we shall see," said Bheji, eyes crinkling. "One wedding often starts off another. Give me a lemonade for Aunt Asha also, please."

Melanie passed biscuits to the embarrassed Nirmal, who took one without meeting her eyes, and with a murmured excuse withdrew to talk to Balwant. Nirmal was a slender girl with thick hair worn on top of her head, and a long, slim neck. There had been hopes, once, of her and Rehal.

Rehal, now being animatedly discussed by Bheji and Aunt Asha, was one of the elder sons of Bheji's elder sister. He was twenty-six and in his parents' opinion ought to be married by now, but Rehal, said the family gloomily, was *difficult.* This difficultness took the form of going to England to read English and History at university, turning himself thereafter into a Fleet Street journalist, acquiring British nationality, and announcing that he intended to stay in Britain for life. His parents had been relieved when, two years before, he paid them a visit and showed signs of interest in Nirmal when he met her by chance at Bheji's house. They all agreed that if Rehal could be persuaded into marrying her, it would be an excellent thing. She was good-tempered and well-educated and nice-looking and adaptable enough to cope with life in the West. She would be a . . . a stabilising influence, said Aunt Prem delicately, wrapping it up because Melanie was present. Aunt Prem did not like what she had heard of the West. Its perfumes and cosmetics were admirable, yes, but its drugs, alcohol, and unregulated sex appalled her. Unlike Aunt Asha, however, she had taken to Melanie and did not express those feelings openly in Melanie's hearing.

But Rehal went back to England neither married nor engaged and Melanie had felt sorry for Nirmal. Rehal had struck her as a young man with considerable magnetism, and Nirmal looked as though she had been duly magnetised. Melanie only hoped that she was not about to be hurt once more.

"He was always a wild boy," Aunt Asha was saying. She cast a glance of approbation towards Saranjit—who was not wild but, on the contrary, rather domesticated and an orthodox Sikh in all respects. "It is getting dusk," said Asha. "Malkit, I can hardly see to talk to you. Balwant, you are nearest the switch. Put on the lights. Now"—she turned back to Bheji—"tell me how it came about, this marriage of Arwin's. I keep on thinking I must ask you."

"Through the Patels," Bheji said. "My husband's friends, who are coming tomorrow. They were his patients before they moved to Bombay. They also knew Saranjit's family, who were their neighbours here. They used to correspond with them. The Patels heard that a match was wanted for Saranjit and they remembered Arwin. So they wrote to us and a meeting was arranged. The two of them took to each other at once. So nice," said Bheji. "We had introduced her to some others, but nothing came of it."

"Ah." Aunt Asha sighed and shook her head. "Now, I am old-fashioned, and so were Balwant's parents. Of course, we allowed her and my son to meet beforehand because things are done that way now. But as for the deciding, that was for the parents. The parents know so much better what they are doing—"

"There I can't always agree," said Ajeet Singh. "Naturally, we should object to someone unsuitable. But one should not push too hard. People should not be forced against their will."

A murmur of mild social argument arose. Saranjit caught his fiancée's eye, and behind his spectacles one of his own eyes closed in an amused wink. "I should make more tea," said Arwin hastily. She rose to gather teapot and used glasses onto a tray. "Who would like some more?" She collected orders quickly and disappeared towards the kitchen. Saranjit chuckled and Melanie managed to exchange a smile with the shy Nirmal, and the lights went out.

Dusk had fallen swiftly, as it did in this part of the world. A stifling darkness, like a blanket of crow's feathers or soot, descended on the room. Overhead, the ceiling fan whirred down to a halt. From the kitchen came a thud and a wail, as if Arwinder had bumped into something.

"Oh, what a nuisance," exclaimed Bheji. "The power is cut *again*."

❧

"This is frightful," said Melanie to Arwinder an hour later as, candles in hand, they felt their way into the kitchen to prepare supper for the party which had now adjourned to the roof, thus compelling Surinder to join it after all. On the roof there was at least some light from the sky, and it was now fairly cool. The same could not be said of the kitchen, where the quality of the darkness suggested a coal cellar in which the coal was quietly smouldering. "We haven't had a cut as long as this before," Melanie said. "What on earth can we give them? We can't see to clean rice."

"Oh, there is chapatti batter standing and some chicken curry from yesterday," said Arwinder. She set her candle on a shelf where it cast an inadequate light over polished stainless steel and aluminium pans, a sink full of used glasses, and a lizard like a painted shadow on the stone wall. "Do we count Avtar in?" she asked.

"Yes, he might come at any time now. I'll do the chap-attis, if you like, while you liven up the curry." Melanie found the basin of pale brown batter and tested it. It was getting dry. She moved to the sink and discovered without surprise that the taps were dry too. She dipped water from the big bowl which was the kitchen emergency supply, and wetted the dough with a slightly irritable slop from a spoon. She began to knead. "I only hope," she said, "that he isn't trying to sew up a gash in someone's head or deliver a baby by candlelight. I think you are lucky that Saranjit is a teacher and not a doctor!"

Arwinder laughed. "I think I am lucky too—but not for quite that reason. Saranjit was almost married to someone else last year but there was some scandal about the girl—did I ever tell you? No, I can't have done, I only knew myself a week ago. She had had an affair or something of the sort and his parents were against the marriage. He didn't want

44

to upset them but he was keen about the match at the time. He told me," she added proudly, "because he said I had a right to know. He is so honest. But I think he likes me a lot, so it will be all right. Melanie, I want to ask you something. It is funny, you have been here three years, and yet there are many things I don't know. Perhaps I didn't like to ask but . . ."

"Ask away," invited Melanie, slapping dough from hand to hand.

"Well, Melanie, did you go against your family when you married Veerjee? You have never said."

"I hadn't all that much family to go against." Melanie shaped dough into small balls. "My parents were dead, remember. My grandfather was a bit startled, but he got over it."

"He minded that Avtar was Indian?"

"He minded," said Melanie dryly, "that I was going to live in India."

～

"It's nothing to do with race or colour!" Gran had shouted, storming round the parlour of Gavin's Cliff like a tornado in ginger tweeds. "Or religion either. That young man of yours hasn't much, if you ask me, which is in your favour and his, if you want to know. People getting entrenched in their religions have caused half the wars on this planet and ruined God knows how many marriages. It's nothing to do with any of those. I nearly married a Hawaiian girl myself, once. . . ."

"Why didn't you?"

"*She* wouldn't marry me. Said she wouldn't be happy in England. And I'm telling you you won't be happy in India. See here, Melanie, I don't care if you marry a white man or a brown man or a little green man from Mars as long as he doesn't warp your life out of true, but this marriage *will* warp it! He's going to take you to a strange country to live among strange people—you that broke up with Robin Selwood because he didn't care for Somerset! You break up with Robin, you do," said Gran, brandishing his pipe wildly in the air, "and you come tearing down here, driving half the night, in floods of tears, all because Robin won't see eye to eye with you about red mud and dripping rhododendrons and moorlands full of sheep whose conversational resources stop at saying baaa—"

"Gran," said Melanie from the windowseat overlooking the sea, "you adore Gavin's Cliff."

"Don't change the subject. We're not discussing me. I am attached to Gavin's Cliff but I'm not demented about it. I'm a reasonable and moderate man," said Gran blatantly, "and I realise that however much I love this place it's not to everyone's taste. But do you realise that? No, you do not. You think it's a blueprint for paradise and you give Robin his marching orders because of it and probably break his heart . . ."

"Robin's thirty-three and he's been through a broken marriage and if that didn't smash his heart up—and it didn't—I'm not likely to manage it, either."

"I said, don't change the subject. I repeat, you think that the west of England is Shangri-la itself and you throw your man over because of it, and now what are you proposing to do? Marry a fellow who wants to take you to bloody Chandigarh!" roared Gran, and stopped for lack of breath.

In the quiet parlour, a peace all the deeper because it was backed by the wind in the pines outside and punctuated by the deep tick of the clock, Melanie said: "Robin insisted on living in London. India's different."

"You've no idea how different," Gran informed her.

46

"Heat, dust, mosquitoes, beggars with leprosy and cows roaming about in the streets . . ."

"Trips to the Himalayas too. It won't be like London. Even Chandigarh won't. I've seen it on film. Wide streets and the foothills of the mountains in the distance. It isn't leaving Somerset that matters—"

"Isn't it?"

"—it's what one gets in exchange. I'll be getting something much better than London ever was. London's a vacuum to me."

"It's been damn useful to you in your career."

"Oh, vacuums can be useful. I'll be taking coffee in a vacuum flask when I drive back to Croydon."

"Now you're trying to be clever. Listen to me. What *about* your work? Are you abandoning that too?"

"No, I can design wherever I am."

"I sincerely hope so. Oh, for God's sake. Your mind's made up. I can see it. Obstinate, the way your father was. I suppose I'm invited to the wedding? What is it to be? Civil?"

"In all senses of the word, I hope. I want you there. As long as you don't *say* anything to Avtar."

"Who, me?" said Gran. "When did I ever *say* anything to anyone in that tone of voice? Anyhow, I'd be wasting my time with Avtar. He'd just respect my gray hairs and agree with me till I felt like punching him one. I shall be the soul of discretion."

". . . so there was no real conflict," said Melanie, after a slightly edited version of this conversation. It was not easy to convey to Arwin the ersatz nature of Gran's rages. Arwin took things at their face value and assumed that people who shouted must really be angry. Reporting Gran, therefore, Melanie toned him down. "He didn't forbid me to marry

47

Avtar, or refuse to know us, or anything like that," she finished.

"But if he had? Would you have gone on with it then?"

"Well, yes. I think so," said Melanie. Arwinder stirred curry, evidently needing to assimilate this—to her—astonishing concept. Like Saranjit, Arwin would not want to upset her family. Gran would have said that her family had programmed her, so thoroughly that not only did she accept their guidelines, but would be virtually incapable of happiness if she ever stepped outside them. And that, in turn, was a concept altogether foreign to Melanie.

Arwinder said at length, still questioningly: "You mentioned this man Robin, that you once considered marrying. Were you engaged to him?"

"Not formally. We'd talked about marriage but we decided we weren't right for each other." Deliberately, she made it sound a cold decision. Even now she did not want to remember the storm of shouting and weeping and recrimination in which she and Robin had finally released themselves from each other. "He was older than I was," she said. "We did the same kind of work—he was head designer in my department at Hallowens—but as people we weren't alike."

"But you and Avtar are alike?"

"In some ways. And even where we're different"—Melanie frowned with the effort of analysis—"we're complementary. The things that interest him, like medical science, seem to fill a gap in me. I like to hear him talk about his work and I think he likes me to talk about mine. It's the same with his Indianness and my Englishness. We give each other a new way of looking at things. Only, the odd thing was, we seemed to know all that at once, before we put it to the test. It was curious."

48

"At that art exhibition in Hallowens," said Arwin, who had heard the story and considered it, sentimentally, to be romantic.

Melanie herself did not remember or regard it as that. To her it was simply a thing which had happened in the face of all reason and probability, like getting struck by lightning. "There's an excellent exhibition of Indian paintings and sculpture in the Gallery," Robin had remarked, strolling among his department's drawing boards one wet April morning. "It's worth seeing, especially if you don't fancy getting drowned in Oxford Street at lunchtime." So at lunchtime Melanie had made her way through the curious labyrinth of passages which was simultaneously the division and the connection between the Hallowens design and production company and the Hallowens retail store, and went into the Gallery, which occupied a mezzanine floor overlooking dining room furniture. It was crowded with a mixture of casual visitors and invited guests, and free glasses of red and white wine were being dispensed to the latter, in a roped-off area at one end. Her attention had been caught at once by a display of small paintings with very clear colours and sharp, in-focus figures. A plaque below them described them as paintings of the Kangra and Rajasthan schools, and followed that with a dissertation on the techniques and materials used. She was staring, rapt, when someone touched her arm. "I think someone is waving at you. You are invited to a glass of wine," said the stranger beside her. "But you are so deep in the paintings, you did not see."

She turned, startled, and saw Robin in the roped-off area, making do-you-want-a-drink? signals. Then she looked at her neighbour, saw that he was Indian and amused by her apparently mesmerised condition, and was . . .

Avtar.

49

She did not know his name but it was as though she knew its owner. She shook her head at Robin, and he shrugged and moved out of sight. She said something—and could never afterwards remember what it was—to Avtar. He answered. There ensued a trivial conversation which was no more than a means of remaining side by side while each of them secretly put the other's face and voice and aura against some private master image, and found that they matched. The conversation emerged from its welter of the trivial and became an exchange of information. He was not normally a frequenter of art shows ("You met Veerjee in an *art gallery?*" Arwinder had said, flabbergasted, when she first heard of it) but had been drawn into this because it was Indian and would remind him of home. Melanie, on the other hand, was a designer herself and worked for Hallowens. His name was Dr. Avtar Singh. Hers was Melanie Purvis. He was just about to get some coffee and a light lunch in the Hallowens restaurant. Would she like to join him?

". . . we were engaged three weeks later, officially," Melanie said. "But we knew at once, I think. It was extraordinary. It was nothing like anything I'd experienced with Robin."

"Were you still . . . not quite engaged to this Robin when you got to know Veerjee?"

"No, that was over, though I had hard work to make Avtar believe it." Melanie turned a chapatti hastily over on its griddle. Talking could make one neglectful. "We were still on speaking terms, of course, because we had to work together. It was really very awkward. We didn't see each other outside Hallowens anymore, but during the day we couldn't avoid it. We were very formal and courteous and neutral. What with being gracious to Robin all day, and then spending the evenings trying to convince Avtar that

50

that was all it was, I wonder I didn't go quite mad. I had to tell Avtar about Robin, of course. It was like Saranjit with you—I felt he had a right to know. He kept saying I should leave the job, but one can't find another job in five minutes. And anyway I liked Hallowens."

"You had to work? Well, you had no parents, of course," Arwin said. "But there was your grandfather."

"Yes, and some uncles and aunts and assorted cousins. But no one to be responsible for me financially," Melanie explained. "I was a wage earner with my own home. England is different."

Arwin nodded. "Did anyone at all mind about you marrying Avtar?" she asked curiously. "I am sorry to be inquisitive, Melanie. But I am getting married soon myself and it makes one want to know about other people."

"I don't mind. No one in the family objected, or if they did, they didn't say so. There were one or two outside it . . ." Melanie's voice became reminiscent. "There was the 'woman in Woolworths,' for instance. Only that was more funny than anything else."

"Funny?" In the bad light it was difficult for them to see one another's expressions, but the pattern of candlelight and dark shadows on Arwinder's face suggested that she was frowning.

"Yes. It was after we were married. We were in the queue at the pay desk in Woolworths—that's a big chain store—and we were talking together. The woman in front of us heard and turned round—I expect she'd heard Avtar's accent. Anyhow, she turned and gave us such a glare and . . ."

"*Funny?*" said Arwinder again, pausing with the sauce-pan in her hand.

"Yes. Because," said Melanie with the satisfaction of one who looks back on a triumph, "there is a way that one

51

woman can look at another that says quite clearly: My dear, you have a smut on your nose and that colour doesn't suit you . . ." Arwinder giggled. "And I looked at her like that and she went red and hastily faced away from us again. There was that occasion and one or two other incidents like it, and we took to calling that sort of person a 'woman in Woolworths,' or 'man' as the case might be. But it was very rare. We might have run into it oftener if we'd had to find a flat—I've heard of couples like us having that kind of difficulty. But we had the flat my father left me, so for us it didn't matter. As for our neighbours, they were fascinated by us and almost fought each other for the privilege of asking us in for coffee. We had nice neighbours."

"They had not seen many Indian people?"

"Yes, plenty. There's a fair-sized community in Croydon. But I don't think they'd met many Indians socially before. Just seen them in the streets and the shops. The communities live apart, on the whole."

"It was like that here during the Raj, I think," said Arwinder. She passed Melanie a cloth in which to wrap the chapattis. "Most of us must seem so strange to most of you. It was brave of you to marry Avtar, Melanie."

"Was it? I don't think it was. It just seemed inevitable. Have we got everything?"

"I think so." Arwinder piled plates and spoons on a tray. "Let's go up. I still think it was brave of you to marry Avtar and come here so far away from your home. I hope you have never regretted it."

"Good heavens," said Melanie heartily, "no!"

∽

Avtar did not come home till midnight. The power was still off and he slipped into a pitch-dark room, trying not to bump

52

into things. Unnecessarily, because in the airless heat, Melanie was still awake.

"Sorry, I disturbed you."

"I'm too hot to sleep. Where did you get to?"

"Over half Chandigarh," said Avtar wearily, shedding clothes into a dark heap by his divan bed. "There was an ectopic pregnancy to get to hospital and then I rushed off again on an emergency call to see a child with scald burns. Overturned a pan of hot water in the kitchen. You grumble about our pans with no handles, but they're safer with children about. This household had some *with* handles and the child caught hold of one and pulled. It was a little girl. She'll be scarred."

"Have you eaten?"

"No. Don't want to, either."

She recognised his mood. Too wound up to eat, too exhausted, paradoxically, to sleep. She moved onto his divan as he lay down and put her arms round him. It was not a sexual advance, but a kindly embrace which could sometimes ease the tautness when he was like this, and help him rest. But tonight it was too hot. Skin in contact with skin burst into a slippery sweat at once. They drew apart.

Rehal

Avtar's family had lived in Chandigarh and its surrounding districts for generations, since long before Chandigarh was built into a town. His father and his grandfather had been doctors, the grandfather a homeopathic practitioner. Earlier generations had been farmers, raising grain and vegetables and herding buffalo on the broad Punjabi plains. Most of Melanie's ancestors had been farmers too, but they were not as respectable as Avtar's. Melanie could trace her origins back as far as an eighteenth-century ancestor called Gavin Purvis, and Gavin had been, quite simply, notorious.

There was a full-length portrait of him in Gran's study

at Gavin's Cliff; it was one of the few things rescued when the original house burned down just before Gran was born. Gavin was a type. His hazel eyes surveyed the world coolly from under brows mounted on expressive mounds of muscle. His cheekbones would not have shamed a Sioux Indian, and his concave profile with its flaring nostrils and the short upper lip below did nothing to contradict the traditional assessment of him, which was that he was arrogant, over-sexed, and unscrupulous.

Gavin had appeared out of nowhere sometime during the last quarter of the eighteenth century, riding into Hever-ton with a full wallet and at once beginning negotiations for the sixteenth-century farmhouse which then stood up on the cliff beyond the headland. He had settled at the Cliff, as it was called in those days before he gave his own name to it. He married a girl called Arabella, the daughter of a local farmer. He then proceeded to dig himself into the life of the locality. His method of going about this included frequent visits to the *Fishing Boat,* the tavern by the harbour. In the twentieth century, the *Fishing Boat* had become the re-spectable haunt of holidaymakers to whom it virtuously refused to sell the potent local draught cider, for fear that unaccustomed heads would get belligerent on it. But in Gavin's day it had had a bad name. There were obliging wenches there, and in an upper room there was gambling for high stakes by the lively young men of Heverton.

Gavin was among the liveliest and most popular. He was popular with the obliging wenches—the Miller family up at Stancross Farm above Amberscombe were said to be his descendants too, through the medium of a *Fishing Boat* girl—and with his fellow gamblers. He also gained approval for a more admirable reason. On learning that Heverton was liable to visitations from the press gangs, and that the lads of the town were in the habit of taking refuge in the woods of Heverton Point, he offered them hospitality at his home if they needed shelter in wild weather. This arrangement lasted for some time and did much for Gavin's reputation, until he chose to shatter both arrangement and reputation simultaneously. At a time when, after several years of marriage, Arabella was at last expecting their first child and he himself was embarrassed by heavy gambling losses in the *Fishing Boat,* he sold his secret out to the press gang. They swooped on the Cliff one windy night and took away ten ablebodied Heverton boys for enforced service in the navy.

It would have been better for Gavin had they taken eleven. The eleventh dived out of a pantry window and escaped into the woods. Three nights later, a party of men, heavily masked, marched up the long red-earth path between the pines and the sycamores and the stunted oak, forced their way into the house and the drawing room where Gavin and Arabella were sitting, and overpowered Gavin. They pushed the protesting Arabella out of the way, telling her shortly not to interfere with men's business, took Gavin outside, and shot him.

Arabella, evidently a young woman of spirit, clearly considered that, whatever her husband's shortcomings, to tell a woman more than eight months pregnant that the death of her breadwinner was none of her business was an impertinence not to be borne. As the firing squad prepared to leave, Arabella leant out of an upstairs window and discharged a blast from the gun that Gavin had used for shooting wildfowl. She killed two of the party outright and injured a third, and in the ensuing confusion their identities emerged as relatives of the lads who had been seized three days before. Arabella herself was flung to the floor by the recoil and the second Purvis, Gavin's son, William, was born that night, delivered by the housekeeper.

No action was ever taken against anyone involved. The moral and legal implications were confused to say the least of it, and Arabella maintained that she had imagined her husband's assailants to be a band of robbers. She lived to be old, and reared her son at their home, which now began to be known as Gavin's Cliff. She was Melanie's ancestress.

With such colourful antecedents, it was to be expected that the Purvis family would be people of character. After Gavin's day they were perfectly law abiding, but they had a strong unconventional streak and were physically courageous. This they turned to good account in respect of the cove at the foot of the cliff, which because of the currents which set into it, and the unpleasant range of rocks which guarded it, and were locally known as the Fangs, was frequently the scene of shipwrecks. The Purvis men were Auxiliary Coastguards as a matter of course from the day the Auxiliaries were formed, and Gavin's Cliff rapidly became a semi-official reception station for sailors rescued from the Gavin's Cove rocks. A tradition grew up, under which the Purvises claimed a souvenir lifebelt from every ship that they assisted.

That traditional connection with the sea still survived. As a child, Melanie could remember being at Gavin's Cliff during a storm, when men were brought in from a wrecked trawler, and she knew that Gran kept a supply of blankets and first-aid equipment against such emergencies. She knew too that he had for a short time, as a young man, been an Auxiliary himself, even though his own interest in the sea was marginal.

His interest in farming, until then the proper business of all Purvis eldest or only sons, had been more marginal still. In Gran, some unlikely permutation of the genes had thrown up a personality quite unlike anything in the family's previous history. It was not, his father was said to have declared grimly, merely that he had not got green fingers. Gran's fingers appeared to be actually infected with blight and aphids. No growing thing throve which was left in his care. But he was bright at his books, and his headmaster said it was worth sending him to university. The result of that was Professor William Purvis, anthropologist, who came to Gavin's Cliff for vacations and then permanently after retirement, but sold off its farmland to the Heatons at Whitehangers, a mile and a half further along the coast.

There was a curious duality in the Purvis nature, of which Gran was a striking example. He was simultaneously a lover of his home, and a born traveller. Researching, he had roamed from Tibet to the Australian outback, yet Gavin's Cliff constantly recalled him. His duality also showed itself in another way, for his two wives could hardly have been less alike. The first, Daniel Purvis's mother, came from a farm in Cornwall and was a sturdy, practical country-woman. She had found Gran a bewildering kind of spouse and eventually divorced him. The second, Leonard Purvis's mother, was a qualified librarian from Hampshire, and was exceedingly bookish. That union was successful and lasted until she died. The dissimilarity of the two women certainly accounted for the almost weird dissimilarity of Daniel, owner of the Ambersford Hunting Stables, and Leonard, manager of Hallowens.

The same duality was in Melanie, although in her it developed late. As a child, she was unusually singleminded. After he and Melanie left Ambersford, Leonard Purvis found it impossible to keep her from making frequent visits to what she still considered to be her home. After an initial resistance, he gave in. They went twice yearly; at Easter for a long weekend, and in summer for two weeks. They went by road, and the journey became a ritual.

∽

It usually started at about four A.M., sometimes in darkness. Melanie loved leaving the house during that silent time when everyone else was asleep. They would drive off through empty roads with the cats' eyes unreeling like a shining thread along the macadam labyrinth and the wayside trees like ghosts of themselves in the white headlights. They would leave with empty stomachs except for a cup of coffee, and at about six o'clock they would reach Basingstoke. There they would have breakfast in a small cafe which they had discovered, where eggs and bacon were served at dawn to people coming off shift in nearby factories.

That cafe became a symbol to Melanie, a sign that they were on their way and would see Ambersford that day. After the cafe, her sense of urgency—which had been responsible for the practice of leaving at four in the first place—would subside and she would enjoy the rest of the drive for itself. They usually stopped at Stonehenge for coffee and biscuits and sometimes for a stroll round the monument, and then they would drive on through the second half of the journey, dropping from Salisbury Plain into the lowland part of Somerset, passing through Glastonbury and on to Taunton or Bridgwater, choosing either route impartially, until the hills rose and the valleys deepened and in the distance they saw the first gleam of the Bristol Channel and the outlines of the distant heights of Exmoor.

As soon as she was old enough, she acquired a driving licence and shared the wheel on these trips. This went on till she was twenty, when her father had the first of the heart attacks which presaged his end. He gave up driving then. He gave up the west country too. But Melanie was welcome to the car, he said. Thereafter, she made the journeys alone, except for two occasions.

One was the time she took Robin to Somerset and found that he disliked it. The other was when she took Avtar. It was with the arrival of Avtar in her life that the other side of her nature awoke. He talked of India, of wide and dusty skylines and bullock carts and white houses and flat roofs and drenching sunshine and Melanie, kindling, desired to see these things.

At one point it seemed that the two sides of her personality were going to pull her in half. The last journey of all that she made to the west country, just before they flew out to Delhi, she made on her own despite Avtar's protests. She went on her own because she did not want him to see what it would do to her. Leaving it, she had to pull off the road five miles outside Ambersford and sit there for half an hour, because she was half-blind with crying and could not see to drive.

～

The weekend brought the first wave of wedding guests. The Patels came from Bombay: husband, wife, husband's younger brother, four children. Soon after them came Aunt Prem, large and soft and exotically perfumed, her small dapper husband, Ram Bhawan, and three teenage sons. This incursion was followed shortly by the eldest Bhawan son and the two Bhawan daughters, all with spouses and offspring. The age range of the children in the house now went from adolescent to toddler and the house vibrated to the thunder of youthful feet and youthful shouting, laughter, and shrieks. "I shall never disentangle whose children are whose," Melanie said to Arwinder. "I daren't call any of them by name in case it's the wrong one."

The Patels had also brought two servants, a man and wife who instantly took charge of the cooking, a complex task in a house so crowded that food had to be served in shifts, and so variegated by religious dietary restrictions. The Sikhs were mostly omnivorous, but the Patels were Hindu and vegetarian except that they would eat eggs, while Aunt Prem and her daughter-in-law were also Hindu and were strict, refusing to eat even cakes with eggs in the mixture. (In England, Rehal had taken enthusiastically to eating meat, which was another cause for head shaking in his family.) When Sita and Kalu, therefore, with palms pressed humbly together and deprecating movements of the head, made it clear to Bheji that with all possible deference to her position as lady of the house they had no intention of letting her into her own kitchen, Bheji said: "What a relief!" and plunged instead into another demanding task: seeing that the sleeping accommodations would go round.

Her methods were simple and also efficient. Ladies and small children went into her and Arwinder's room; males into Surinder's. Any overflow would have to camp in the sitting room, which now contained a couple of extra divans. Bags, baskets, and suitcases began to proliferate amid the furniture, and Leela, after a few ineffectual dabs with her broom, unaffectedly gave up trying. The only sacrosanct room was that shared by Melanie and Avtar. A doctor was a paradoxical being who needed all the undisturbed rest he could get, and also needed a phone at his elbow when he was taking the aforesaid rest so that he could be summoned back to work at a moment's notice. Either way, intruders were unthinkable.

Melanie made a few more halfhearted attempts at design work and then gave up in favour of the Sangeet wall decorations. She found even that an effort. The heat was draining her vitality. The continuing power cuts were also a nuisance. They had a diabolical knack of occurring at awkward moments: just as ten people sat down to a late evening meal, or just as Melanie had washed her hair and settled down to dry it under a fan because the sun outside was too hot. When it happened in the midst of a semiformal viewing of the saris and jewellery which constituted Arwin's dowry, and the room was packed with guests, the failure of the fan instantly converted the place into a breathless hothouse, causing Aunt Prem to remark to Aunt Asha that she could not imagine what life had been like before there was any electricity at all, and Aunt Asha, wiping her forehead, to tell Balwant to prop the door more widely open "and open the door across the landing too. More air circulation we must have."

"I've already done that," said a strange male voice from the threshold, in flawless English. "I looked at it as I came up the stairs and thought, *Whew!* What a temperature! The bus which brought me to Chandigarh was nothing but an oven on wheels."

Everyone turned. Balwant, halfway to the door, veered apologetically away, pulling her sari round to shield her face. Arwinder's friend Nirmal, who was curled on a divan beside Arwinder, an embroidered sari half-unfolded in her lap, said: "Oh!" and looked fixedly down at the peacock silk between her fingers. Arwinder leapt off the divan and flung herself into the stranger's arms with a joyful shriek of "Rehal!"

"Hallo, all," said Rehal, patting his cousin, helpfully

kicking the doorstop into a better position, and then moving forward to embrace his relatives in rapid succession. "I got here, you see. I landed in Delhi yesterday and travelled on this morning. Mother, you look lovely. Father, it's good to see you . . . who's this, not my little niece Dili? I don't believe it, you can't have grown so much. Hallo, Avtar, still a busy G.P. And of course, this is Melanie . . ."

To Melanie he gave his right hand, Western-style, and the handshake itself was strong and uninhibited. He had thick blue-black hair and skin the colour of copper, and he had switched from English to Punjabi. But he carried with him an atmosphere as headily European as tobacco smoke or fish and chips. As well as being distinctive, the aura was also overpowering. Balwant had receded from it at once, retreating to the back of the gathering, where she was quietly refolding some of Arwin's spread-out saris. Nirmal too was moving unobtrusively into a corner. Bheji stopped that.

"Nirmal, you and Arwin fetch us all some cool drinks. Don't let Sita bring them, she runs up and down stairs too much these days. Bring lime juice and some campa cola, and hand them round. You remember Nirmal?" she added to Rehal as the girls went out. "Arwin's friend? She is studying for B.A. now. English language is involved; since you are a journalist in English, you must talk to her about it. Her parents are so pleased with her. She will have an even bigger dowry than Arwin's when she is married."

"Indeed?" said Rehal courteously, as he took a seat on the nearest divan. There was a silence. Rehal's eldest sister and Mrs. Patel started to speak at the same moment and stopped. Rehal's father regarded his son with disapproval and cleared his throat. "Well, how is life in London these days,

Rehal? You have the same house still, in Southall? You write for a living but not often enough to us. Tell us, what work you are doing now?"

◦

"But I cannot see," said Rehal's father, Ram Bhawan, half an hour later in the persistent voice of one who feels he hasn't made himself clear and is obliged to press on until he has, "how an Indian journalist in a foreign land can detach himself from being Indian. He must all the time want to put the Indian point of view."

Arwin, sipping campa beside Melanie, whispered: "No sooner Rehal is inside the door than we have argument. Sometimes the family begins it, but he encourages them. I wish he wouldn't."

Melanie smiled without replying. To her, it was stimulating.

It was even nostalgic. This kind of conflict had been a constant part of the society at Gavin's Cliff, but she rarely encountered it here, at least in the feminine circles where she spent most of her time. The argument had begun to develop within a few moments of Rehal beginning to talk about his work. Nirmal's return to the room had effectively kept the subject from shifting or being shifted back to the matter of Rehal and herself, yet that question, already hinted at by Bheji, was waiting to emerge, and it was certainly the reason why Ram Bhawan was now nearly making an attack upon his son.

If Rehal were to be steered into a conventional Indian marriage, Ram was implying, he must first be made to recognise that he was a conventional Indian man.

Only the son, sitting ankle over knee, campa glass in left hand while he gesticulated with his right, the glitter of

64

battle in his diamond-shaped eyes, had not the slightest intention of being made to recognise anything, unless he chose. On the contrary . . .

"A journalist's first duty," he said firmly, "is to be objective. Besides, my chief subject is economics. That doesn't change much, East or West."

Mr. Patel leaned forward to join in. "But Rehal, you must surely feel you should use your talents to promote the interests of your fellow countrymen in England where we hear there is so much prejudice."

"But what you are saying, and what my father is saying, is that when I write I should do so as though I were a kind of public relations department for the Indian community in Britain. But if I do that, where is my objectivity? I should have to pretend to be 'pro' the Indian community all the time."

"Pretend?" said Ram Bhawan.

"Yes, pretend. Because I don't always necessarily agree with them. And I can't tell lies with a pen in my hand."

Aunt Asha, sitting on a hard chair by the window which led on to the roof of the one-storey kitchen, turned from opening the window wider. "You have grown too westernised, Rehal. Now, when my father visited England as a young man, he took with him supplies of ghee and chapatti flour and lived as an Indian all the time. I think that is right."

"I think it's insular," said Rehal. Balwant raised her eyes from her self-imposed task of tidying Arwin's dowry wardrobe, and gave him a glance of sheer astonishment. Arwin smothered a chuckle. "When visiting someone else's country, one should make a few adaptations," Rehal said. His eyes rested on Avtar's short hair and Melanie's cotton sari. "Or you may create prejudice instead of soothing it.

For me, I feel I can achieve more by being a journalist first and an Indian afterwards. It takes people's minds off my foreignness and encourages them to listen to what I am actually saying. Melanie"—his eyes had scanned the room again but this time paused when they reached her—"you listen with great interest, but what are you thinking? Tell us your opinion."

"I think," said Melanie, "that it would have been rude of me not to make some adaptations since I am living here. So I wear Indian clothes here and eat Indian food."

The expressive blankness of Aunt Asha's face made it clear that in her opinion, people should remain where they did not need such chameleon antics. Avtar looked mildly irritated. He always slightly disliked it when his wife drew the attention of another male. He said: "You have not altered so much, Melanie. It's on the surface only, with you. You are as English as you ever were, half a millimetre down. With Rehal, I think the change goes deeper."

"Maybe," said Rehal. He glanced once to where Nirmal was opening a fresh lime juice bottle. Her head was averted. Melanie studied his face while he was not looking at her and thought that Avtar was right. Rehal had classically Indian features, with slightly pointed ears and a faunlike smile. But his expression, the lines at the corners of mouth and eyes, were indubitably Western. It was the result, perhaps, of thinking and talking as his fellow journalists in Fleet Street did. Despite his defiant haircut, Avtar's face with its long almond eyes and moulded bronze cheekbones still possessed the Oriental calm characteristic of Eastern art from the Nile Valley to Nepal. First thing in the morning, with nothing on but a towel wrapped round his loins, Avtar might have stepped straight off the wall of a pyramid. Rehal would never look like that.

"Listen," Rehal was saying, "it's a matter of self-defence as well as conviction. I have actually been picked on in the street in a London suburb—by picked on I mean subjected to rude remarks, ruder gestures, and the threat of imminent violence—by a bunch of disagreeable youths with crewcuts. There were six of them and only one of me and their complaint, apparently, was that I looked too different from them. Being outnumbered, I had to run for it, which was undignified. I jumped on a bus which was just pulling away from some traffic lights. What made me really furious was that the rude remarks were couched in the most execrable English. If I can speak the language properly . . . can I, Melanie?"

He was using English again now. "Yes, very much so," Melanie said.

". . . if I can speak the language properly when I only started to learn it at the age of ten, then people who were born to it ought to be able to speak it properly too. I say that to make it clear that I don't feel in the least forgiving about those youths. But I could see the mechanics of what was happening. Noticeable differences breed prejudice. The fewer the obvious differences, the less the conflict. The human race has this disastrous habit of banding into troups and flinging missiles at other troups which don't precisely resemble the first one . . ."

"It sounds," said Melanie, "as though you've been reading my grandfather's book."

"*The Organic Computer*? I have. Have you, Father? You, Mr. Patel?"

They shook their heads. Arwin said: "Melanie has a copy but I am shamed to say I have not read it. You must lend it to me, Melanie. Does it say something about . . . troups, was it?"

"What it says," said Avtar, "although to my way of thinking it goes too far, is that human beings are what they are because they are descended from troup-dwelling anthropoids. Melanie's grandfather thinks that this accounts for the instinct to band into groups and engage in rivalry with other groups, and also to train or program their young to believe that the home group is right and the rest are all wrong. Where he went too far in my view was in saying that all political parties, religions, or even clubs—"

" '*Labour versus Conservative, Christianity versus Islam, and Sunderland versus Sheffield United,*' " quoted Rehal. " '*are all manifestations of the same group mentality.*' When I read that for the first time, I was on an underground train. I laughed so much that I went straight past my stop."

"It is quite wrong," said Aunt Asha decisively. She had been listening with deepening indignation. "Quite wrong. People should not think in that kind of way. It is saying we are just animals and tradition does not matter."

"And does it?" asked Rehal.

Aunt Prem, Mrs. Patel, and Aunt Asha all simultaneously burst into speech. As when Rehal had first arrived, the voices attempting to retrieve the situation became entangled and stopped. Rehal said calmly: "Because a thing has been done a certain way in the past is no reason why it should always be done that way. The criterion should be: Which does a tradition contribute to the most—human happiness or human misery? If the latter, away with it."

Balwant, who had been silent for a long time, her task completed, suddenly put out a small hand and touched Melanie's arm. Turning, Melanie saw a deep crease between the luminous brown eyes. Balwant's other hand was pressed against her temple. "I am so sorry," Balwant whispered.

"But it is so hot in here. I have a migraine. Melanie, could I lie down for a little?"

⌒

"Take these two tablets," Melanie said, tiptoeing into the darkened room. "Avtar gave them to me for you. They'll ease the pain and help you to sleep. How do you feel now?"

Balwant was lying on her back, one wrist over her forehead. "Not so bad, now I am lying down. I am very sorry, but the heat made me dizzy and then this pain began."

"Well, swallow these. I've brought some water."

"Thank you." Balwant sat up cautiously. "What a bold young man that cousin of Arwin's is. How he answered my Bheji back. Did you notice? He has made her cross, I think."

"She'll get over it," said Melanie. "Now go to sleep. Your head will be better when you wake."

An Attack of the Occidentals

"Melanie, that looks so nice," said Arwinder, surveying with pleasure the effect of Melanie's decorations on the wall of the Sangeet room. "What wonders you have done with some shiny coloured paper and a pair of scissors. I hardly recognise the room, even."

The bedroom, which a short time ago had been a crowded muddle of divans, baggage, and the personal clutter of nine or ten female guests, had been miraculously transformed. Sweating, heaving, and from time to time colourfully cursing, Kalu (whose skeletal physique concealed a surprising amount of strength), Rehal, and Rehal's younger brothers had shoved all the furniture and miscellaneous

70

belongings out onto the kitchen roof. Over the floor of the room they had spread clean white sheets. Anyone wishing to enter thereafter left their footwear at the door. Tacked into place round the walls were Melanie's contributions. The idea that would not burgeon as a fabric design had done so for the Sangeet. Melanie had used a strong, gleaming paper in primary colours, from which to cut arches with tapering apexes. Framed in each were silhouette figures. In the first was a girl with trailing skirts and downbent head. In the second stood a young man with sword and turban. In the third both were shown, walking to meet each other. In the fourth, they were seated side by side and musicians with tinsel sitars attended them. Then the sequence was repeated. The figures were three feet high and the sequence repeated only three times round the walls. Melanie had gone for boldness. Above the arches was a frivolous frieze of elephants, prancing in single file, each trunk holding the tail of the animal in front. "The elephants are *lovely*," said Arwinder.

"Those arches," said Rehal, prowling round the room with a hammer, to make sure that all the tacks were firm. "You've used the Taj shape, haven't you, Melanie? It's Moghul, anyway. Most effective."

"You're right, it's the Taj." Melanie surveyed her handi-work—not without satisfaction—as the first of the Sangeet guests were heard on the stairs. She had gone away from it in order to change, and on returning had herself been im-pressed by the effect when the room was viewed from the doorway. "I had some photographs to work from, though I could almost have done it from memory. It's such an in-credible building that it prints itself on the mind. It gave me a tremendous shock when I first saw it."

"A shock?" Arwinder asked. "I have seen it once. I thought it was such a sad place. Shah Jehan must have loved his wife so much to build her such a memorial. I didn't like thinking of him dying a prisoner on the other side of the river, where he could only just catch a glimpse of her Taj. They might have put him somewhere where he could see it clearly. But shocking . . . no, that I don't understand."

"It was sad as well," said Melanie, raising a hand to greet Balbir and Nirmal as they came in together with Aunt Prem. "It was full of atmosphere. You could almost feel them, down in the crypt where their tombs are. But the shock is something else . . . I meant an architectural shock. It's the proportions, I think. That double line of white columns that leads to it makes the eye expect something at the end that's been dwindled by distance. Instead, you get the Taj on its plinth, rising up at you, huge and powerful. I could hardly get over it. Avtar says I didn't utter a word afterwards for four hours, all the way from Agra back to Delhi . . . I didn't come back to earth till we met an elephant. That's the elephant, in the frieze."

"But Auntie!" That was Dili, Aunt Prem's eldest granddaughter, eleven years old and acutely interested in all the preparations (just beginning, Aunt Prem had said fondly, to think of how her own marriage would one day be). "You had seen elephants before. They are in London Zoo, aren't they?" Dili had danced into the room behind her grandmother and was now hopping excitedly from one foot to the next, as the arrivals gathered round Melanie and Arwinder, murmuring their admiration of the room.

"Yes, I'd seen them in London," Melanie said, seeing that everyone was interested in her answer. "But they were curiosities, not everyday working elephants. The elephant outside Delhi was plodding along under a load of hay so enormous that it looked like a colossal haystack on four big grey legs. And there was a diplomatic limousine doing five

miles an hour behind it. We all laughed! I always think of
elephants in the same breath as the Taj now. So there they
are, up on the wall above the arches."

"You've made a very quick job of it," said Rehal. "There
are just the sandalwood tapers to put in place now, and then
we boys will leave you ladies to your party. It's all parties
when someone's getting married, isn't it?" He grinned at
Arwinder. "I hear your female guests are even going to have
a special one the day before the wedding for making the
garlands. Arwin, where did you put those tapers?"

∽

The Sangeet was almost an Indian equivalent of a stag party,
except that it was a hen party and strictly nonalcoholic.
There would be about fifty guests at this one. They would
sit on the white sheeting and Arwinder would sit enthroned
on cushions in their midst. Then they would sing to her,
songs to put a bride in the right mood for marriage. There
would be lighthearted innuendo and much laughter, for if
some of the songs were sacred, others were romantic or
broadly comic. The menfolk would stay as far out of
earshot as possible. They were quite aware that if they were
to bug the Sangeet, they would be considerably startled and
quite possibly shocked.

The guests were arriving now in force, a constant
stream of festive colour on the stairs, led up by Bheji and
Aunt Prem in turns. Aunt Asha arrived, doing honour to
the occasion with ivory brocade, and at her heels walked a
very beautiful young woman in a powder blue sari, whom
Melanie at first completely failed to recognise until Dili,
giggling, said: "Oh, Auntie! That's Auntie Balwant!" and
Balwant laughed.

Today Balwant did not look as though she knew the

73

meaning of the word migraine. The powder blue silk changed her, taking away the queer taboo look of the white mourning garments. She had a little blue on her eyelids and under it her eyes were more huge and lustrous than ever. There was a subtle alteration in her personality too. Her back was straighter, and her walk more confident.

The aromatic fumes of sandalwood began to pervade the room; Rehal had set the tapers and lit them. He strolled to the door and paused, to make sure that all of them were burning properly. Satisfied, he rested a hand on the doorpost while he retrieved his footwear from the growing heap on the threshold and said: "Our efforts have been worthwhile, Melanie. The room's a success." Balwant, whose eye had been caught by the frieze of elephants, turned from them and said shyly: "Are these the decorations that Melanie made? I like them so much," and smiled directly at Rehal.

Afterwards, Melanie remembered that moment as though it were in three dimensions, standing out from surroundings which were flat. She remembered how on Rehal's forearm, bared because he had rolled the sleeves of his white shirt up above the elbow, the muscle suddenly stood out like steel cord as he braced himself against the doorpost. She remembered the black hairs on the brown skin. She remembered that a light appeared to come on behind his eyes as they took in this new and exquisite Balwant, and that Balwant's own widening gaze responded, growing still larger and more lambent as she observed the shapeliness of that arm and of the hand on the doorpost, and interpreted the message in his face. Her smile faltered and a small hand came up to draw the blue sari further over her smooth head, as if to shade her eyes from the sun. There was a tiny tremor in the hand.

Oh no, Melanie thought. No, no, I am imagining it. It

is not as it was for me and Avtar in front of the Indian paintings in Hallowens that day. It is not . . .

Not love at first sight, no. That was a romantic cliché. What had happened in Hallowens—and what was now happening here—was infinitely harder and stronger, more fundamental than that. It was recognition, perhaps pre-cognition. It was the resounding certainty that the person at whom you were looking, perhaps seeing for the first time, was part of you. It was as though you remembered the future. Melanie·had experienced it, and Melanie could not now be deceived.

Furthermore, Bheji had seen it. Smoothly, she had moved between Balwant and Rehal. "Rehal, this is Balwant, Aunt Asha's daughter-in-law. Her son's widow. She was here when you arrived but in the crowd I think you were not intro-duced. Melanie, I think we can start. Only a few are still to come. You have been so helpful, Rehal. Go and see Arwin; she wants to thank you. Balwant, dear, come and sit down."

Rehal was already moving away, accepting a tactful dismissal. Melanie took her own place on the white sheeting, mind spinning. Had she seen what she believed she had? Had Bheji believed it too or was that socially graceful in-tervention just by chance? Rehal had gone. All the men had gone. The ladies were settling down amid a buzz of small talk, and Bheji, seated in the middle of the room, was beginning to tap out a rhythm on a small drum. Nirmal was accepting compliments on what Melanie now observed to be an exceptionally elegant sari, and somewhere to Melanie's left, a voice was remarking amusedly: "Well, of course, *Rehal*'s home . . ."

Melanie suddenly remembered that when Rehal arrived, though he had not taken Balwant in, she had probably had a good look at him. And there had been hints of a marriage negotiation between him and Nirmal, and at the same time they had all been looking at Arwinder's trousseau. And then Balwant had been struck down with migraine.

No, she had not imagined that atomic encounter.

Poor Balwant. And poor Nirmal.

⌒

Arwinder had fifty-seven guests for her Sangeet at the final count, and they covered the white floor like a garden of vivid, scented, silk-petalled flowers. Arwin, still in her old clothes and still beautiful in spite of them, sat cross-legged on her stack of cushions, the only person in the room not singing, clapping, or gossiping, and tried not very successfully to look shy. The little hand drums which beat out the rhythm for the songs tapped gently and persistently below the voices. Bheji had one; Aunt Prem had produced another and had sent it passing from hand to hand round the company. Nirmal had it now. Sita moved to and fro with offers of cold drinks, stepping over the feet and spreading skirts of the guests. "This is fine party," said one of Melanie's neighbours in her ear, a girl she did not know. "My Sangeet was not so big. We have not met, I think. I was married and moved away from Chandigarh just before you came. We are visiting my parents just now. I have a baby son and another baby coming. How many children have you got?"

Indian women invariably put it that way. They did not enquire if you had children; they merely asked how many. Melanie had had to harden herself to it at first. Later, she had grown used to it. "We haven't any," she said. "I can't have them." And then added, forestalling the next question: "Avtar doesn't mind. He's a doctor and he sees so much poverty and overcrowding in his work. He says that to have too many children is far worse than having none."

"Oh, but it must be very sad for you," said her neighbour with sympathy.

"One gets accustomed. There are sadder things," said Melanie.

She was watching one. Bheji had passed her drum now to Aunt Prem, and Aunt Prem and Nirmal, with a drum each, had embarked on a comic duet. For the moment they had become a mother and daughter-in-law who disliked each other. Glowering with a histrionic verve which Melanie had never seen bettered even at the Old Vic, they were singing acid and hilarious comments into each other's faces while the rest sang with them, now and then dissolving into laughter. Nirmal was letting herself go, speaking her dreams through the licence of this day. One day I shall be a daughter-in-law too. And there will be a Sangeet for me, and my friends will sing this song—but only for fun—for perhaps I shall be saying *Bheji* to Aunt Prem, and I shall say it with affection for we like each other. And anyway, if I marry Rehal I shall live far away, in London. To live with Rehal . . . Rehal . . .

And in all probability it would come true. Rehal would not be allowed to have Balwant. The family, kindly, loving, and completely determined, would gather round him like white corpuscles round a potentially dangerous virus and steer him in the direction in which they thought he ought to go, to Nirmal. And Balwant knew it. She was sitting against the wall, near Arwinder. She too was watching the performance in the middle of the room and she too understood it.

⌒

Living in a country, in a culture which was not her own, Melanie was accustomed now and then to experience a

77

phenomenon which to herself she called an Attack of the Occidentals. It had descended on her for the first time at that dreadful initial meeting with the family in Delhi. Since then it had made occasional comebacks, like recurrent malaria. It was a sense of alienation, an acute awareness of being half a world away from her physical homeland and several whole worlds away from her mental one. She was conscious of being a European among Indians, her mind as different from theirs as was her build and her skin. She felt, even, as though her heavy Anglo-Saxon bones were growing, as if she were turning into something huge and obvious and out of place, like a hippopotamus or a giraffe. It was happening now.

She murmured something to her neighbour, about the heat. She got up. People often grew stiff, sitting on the floor, and wandered out to stretch; no one would take any notice. She trod on the hem of her sari (one of the symptoms of the Occidentals was a sudden inability to manage Indian dress, and a tendency to burn one's fingers when using them to eat with), stumbled and apologised, and got herself out of the room.

On the landing she stopped to listen. From below came a muttering of male voices; the men were keeping what was no doubt a bored vigil downstairs. She did not want their company, either. She turned to her own room. There she could be alone.

There were two unopened airmail letters on her bedside table: today's post which she had had no time to look at yet. She would look at it now. She sank into the basket chair, and picked up the top letter.

It was from her friend Jane Hanworth in London. Jane was a well-dressed and well-paid secretary employed by a firm of iron and steel importers. She was in her thirties, unmarried but apparently content to stay that way. She was extremely attractive and had had numerous men friends, and presumably found that sufficient. Her letter was like its writer —good-humoured, impersonal, just a little astringent—a nice relief from the sultry atmosphere now gathering round Balwant and Rehal. Jane wrote of amusing people encountered on a coach tour in Yugoslavia, and of the latest government proposals for a new immigration policy, which had caused a demonstration which in turn had caused Jane to be late for a conference because, said Jane with suitable detachment, it blocked the road along which she wished to drive to get there. She was no longer seeing the advertising executive who had been her steady companion for the last eighteen months, but now she had an interest in another direction. More of that later, said Jane. She would tell Melanie all about it in her next letter if the relationship prospered.

Melanie grinned. Typical Jane. She took up the other letter. This was from Frances, giving family and local news. Molly, Frances's daughter, had won a swimming prize at school. Up at Stancross Farm, Sheila Miller had had an illegitimate baby. ". . . quite a feat, considering what that old father of hers is like. He could have taught Barrett of Wimpole Street something, or that's what your grandfather says," said Frances. That was the authentic voice of Ambersford as well as Gran: inquisitive but not censorious, regarding Sheila's unpremeditated motherhood as a tribute to her spirit and resourcefulness in evading her disagreeable parent, rather than as a sign of moral downfall. Melanie vaguely remembered Sheila at school; she had even been to the farm to play with her once or twice—a downtrodden sort of girl with frizzy fair hair and an expression older than her years. She turned the page. They had had a wet summer and

79

Old Harry, the bog on the moor above Stancross, was threatening to overflow. Disquieting. But the end of the letter was more disquieting still. "Your grandfather hasn't been so well lately. He seems to be having digestive trouble again. He says it's nothing, that it runs in the family, but he has agreed to go into Heverton Hospital for a check-up. He says he'll write to you himself presently. . . ."

Melanie put the letter down. Gran was . . . what? . . . eighty? It was always worrying when the word *hospital* arose in connection with someone of that age. The digestive weakness was a family failing, yes. Melanie had suffered from it as a result of sheer nerves when she first came to India, and had raised Bheji's hopes considerably as a result. In all likelihood, this illness of Gran's meant nothing.

She shook herself. The next news would probably be that Gran was back in Gavin's Cliff, having been in the hospital, put on a diet, bullied his friends into smuggling him all the things he wasn't supposed to eat, and then confounded medical opinion by getting better anyhow. It was silly to feel so anxious. She should pull herself together and go back to the Sangeet.

She raised her head, listening. She could hear the singing and the drum music from across the landing. But there was nothing there to assuage her unease. It could not soothe her as Western music could; its cadences were not recorded in her genes; she had no race memory of it. Nor, in the face of Balwant's unhappiness, could she wholly rejoice in its purpose.

She did not go back to the Sangeet. She shut the door instead, to keep the music out. Then she sat turning Frances's letter over in her hands, longing to see one come addressed in Gran's own writing, and wishing uselessly that she could be with him, in Gavin's Cliff, at home.

Marigold Garlands

On the night after the Sangeet there was another prolonged power cut, and Rehal rebelled. He had been trying to write a letter at the time, he said, and had had to finish it by candlelight, which made his head ache. "Arwinder's friends are holding their garland-making party tonight," he pointed out. "What if the lights go out in the middle of all that? And what about the rest of us? We'll be all over the house finding odd jobs to do. A blackout we just can't put up with. I'm going to do something about it."

"Oh, we are all used to these things," Arwinder said with amusement, across the breakfast table. "You have forgotten what India is like."

"And I don't propose to tolerate the reminder. Wait and see."

He then departed into town in a rickshaw, and returned that afternoon in a taxi, so heavily laden that the back axle sagged visibly under the weight. He and the taxi driver unloaded a mass of equipment ("Hired," said Rehal, in answer to astonished questions), including large portable batteries, portable lights of the footlight variety, and several enormous rolls of cable. "We'll need to take all this upstairs," Rehal said.

Melanie, roused from a siesta by an escalating uproar outside, pulled on a dress and wandered out to the kitchen roof to discover what the noise was about. She looked down on a scene of confusion. Rehal's arrival had coincided, it seemed, with the arrival of the caterer's men who were bringing in trays of sweetmeats and crates of soft drinks, and the deliverymen who were bringing the sacks of marigold heads for making garlands. The electricians who were to festoon the front of the house with fairy lights were already there, and the drive and hallway were an obstacle course of ladders and boxes. Rehal was loudly requesting the removal of a ladder, a sack, and several crates of coke from his path to enable his gear to be carried in, while an indignant chorus in mingled Punjabi, Urdu, and English protested that they had only put them there just this minute. As Melanie watched, Rehal, by sheer force of personality, overcame the opposition and the offending objects were shifted out of his way. Behind her she heard a light footfall and then Arwinder was beside her, laughing at her bemused face. "This is how it always is, at our weddings. Last-minute panic is obligatory. It is exciting!"

"They'll *never* get everything straight in time. And what on earth is all that stuff that Rehal's bringing in?"

"They will get straight," said Arwinder tranquilly. "As for Rehal's things . . ." She made a none-of-my-affair gesture, and laughed again. "Let there be light, he says. Rehal is very determined."

Whether or not due to Rehal's determination, by evening there was order and there was light. The deliverymen and the electricians had gone. The crates of bottles and trays of sweetmeats were tidily stacked in the hall, piled on charpoy cots whose legs rested in saucers of water to discourage ants from attacking the sweets. The sacks of marigolds were waiting on the kitchen roof, chosen for the garland party because although it was smaller than the main roof, it afforded a better view of the front garden, and the front garden was well worth looking at. A gold net canopy had been raised over the drive, and this, like the doors and windows and the low parapet round the kitchen roof, had been strung with small coloured lights. It was being announced to all the world that the Avtarsingh residence was today a place of rejoicing. A hundred yards along the road, on a useful piece of waste ground, more fairy lights shone on a vast red and white marquee, which had appeared like a monster mushroom in the course of the afternoon. Tomorrow's marriage ceremony would be held there. Melanie, leaning on the parapet while Rehal fiddled with the lighting gear which he was arranging round the roof, said: "Arwinder's right. It *is* exciting."

"Or exhausting," said Rehal. He glanced up from the screwdriver he was using. "I'd forgotten what this heat was like. Does it worry you? Avtar said you weren't too well today and were taking some rest. Is it the climate?"

"Yes." She supposed that it was, anyway. "It's been especially hot this year." Melanie found that she wanted to change the subject. "Arwin's gone off to the beautician and

83

Avtar and Bheji went with her, so Aunt Prem and I are doing the honours for the garland party. You'd better show me how all these lights work."

"If I can make them work myself, I will . . . ah!" He pressed a switch and the roof was flooded with bright white light. "Good. Okay, I'll demonstrate. If there's a power cut, this switch controls lights here and in the bedroom . . ."

He had arranged battery-operated lights for the kitchen roof and the bedroom and landing behind it, the main roof, and the kitchen. "I've shown Sita and Kalu where to find the switches indoors," he said. "I could have done with more gear but it wasn't available and it wouldn't have gone into the taxi if it had been. If my paper ever folds, I'll make a living as an electrician. I'm better than some so-called professionals."

Outside, the engine of a motorised rickshaw lost momentum at the gate. Melanie strolled out to the open air. "I think our first guests are here."

"Ah. Aunt Asha and Balwant." Rehal joined her. He watched the arrivals detach themselves from the rickshaw. "I see Balwant's in white again. That's an intelligent girl, Melanie, once you get her to talk. I did talk to her for a while last night, after the Sangeet. She reads the papers and she knows what's going on in the world. I'd like to tear that damned mourning robe off her," said Rehal. And meant it.

Melanie said nothing. At the grating undertone in his voice, her stomach had gone cold. Her sense of alienation, soothed for a time by a day of relaxation, had returned. It was harsher and stronger now than before. Did either Rehal or Balwant have a chance? Everything in Melanie wanted them to have one. Yet it seemed to her that the entire weight of their history, the full pressure of this massive subcontinent, top-heavy with tradition and overpopulation, pressing individuals so closely together that they almost lost individuality, stood against them.

Rehal seemed to expect her to speak. When she did not, he turned sharply away as if in anger and went into the house.

∽

Even more than the Sangeet, the garland party was romantic. They were well away now on the fragrant task of pushing stout needles through the fat green bases of the marigold heads, to string them into thick ropes of flowers; Melanie, lifting a hand to scratch the tip of her nose, found that even her fingers were scented.

As the sky dimmed, the lights had been turned on. The house front and the canopy were festive with dots of luminous azure and amber, crimson and violet and green. Up on the main roof some of the older women, Aunt Asha and Aunt Prem among them, having decided that the garland party was large enough without them, were having an impromptu continuation of the Sangeet. The tapping of their drum was low and persistent and troublesome. What did Balwant feel tonight, stringing garlands for another girl? Balwant seemed much as usual, her fingers deft on her work and her light voice, making small talk to Nirmal, apparently cheerful. But Rehal was somewhere in the house; was she secretly aware of him? Behind that serene facade, was her mind reaching out for his, like a hand stretched between the bars of a cell window?

In the effort not to stare at her, Melanie fixed her gaze on the fairy lights instead and was reminded of the coloured lights which were strung along Heverton promenade in summer, for the enjoyment of the holidaymakers. Almost, looking at them, she could hear the sea murmur on the darkened beach, and see the outlines of the seafront hotels against the sky and the lamplit windows of the few houses among the trees on Heverton Point. She was far away in memory at the moment when the lights did what everyone had subconsciously been waiting for them to do, and suddenly blinked out.

For a moment she was confused, as though she did not know where she was. All round her there were exclamations of annoyance, and she was aware of people scrambling about. Up on the main roof, the drum taps had ceased. Somewhere in the depths of the house, Kalu's voice was heard calling to Sita to wait, he would attend to everything. Melanie pulled herself together, back from her lost vision of Heverton to the present tense and the blacked-out kitchen roof in Chandigarh. "Just a minute," she said. "The switch is here. Rehal showed me. Let me put it on."

She found the switch and pressed. At almost the same moment, lights shone out again in other parts of the house. There were cries of joy. "That is very fine," said Balwant. She smiled at Melanie. "I saw that you were admiring our fairy lights. It is pity they are gone. But at least we can now see what we are doing, no matter how long the cut lasts."

As though the authorities had heard her and abandoned their neutralised joke in disgust, the power was abruptly restored. Windows, lampposts, fairy lights glowed forth once more. "Oh, good," said Melanie, just as somebody screamed.

There was a crash, as a human body was flung against the frame of the glass doors. Nirmal's voice cried: "Balwant!" Melanie sprang from her chair to kneel beside the huddled white heap in the doorway. There was a clatter and a thudding of feet from inside the room, and on the other side of Balwant, Rehal was kneeling too. "What happened?" he demanded.

Balwant was lying half on her side, eyes distended, gasping. The others crowded round, exclaiming.

"My God, what has she done?"

"She had her hand on the fairy lights, she was saying it was pity they had gone off. She has had electric shock."

"Electric shock from the fairy lights? Oh God, I knew they were rotten workmanship," said Rehal. "I did the plugs ... I should have checked the strings of bulbs too. Balwant, it's over, you're safe." He took up one of her hands and then the other. "There are no burn marks, Melanie, at least there are no marks."

"Oh, why is Avtar not here?" somebody lamented.

"We must manage without him." Balwant's breathing was easing. Rehal gathered her into his arms. "It's all right, you'll be all right. Melanie, Avtar's got drink somewhere; he gave me a whisky the night I arrived. Where is it?"

"Sitting room sideboard. Brandy, whisky, and there's beer in the fridge as well."

"Brandy'll do. Bring a good thick shawl down there, will you?" said Rehal and strode away with his burden which was now faintly protesting that it could walk. "Maybe, but you're not going to," they heard him say as he went.

When Melanie, shawl in hand, reached the sitting room, Balwant was sipping brandy while Rehal sat with a supportive arm around her. The tenderness in his face caught Melanie like a jab under the ribs. Like the grating note in his voice earlier, it meant only one thing. This was real and deep with him, not a brief attraction that would pass. She was sick with concern for them and anger on their behalf.

But it was the wrong moment for a serious discussion of Hindu orthodoxy. She took refuge in flippancy. "Opportunist!" she muttered at Rehal, handing the shawl.

"It's the secret of success," said Rehal. "Alexander, Napoleon, and Genghis Khan were all brilliant opportunists, I bet." He wrapped the shawl round Balwant, who was still shivering. "So sorry," she whispered. "I feel so cold."

"Finish the brandy. It'll warm you," he said.

Balwant sipped the tawny liquid again, doubtfully, and coughed. "I ought not. My Bheji would say . . ."

"Your Bheji isn't here. I'm here instead and I'm your doctor and I say drink." Balwant took another obedient mouthful, choked again, and swallowed. Melanie prepared, tactfully, to leave.

"I don't mind if you stay, Melanie," Rehal said. "I can't think why they haven't all poured downstairs after you, though."

"I said, in the most authoritative voice I could manage, that Avtar always insisted that cases of shock should not be surrounded by crowds. I asked them to stay where they were," said Melanie. "I thought you might like some privacy. But I'd better go and tell them how she is."

"Oh, pour yourself a drink first. You might pour me one while you're at it. We could all do with it. This could have been serious." Rehal's face was grim. "Avtar must complain officially to that company. Balwant is an adult, but if Dili or any of the children had touched that wire . . ."

"What is this? They said an accident, an accident to Balwant, and from the roof we heard a scream!" Melanie stiffened and Rehal quite audibly groaned. Aunt Asha had arrived, with a patter of rapid sandals and a white-draperied swish. She regarded them suspiciously from the doorway.

From where Aunt Asha was standing, Melanie thought, the scene probably merited suspicion. There was Balwant in the middle of it, a glass of brandy wavering at her lips, while Rehal stood on one side of her with an arm round her shoulders, and on the other side was Melanie, bottle in hand and two glasses dangling from her fingers. To Aunt Asha it no doubt looked like the opening stages of a bacchanalia.

"Balwant has had a severe electric shock," she said.

"She was thrown right across the kitchen roof," said Rehal. "The fairy lights were faulty."

"But what is this she is drinking?"

"Brandy," said Rehal. "It's a stimulant."

"Stimulant!" Aunt Asha dismissed the medicinal properties of spirituous liquors into the realms of legend with a single abolitionist gesture. "Why you did not call me? I was just upstairs. I know what to do, I have had such shocks myself. She should rest and keep warm, nothing else. Balwant, come with me!"

Advancing, Aunt Asha plucked the unprotesting Balwant from between them, dispossessing her of the glass. She swept her daughter-in-law from the room. As they ascended the stairs, Rehal and Melanie could hear her scolding. "But Rehal only wanted to help," said Balwant, halfway up. "Rehal, is it? You call him Rehal? What else he has helped you to do, eh?" said Asha with unbelievable crudity, and with that passed out of hearing. Rehal uttered a single, very obscene, Anglo-Saxon monosyllable.

"I know," said Melanie. "I feel just the same."

"Do you? I doubt it. You can't possibly feel just the same as I do. You may have got the impression, Melanie, that I want Balwant. If so, you are right."

Melanie said, with difficulty: "It will be hard for her,

you know. She'll be like an ear of corn between two grind-stones if you and Aunt Asha join battle. Be careful."

"My dear girl." Rehal drained his glass and stretched out his arm for the bottle. "Mind your own business. And now I think you'd better go away. Because I intend to sit here, all on my own, and get very thoroughly drunk. And probably belligerent with it!"

∽

"What on earth," said Avtar half an hour later, striding into their room, "is going on here?" Melanie eyed him from the edge of her bed, her own glass still in her hand although it no longer contained any brandy. "Arwin and I leave you all settling to a nice happy garland party, and when we come back, the place is in a ferment. Balwant laid out on Arwin's bed. Rehal glowering and muttering and pushing past people on the stairs without a word, and reeking of brandy. Now I find you here"—Avtar marched across the room to sniff at the glass his wife was holding—"apparently having a little booze-up all on your own. Why?"

"I'm not having a little booze-up," said Melanie. "I had one brandy and I needed it. Rehal is in love with Balwant."

"I beg your pardon?" Avtar's face expressed disbelief. "That is only brandy you are drinking, I hope? Not methylated spirits or Irish poteen? How can Rehal be in love with Balwant when he has only just come home?"

"I can't help it, he is. It happened when she came to the Sangeet. It does strike like that sometimes. Look at us. Then today, Balwant got an electric shock from the fairy lights on the kitchen parapet——"

"Yes, I've had a look at her. She is recovering, I'm thankful to say."

"—and Rehal took charge of her and gave her a drink to revive her and Aunt Asha caught him at it, and . . ." Briefly and pungently, Melanie described the rest. Avtar threw himself into the basket chair and stared at her.

"I see. And may I know why you're glaring at me about it?"

"Am I?"

"Yes."

There was a silence. Then Melanie burst out: "Well, is anyone going to help her? Help them? Will anyone back them up? You didn't hear Asha. She was . . . she was coarse, monstrous! As if Balwant weren't a grown-up woman and a free citizen of this country. Is anything going to be done about it or not?"

"Oh, for the love of God," said Avtar, "what do you take us for? We're not living in the Middle Ages. You think we are, don't you? My family lives in the twentieth century, I assure you. This is not some backward village. If Rehal wants it and Balwant wants it then yes, we shall help. If. Rehal may know his own mind, yes. Even so quickly, he may know it. Rehal has always known the time of day. But Balwant? You say he's in love with her. Is she in love with him? Can she even know if she is? She's inexperienced. She's not used to making such decisions. And I tell you this, Melanie, something you ought to know but it seems you don't, there is such a thing as cultural security. It may be that Balwant won't want to defy the laws she has been brought up with, because for her, happiness doesn't lie that way. The mere fact of being outside the pattern she knows may overturn her. I said she was inexperienced; I didn't say she was a fool. You think she is because she's so quiet, but that girl is actually very intelligent—"

"That's what Rehal says."

"—and she may be intelligent enough to know what is best for her. You broke away from your own traditions, coming here with me—and with you tradition is not so strong—but I sometimes think you are not happy. As for Asha, she is certainly not a monster."

"You should have heard her!"

"When I came in just now," said Avtar, "I was called to see Balwant, as I said. Asha was with her when I went in. For your information, though Balwant was crying, she was doing it into a cup of tea which Asha had brought her, and Asha herself was sitting on the end of the bed, massaging Balwant's feet and crooning to her. Half that blustering you heard was panic, fright over the accident. Asha's a kind woman at heart."

"*Kind!*"

"Yes. She nursed Balwant through typhoid two years ago, and it was devoted nursing and very competent once I got her through the panicky early stages. I went to Delhi to see if I could help, you remember? And stayed there for some days. She takes great care of Balwant when Balwant gets migraine attacks too. The fact is that Asha had a wretched marriage and she had no chance, ever, of escaping and starting again, even after the marriage ended, and if it's too much for her to bear, seeing other people have what she couldn't, well, that's human. You're human too. You told me once that you were jealous of your cousin Frances because she was living in Ambersford and you weren't. I tell you, Asha and Balwant get on all right when they're by themselves. In fact, they're fond of each other. You don't know everything."

"What was wrong with Asha's marriage?" Melanie asked, partly out of genuine curiosity, and partly by way of damping down what seemed to be turning into a quarrel. "I knew it was unhappy but I never heard why."

Avtar came to sit by her on the divan. "These things are hard for you to understand, I know. Her husband was mentally sick. It wasn't obvious at the time of the marriage, though I think his parents must have suspected. They probably pushed the marriage ahead because of that. They wanted him to have a son while he could. They got the son. She started him in the first month of the marriage. Then after the child was born, Asha's husband tried to kill both her and the baby with a knife. His father and uncle heard her screaming for help and they ran into the room and took the knife away. Her husband eventually went into a hospital and died there—he got a growth a few years later. His family wasn't very kind to Asha, but we were able to help her. We got a flat for her in Delhi, and later on, of course, she inherited the house she has now in Chandigarh. Her husband's family said she drove her husband insane, because after her pregnancy was confirmed, she refused to share his room, and she went on refusing after the birth. But she told my father that she refused because she knew he was abnormal, and she was afraid of him. She hadn't met him before the marriage, of course."

"That's . . . horrible," said Melanie.

For the first time she felt sympathy with Aunt Asha. There had been a neighbour once at Ambersford, a woman who had lived alone in the small cottage opposite Roadend. She had eventually been taken into a psychiatric hospital. Melanie had been glad when she went, because she had found her very frightening. She had had a trick of beckoning people to her—children, passersby, tradesmen, it made no difference—imparting absurd pieces of information to them as though these were secrets of the utmost importance, and obviously expecting a reply in the same bated-breath vein. Even grownups, let alone little Melanie, were hard put to find an answer when told with wide eyes and a furtive whisper that the milk had gone sour by *ten o'clock last night,* or that there was a tabby cat on the roof of the Ambersford Arms yesterday; *it just shows, doesn't it?* What Melanie remembered most vividly about the woman was that she generated not only discomfort and fear, but actual physical repulsion. Melanie had learned early that pity for mental abnormality could not thrive if you were in any way at its mercy. If Aunt Asha had been forced into sexual intimacy, that closest and most surrendering of all intimacies, with *that* . . . then it did much to explain Aunt Asha. The very sight of Melanie, who had chosen so freely that she had chosen a stranger from another hemisphere, must be like a continual jeer.

"I'm sorry," she said sincerely. "For Aunt Asha, I mean. But . . . it doesn't help Balwant, does it?"

"Balwant will help herself," said Avtar. "If she can't take this decision alone, she is better off as she is."

A Beginning and an End

In the household of the bride, Melanie discovered, an Indian wedding started before dawn.

She woke reluctantly as Avtar shook her. The house was alive with sound but the light was on and the windows were dark. Avtar was dressed already in his best grey suit, his chin satiny from shaving. "Come on, Melanie. It's quarter to five."

"Quarter to *five?*"

"I left you as long as I could. Here." He held out a dressing gown. "Put this on. You can dress properly later. You're feeling all right, aren't you? Bheji says you've been shutting yourself away a lot lately. I said to her that it was just the heat and family worries, but . . . you are all right? You want to come down to the bangle ceremony?"

"Yes, darling, of course." Melanie pulled on the dressing gown and tugged a comb through her hair. "Will this do?"

"Yes. Come along."

Downstairs, the ground floor was already busily populated. Mrs. Patel, also in a dressing gown and yawning so that Melanie's jaws ached in sympathy, appeared from the kitchen with a laden tea tray. "Tea? There will not be formal breakfast today but Sita has put out some cut bread and some fruit if you feel hungry."

"No, thank you. Tea will do." She drank it standing beside Avtar in the hall, since there seemed to be no room anywhere else. Then Aunt Prem rustled out of the sitting room, fully dressed for the day, wafting a cloud of Nina Ricci before her, her still-dark hair glistening with oil and convuluted miraculously on top of her head, her complexion a wonder of pale gold and rose tinting, her sari a gold-bordered emerald vision with knife-sharp pleats. "We are ready!" Melanie put her teacup down on the hallstand, and went with the crowd.

The dawn was bleaching the sky, as the gold and ivory bangles that Arwinder would wear throughout her married life were given to her by her uncles and aunts. She knelt in the middle of the sitting room, dressed in a blue silk salwar kameeze which she would use for this ceremony only, and her usually impish face was grave. The small hands which she extended to receive the bangles were patterned, palms and backs, with a pale brown design in henna, put there by one of her cousins the evening before, and they were not absolutely steady. This was a serious moment. Arwinder's position in society had begun to alter. She was being dedicated now to another life and another family. Melanie herself was

96

unexpectedly struck again by a sense of loss. Arwinder would be less of a sister to her henceforth. She had relied very much on Arwin's company since she came to India.

When it was over, there were more trays of tea ("I didn't know we had so many trays," said Melanie. "We haven't. I borrowed five," said Bheji) and then, like a gracious cavalry charge, the ladies surged up the stairs so that those whose toilettes were still incomplete could amend this before the groom arrived.

Melanie got ready in her bedroom, washing in a bowl of water thoughtfully placed there beforehand by Avtar ("Everyone will want to get into the bathroom at once"), and wondering at what time Aunt Prem had had to get up to achieve that fantastic coiffure, or if she had ever found time to go to bed at all. Melanie dressed rapidly. Blouse, heavy cotton underskirt with drawstring, sari . . .

The sari was new for the occasion. She had ironed it but it still wanted to pleat itself along the line of its packing creases, and the embroidered border was stiffly resistant to her fingers. She forced the recalcitrant folds into some kind of order, applied perfume, and then, hearing someone call her, pulled on a pair of gold sandals, and ran.

The women's bedroom had become a shrine dedicated to Venus, with that acknowledged beauty expert, Aunt Prem, as the high priestess. Arwinder appeared to be somewhere in between the deity to be worshipped and a human sacrifice. She stood obediently, while Aunt Prem painted and powdered and told her to keep her eyes closed until the mascara had dried. "Lip brush!" said Aunt Prem, in the tone of a brain surgeon saying: "Scalpel!" She smoothed eye shadow into place with the delicacy and precision of one who writes the Lord's Prayer on a postage stamp. The make-up completed, Bheji, Aunt Prem, and Rina Patel, their mouths full of pins, prowled round and round the bride, winding and draping the gleaming red and gold sari. Last of all, Bheji brought out the jewellery and Aunt Prem tenderly arranged it. A headdress to overhang Arwinder's forehead; gold chains to enmesh the slender hands. A gold chain looped from ear to nostril . . .

Outside, strident music had started up. Someone pounded on the door. "Is she not ready yet? The band is playing and the bridegroom's party is in sight!"

"In a moment!" shouted Aunt Prem. "She will come in a moment. Will he run away if she is not there instantly?"

Saranjit had chosen not to come on the traditional white horse, for which Melanie was glad. The white horse sounded romantic but like most horses in India, all the ones she had seen were depressed-looking animals. She never saw one without thinking of the well-muscled, glossy occupants of Uncle Daniel's stable, and making a sad comparison. But Saranjit had followed custom in other ways. His turban was topped by a gold-fringed headdress and he carried a cere-monial sword. He raised it slightly in greeting as he came near enough to the house to recognise those who had come down to the driveway to meet him. He handled the sword well, without diffidence. Moving through the rituals of his people as a man might walk through the rooms of his own house, Saranjit's stocky, bespectacled figure was full of dignity.

Arwinder would be happy, Melanie thought, standing among the people in the drive, having hurried down at the summons of the raucous band. The sense of loss was on her again, more strongly this time. She looked over her shoulder. Arwinder, in the midst of her family and her close friends, was moving slowly out of the front door and under the golden net canopy to meet her husband. She too was walking with assurance on a path rightly her own. But it was not Melanie's. It was taking her away from Melanie now.

⌒

The temperature in the marquee must, Melanie thought, be at least a hundred. She sweltered inside the heavy silk sari, the underskirt sticking to her damp legs. She was starting a headache. One could all but hear the sun battering on the red and white plastic overhead. The fans which had been placed at intervals round the walls of the marquee had no effect whatever on the throbbing air in the midst of it.

The ceremony was nearly over. The men, dark suited or white shirted, were massed on one side of the canopy under which the priest sat behind the Holy Book with its jewelled cover. The women sat opposite the men, vying, clashing, harmonising, in a dazzle of rainbow silks and multiple bangles. The white-turbanned priest had already read from the scriptures and had instructed the couple to rise and proceed, Saranjit leading, four times round the Book. They went slowly, heads bent, as if climbing a steep hill. Their relations, standing in a circle round them, guided them with pats and murmurs of encouragement, helping them on these last few steps that they would ever take in single life. Melanie curled her feet under her, ready to get up quickly at the right moment and fling flower-petal confetti over the pair. She was moved, as everyone was, by that solemn procession. But at the same time she wished they would go faster. If she did not throw her handful of petals soon, she was sure they would stick fast to her sweating palms. Twice round. Three times. *Now.*

Petals showered, a scented snowstorm. The couple sat once more before the priest. Someone—it was Nirmal—

pushed a rope of marigolds into Melanie's hands. "Come and garland them." A photographer, darting about in search of a good angle, stepped on Melanie's sari and that, she thought, was the end of the hard-won pleats. She joined the queue of garland-throwers and made her contribution. She found Nirmal beside her again. "Melanie, you look so hot and weary. There will be something to eat in a moment and then nothing more will happen for hours. Doli is not till four. Come home with me and lie down. I am going home to rest myself. It will be quieter there. Everything will be hurly-burly at your place."

"I don't think I should."

"You go." Avtar had appeared. The division between men and women had broken down in the rush to offer garlands. "Then Arwin can change in our room, ready for the Doli. Nirmal will bring you back in good time. You do look hot. You ought to have a sleep."

"I'll lend you a cotton sari for the afternoon," added Nirmal kindly. "That silk is all creased with the heat. Come."

Nirmal's home was bigger than Avtar's, built on an open plan with wide, high rooms leading in and out of each other through tall archways. The sun was never permitted to stream into this house; the building was designed to exclude his tyrannical majesty as far as possible. Here the blaze of the sky was defeated by latticed shutters which broke it into little, subtle shapes and then dispersed it harmlessly on un-occupied areas of floor. They sat on divans round a low table in a shadowy corner, and Melanie's impending headache withdrew as they slowly sipped the tea that Nirmal's mother brought. She was a graceful woman, an older edition of her daughter. You could see that through the years, Nirmal would mature into greater and greater elegance. Curious, that the sophisticated Rehal had preferred Balwant. Forbidden fruit? Or was there more in Balwant than was apparent? Melanie did not know.

She finished her tea. Nirmal smiled and said: "Now we rest," and led the way through an arch to where two more divans waited invitingly. Divesting themselves of their crumpled saris, they stretched out. "Nirmal," said Melanie, "*thank* you."

"It's nothing. You were ready to faint, I could see it. This climate is hard on Europeans. In the days of the Raj, ladies would go to the hills in summer. But you are here all the time. You should go home one summer to England. The Indian sun is too demanding for you."

"I did suggest it once, but . . ."

She let the sentence trail away. But. Avtar had walked out of the room, slamming the door. When pursued and cornered and requested to explain himself, he had said that he could not leave his patients to come with her, that her home was now with him, and that under the circumstances this meant India, and that he did not want her going to England alone. Further pressed to explain why Melanie on her own in what was after all the land of her birth was so unthinkable, he had finally uttered just one word.

Robin.

"I'm not going to see Robin!" Melanie had said. "I should go to Somerset at once, to be with Gran. What on earth are you talking about?"

"I know what I'm talking about," said Avtar. "You slept with him before you slept with me, and he writes to you, doesn't he?"

"He wrote one letter. A business letter to say that he hoped Hallowens would still get some designs from me now and then. He does run a design department, after all. As for our love affair, that was all over before you and I ever set eyes on each other. For God's sake, you *saw* that letter!"

"I saw one letter."

"And just what does that mean?"

"You have many letters from England. You don't show them all to me. You are not going, Melanie."

And after that it was no use to say any more, because he would not listen.

❦

"I had hoped to see England myself one day," Nirmal observed, lying on her back, eyes closed. "But I expect I never will, now. There was talk of a match between me and Rehal, you know."

"I . . ." Melanie raised herself on one elbow. "Yes. I know. Is it . . . I mean . . .?"

"My parents," said Nirmal calmly, ignoring Melanie's stammers, "think it would not do. There's a boy in Delhi—I have met him once or twice—a very nice boy, good-natured and in this good engineering post. I think they will settle things with him. So I shall go to Delhi instead."

Nirmal's eyes were still closed. Her countenance was as serene as her voice. Two days ago she had been like a living beacon for joy at the hope of marrying Rehal. Now she was giving him up for a boy she scarcely knew, and yet Melanie could see in her not even the least trace of emotion, let alone rebellion. Did she feel nothing at all? Where was the racking loss, the agony of hope wrenched away? *But don't you mind?* Melanie wanted to shout at her.

But it couldn't be done. That question could not be addressed to that tranquil face. Melanie relapsed onto her

102

divan. As Arwinder in her red and gold sari had been, Nirmal now was a stranger, as if she came from another planet. Little Dili, she too would one day fit into this calm preordained pattern, surrender to it, almost. . . . What in the world did it feel like, to be so certain of where you were going that you did not even wonder if there were other destinations, did not even notice the absence of choice?

Nirmal's eyes opened at last. She put up a hand to move her pillow and turned her head sideways to look at Melanie. A little ironic smile appeared on her face. "It must be difficult in the West. If the man you want doesn't want you, you can't pretend it was just that your parents were against it, can you?" she said.

∽

Because she went to Nirmal's house to rest, Melanie missed the arrival of the daily post. But it was there when, dressed in borrowed clothes, she returned for the Doli, the car which would take Arwin to her new home. There was one letter in the postbox, from Frances. She read it through quickly, while Arwinder was finally made ready. When she had folded it up and joined the others, Arwin was downstairs, and being helped into the back seat of the car beside her husband. She was crying, because at this point it was expected of her. She was supposed to be grieving at leaving her mother and her home, supposed to be afraid of the strangers to whom she was going. Arwin was not, as Melanie perfectly well knew, either grieved or afraid of anything, but she had burst punctually into tears, following the ritual, because she was at home in it.

As the car moved away, others began to cry too. Bheji, Aunt Prem, Nirmal, Rina Patel, even Aunt Asha. Melanie let herself weep with them, relieving the ache within her, losing it amid the general sorrow as if she were a river, abandoning herself to the sea.

"You surprise me," said Rehal's light voice beside her. "Anyone would think we were burying her instead of marrying her. Come on, Melanie. I bet you didn't carry on like this at your own wedding."

"We had a ten-minute civil ceremony. It doesn't generate the same amount of emotional voltage," said Melanie, and tried to smile.

And: "You do surprise me," said Avtar, as they went to their room to tidy themselves. "All these tears. Melanie, are you really all right? This is unlike you."

"No. I'm not all right." She had pushed the letter into her waistband. She drew it out. "This came today. Read it. I read it just now, before the Doli. It's from Frances, about Gran. Gran's dead."

The House on the Cliff

"I am sorry to tell you," Frances had written, "that your grandfather collapsed on the evening of the day when I last wrote to you. He was not at Gavin's Cliff at the time but here in Ambersford having a meal with us. So there was no delay in getting him to Heverton Hospital—I want you to know that everything that could be done, was done. But he did not come out of his coma and passed peacefully away in the early hours of the next morning. It was a heart attack, apparently. He is to be laid to rest in St. Oswald's Churchyard here in Ambersford at his own wish, although Heverton of course is nearer his home. . . ."

Passed peacefully away. Early hours of the morning.

Laid to rest. Frances, instinctively trying to make the unbearable into something that could after all be borne, by wrapping it in phrases worn soft with much use. But nothing made it able to be borne. Gran was dead, and no words, however soft and smooth, could disguise the outlines of mortality.

"You should lie down . . . Bheji is bringing some tea . . . we are all so very sorry, Melanie; even Sita is crying in the kitchen and Leela too . . . but eighty is a good age and if the end was peaceful, that's a comfort. So brave of you to keep it to yourself until Arwin had gone . . . you should have an aspirin . . . a Valium . . . a sleeping tablet . . . more tea . . ."

I don't want an aspirin, a Valium, a sleeping tablet, more tea. I don't want to lie down. I want Gran. I want his ginger tweeds and his smelly old pipe and his opinionated voice laying down the law on everything from human institutions to the idiocy of falling in love with Indian doctors or little roan mares. And if I can't have Gran, I want to be there in Ambersford when they say goodbye to him. Oh, God, it's probably been done already. Letters take days to get here. They should have cabled me. But if they had and I'd gone at once, it would have clouded Arwin's day. I wouldn't want that. There's nothing I do want. Just Gran. *Gran.*

Avtar, coming to bed in a house which although still full of people nevertheless felt oddly empty now that Arwinder had left it, found Melanie leafing through old snapshots, searching frantically for a photograph of Gran. "It's his face. I can't see his face properly in my mind, and I want to see him so much. Here's one." Melanie held up a picture taken one sunny afternoon during her last year in England. She had taken it without Gran's knowledge. He was sitting in a deck chair on Daniel Purvis's small lawn, talking to someone out of the picture. His jaw jutted and his eyebrows were quirking, and he was gesticulating with his pipe. It was quintessential Gran, a perfect summing-up of him. Melanie offered it to Avtar, looked at it again herself, and burst into tears.

"Come to bed. You must sleep," Avtar said.

During the night, moving restlessly under the sheet which was the only tolerable covering, she rolled towards Avtar on the adjacent divan, and found that he too was lying awake.

"It's because of Arwin," he said, as Melanie slid into his arms across the divide. "It's in the air. But I don't want to worry you tonight. Go to sleep."

"It won't worry me. It might help. Please." They hadn't made love for about three weeks, in all the rush and confusion of the guest-filled household. It might, Melanie thought, assuage this awful sense of loneliness.

Temporarily, it did. Enough at least to let her sleep an hour or two. Her usual vigorous response was lacking, but she clung to him and he was warm within her. But in the morning, the grief and loss were back.

They would have been beyond endurance except for the sense of unreality that now enveloped her, like a glass case over a stuffed parrot, she thought wryly. People came and tapped on the glass. Again she lacked in response although she tried to produce it in gratitude for so much unfailing kindness. Arwinder and Saranjit came to visit, trying earnestly if not very successfully to hide their new happiness, out of respect for Melanie's sorrow. The business of response became a duty, a matter of sheer good manners; she drove herself. "I'm quite all right. It was to be expected, at Gran's age. You must tell me, Arwin, how are you settling down into Saranjit's family . . . ?"

107

Arwinder was willing to be reassured; the more experienced Bheji was clearly worried about her. She coaxed
Melanie to work with her about the house, in the quiet which
had fallen now that all the guests except Rehal had gone
and Bheji, not without satisfaction, had resumed control of
her kitchen. They sat side by side in the kitchen or sometimes on the roof when it was cool enough, cleaning rice or
pounding chapatti batter, and Bheji talked of everyday things,
trying to bring her unhappy daughter-in-law back to the real
world again. Melanie did her best, but gave herself away by
constantly reverting to English in mid-conversation. Her
Punjabi had regressed under the strain.

Letters came, which had to be answered. They brought
some relief, giving her an occupation which was linked to
the loss which possessed her mind, and did not, therefore,
cause pain by wrenching her away from it. Uncle Daniel
wrote, telling her of the funeral in the churchyard under the
butt end of Ravensridge. People had come long distances to
attend it, he said; Ambersford had rarely seen such a crowd
at any funeral. Letters came from people Melanie had known
in Ambersford, including the vicar and his sister Mrs. Viney,
who was a local character. Dear, dictatorial Amanda Viney,
thought Melanie, the terror of the St. Oswald's bellringers.
She insisted on being a bellringer although her aptitude was
limited, and Ambersford would not quickly forget the peal
of Grandsire Triples which had been ruined in the first
thirty seconds because Mrs. Viney had mixed up Grandsires
with Stedmans. She was a terror in her family too. She had,
Melanie remembered, taken violent exception to the girl
her son chose to marry, made the couple's life a misery with
a campaign unashamedly aimed at breaking them up, and
then, on finally recognising that they were not going to
yield, taken such relentless charge of the wedding prepara-

tions that the unfortunate pair had come within an inch of eloping out of sheer desperation. But there was no trace of that militant busyness in this kindly letter, full of admiration for Professor Purvis's character and intellect, and friendly recollections of Melanie herself. ". . . although you moved from Ambersford so long ago, you have always remained part of our community. We all hope that we may see you here again one day . . ."

Bill and Mary Heaton wrote from Whitehangers Farm, and Ivor Winnaford wrote too. ". . . a dear friend and a still dearer opponent. I shall have no one to argue with now. I have been thinking that a biography of William Purvis could make a lively and interesting book, and that now that I am retired, I would have time to undertake it." Jane Hanworth did not write, because her paths did not cross those of Melanie's family. Melanie had to send the news to Jane instead, a hard letter to compose since the fact of Gran's death became suddenly more real when she herself was the announcer.

Withdrawn as she now was from the affairs of Avtar's family, she was aware, without any sense of personal involvement, of other dramas in and around the house. She noticed, without questioning it, that Rehal had remained in Chandigarh instead of returning with his parents to their home in Jaipur. She learned by hearsay that he had formally expressed a wish to marry Balwant, and that Aunt Asha, along with some of the older family members, had been exceedingly displeased. A few days later, Melanie heard that Balwant, in an interview with a stiff and embarrassed Avtar, acting as Rehal's spokesman, had declared that she too would prefer to maintain tradition and had decided not to remarry. No, she had said in answer to Avtar's conscientious questions, it was not that she was unable to forget her husband. She had not even known him well. She had met him only twice before marriage and during their year of married life he had been away for most of the time. But she did not feel that such an unprecedented step would be right for her or for her family. Hearing that, Melanie did emerge briefly from her glass cage, to regale Avtar with her forceful belief that wrong did not become right because it was the custom and that Balwant had been brainwashed. "All right," said Avtar wearily. "You go and un-brainwash her if you can. I can't. And I'm too bloody tired to try."

But that one spurt of protest had used up all the altruism of which Melanie was now capable. She was aware, as if from a distance, of Rehal stalking about the premises in a silent fury, of Rehal packing his cases in a series of slams and thuds audible all over the house, of Rehal consulting airline timetables ostentatiously at breakfast, of Rehal departing with a vicious whoosh like the exit of a demon king, bound for Delhi and the first available flight to London. After he had gone, whenever she encountered Aunt Asha and Balwant, she was aware too of Balwant's closed-in, not-to-be-questioned face, but she was at a distance from that also. Her instinct was to avoid Balwant.

After a fortnight, though the flood of letters was easing, it had by no means ceased, and the mailbox was still a major point of interest in her life. Wandering into the garden on a burning Saturday afternoon, because Asha and Balwant were visiting and she did not feel like sitting with them, she found two airmail letters in the box at the front gate. They meant simultaneously the voices of friends from home, and an excuse to stay retired from the company while she read them in solitude. She carried them upstairs.

One was a further communication from Ivor Winnaford. Gran's own publishers were enthusiastic about the biography project and he hoped that Melanie would allow him access to Gran's papers. He understood that these were to be her province. Some of the professor's professional colleagues had already offered samples of their own correspondence with him and indeed he had some excellent material of that type himself. If Melanie . . .

Gran had been an incurable squirrel. He not only kept nearly all the letters he received, and all his own old manuscripts and conference papers and field notes, but he also kept carbons of all the letters he wrote. He had possibly foreseen posthumous interest of this sort. But she did not know why Ivor should approach her on the question of access. Surely Uncle Daniel . . . or perhaps Gran's solicitors, what was their name?—Barnes and Chaldicott, if she remembered rightly—surely they were the people he should contact. Still frowning, she undid the second letter by feel. When she at length turned her attention to the typewritten sheet with the printed letterhead in its curly Victorian typeface, she jumped.

Barnes & Chaldicott, said the letterhead. *107a, High Street, Heverton, Som.* The sight of the printed address brought a visual memory of the premises concerned clearly into focus. A brass plate on a door squeezed between two shops, because Barnes & Chaldicott lived over the top of Dolcis Shoes and next door to Sainsburys. She blinked, and then read the letter.

It began with expressions of sympathy but swiftly changed its note to the purely businesslike. It then stated, in calm and unambiguous English as though making the most reasonable of remarks, that Gran had left her not only a modest sum of money—she could have foreseen that, had she thought about it at all—but also his house. He had left her Gavin's Cliff, with all its contents.

There would, of course, said Mr. Vincent Barnes, who had signed the letter, be a lapse of time while probate was obtained, but no difficulties were anticipated since Professor Purvis had acted with the full knowledge and approval of other members of the family, notably his son Daniel Purvis and Daniel's children Roy, Dick, and Ellen. Barnes & Chaldicott had been named executors, and would be glad of Melanie's instructions in respect of the property which presumably she would wish either to sell or to let. They would be happy to advise her in any way if she required it. The house was in moderately good condition although some exterior repairs might be needed. Its value, given that these were attended to, would be in the region of—

"I'll never sell it," said Melanie aloud. "Never."

"But it would be an excellent idea," continued the letter serenely, "if your circumstances allow, for you to visit England and inspect the house for yourself." There was more, about arranging an advance from Gran's legacy to cover the expenses of such a visit. Barnes and Chaldicott were anxious to give all the help they could and they remained, yours faithfully. . . .

Below Mr. Barnes's signature, justified left, was one abbreviated word: *enc.* Melanie found that the envelope still in her hand was not empty. She scrabbled in it and drew out another, smaller envelope, with her name on it in Gran's writing.

His letter was dated more than a year ago and the ink was already dulled. She had wanted to see his writing again so much, but not like this. This was like receiving a message at a seance.

"My dearest Melanie," said the disembodied voice of Gran, "I have today signed my will. This will has been made with the complete agreement of all the rest of my family. I am dividing my estate as fairly as I can among my descendants. That part of it which is represented by Gavin's Cliff, I am leaving to you.

I am doing this because:

(a) You love Gavin's Cliff. Daniel has no feeling for it and his family still less. Frances says it is lonely, windswept, and damp (it is *not* damp, by the way). Roy says he would sooner live in a lighthouse and Dick took the trouble to ring me up from Gloucestershire to say please would I kindly not leave it to him. Ellen is comfortably married and has a nice home in Taunton and makes no bones about the fact that she would prefer a monetary legacy without the boring nuisance of having to sell a house in order to get the money. It would never occur to her to do anything with Gavin's Cliff, other than sell it. They are all more likely to commiserate with you than to contest the will.

(b) Although you are, of course, perfectly entitled to sell the house yourself if you wish, I want you to have the chance of a home, a stake, in England. Since you disposed of the flat your father left you, you have not had one. I ask you, please, to think carefully what you wish to do with Gavin's Cliff.

I am leaving you a little money, which may help with upkeep. I am sorry there isn't more, but I wish to create no dissension in my family and alas, if I have been a successful man, I have also been a spendthrift one.

What else is there to say? I have always been at ease with words but this is an extraordinarily difficult letter to write. It is like putting a message in a bottle and floating it out to sea. When you read this, we shall be on such widely separated shores. . . ."

Despite the heat, Melanie was shivering. She was being overwhelmed by a grief which extended far beyond simple grief for the dead who cannot return. There was in it a fierceness of longing for that which is lost but may be found again if one is willing to search for it. The two were connected but they were not the same. As grief for her bereavement deepened in her, the need for the healing of her own place had apparently deepened too. Deepened and matured. Gran's death had increased this other unhappiness but not created it; turned a yearning into an imperative need but not inspired the yearning. Long before she even knew that Gran was ill, she had begun to want to go home. Now, that summons deafened.

Below, the front door slammed, and she heard Surinder, who had been out visiting friends, propping his bike up in the hall. From the sitting room, Bheji called to him, and Aunt Asha's voice spoke too. Surinder said something briefly in reply, and his voice changed pitch as he drew away from the sitting room door towards the stairs. Through her open bedroom door, Melanie caught a glimpse of him leaping up them like a deer which has heard the distant cry of the Devon & Somerset Staghounds, making for the roof and sanctuary from the guest he most detested. He had a textbook under his arm.

She must go to England. She could not stay here any longer, in this place of relentless heat and thick dust and perpetual water shortage, in this place where Balwant's young life was being burned out and choked before her eyes by the influence of Asha. She thought of peat streams gurgling deep in their beds as they found their way down from the heather slopes of Exmoor, and of white sea mists lying on the shoulders of the hills. She thought of telling Frances, or Uncle Daniel, or Mary Heaton of Balwant's plight and being comforted by their indignation. She could find no indignation here. People said: "Oh well, this is how it has always been.

One accepts it." Melanie longed, passionately, to be among people who wouldn't accept it, not on any account.

What would Avtar say?

The prospect of telling him made her stomach shrink and curl into itself, but she quelled the sensation firmly. He would say a great deal, no doubt, but she was going all the same. She rose to her feet and looked about the room. Somewhere, she knew, she had a supply of airmail forms.

"There Ought to Be a Way"

Avtar was eating breakfast, his mind far away, concerned with the difficulties of convincing an uncooperative diabetes patient that his high-calorie diet *must* be adhered to, and the even greater difficulties of convincing the patient's wife that if she loved her husband then she should side with the doctor, when Melanie's airline ticket arrived. The clumsy and nervous way Melanie handled the envelope drew his attention, and his eyes were on it when the ticket fell out onto her fortunately empty plate. It lay there in its aggressive scarlet and royal blue, shouting *British Airways* at the top of its voice to everyone at the table. Melanie looked up, met his accusing eyes, and looked away again.

"Are you going to England, Bhabi?" said Surinder interestedly, for once distracted from his eternal textbooks. He spoke without surprise. Surinder never expected to be in his elders' councils. If his family had suddenly announced that they were all off to Timbuctoo next week, it would not have occurred to him to complain that he hadn't been consulted.

"England?" Bheji paused with the sugar basin in her hand. "Are you, Melanie? Will you be away long? I shall miss you so much." Bheji was missing Arwin, these days. Arwinder came to see them often but it wasn't the same. She was always watching the clock, eager to get back to Saranjit or, if he were with her, to be alone with him. Since Arwinder's marriage, Bheji seemed older.

"*England?*" said Avtar.

He was furious.

∽

He loved Melanie so much, and the moment of fusion in Hallowens that day had come as such an astonishment to him. Equally an astonishment had been the day when she actually said in words that she would marry him and come with him to India to live. It was difficult for anyone, man or woman, to throw off attitudes inculcated in early youth. Avtar and Melanie alike had been born only shortly after the end of the British Raj. He had grown up among people in whom it was still an active influence, whose speech and thought were still coloured by it, and so too had Melanie, albeit in a much lesser degree. More than once, especially during their early courtship, he had had to slap down the thought: *I am doing a remarkable thing, convincing an English girl that she should marry me, and she is doing a remarkable thing to consider it.*

Utter rubbish, of course. He was a well-to-do professional man and a good matrimonial prospect by anybody's standards. But the stupid out-of-date concept of Europeans as being somehow, mysteriously, superior to others lay like a sediment deep in his mind, and whenever they quarrelled it would be stirred up, to cloud the argument with its swirling irrelevance: *What if she now regrets what she has done?* It was clouding the argument now; he could not himself fight through to the real cause of this anger, which was also fear. It was partly, he told himself, groping for reasons, sensible reasons to support his rage and his alarm, that she had made these far-reaching plans without him. And partly that she knew very well that he did not want her to go. Here in his home she had everything she could wish for, hadn't she? She had only to express a desire for new clothes or an outing, and he did his best to meet it. He stared at her angrily.

"I heard from Gran's solicitors a little while ago," she said shakily. "He's left me his house—Gavin's Cliff. The solicitors want me to go and see it and tell them what's to be done with it. So I asked them to get me a ticket. I shan't be gone long. A week or two, perhaps."

"I have to be at the surgery in half an hour," he said, pushing back his chair. "We will talk later. Be here when I come back."

He returned punctually, having done a morning's work without noticing how. Patients had come and gone. None of them had fled from his presence in terror and none of the convalescent ones had had instant relapses at the sight of him; presumably he had reassured and advised and prescribed as usual. But all he actually remembered of the morning was the unuttered dialogue which had clattered back and forth in his head as he lived in advance through this interview with his wife. If Melanie went to England . . .

He had never yet pursued that thought to its conclusion. At its conclusion was something that he dreaded——had begun to dread while they were still engaged——so that he had not been sure, until the very moment when the registrar pronounced them man and wife, that they ever would be. He ate his lunch in an ominous silence, ignoring the fact that both his wife and his mother were studying him uneasily. Then he rose and made for the door, signalling Melanie with his head to follow him. He led her to the sitting room, held the door politely open for her, and shut it after both of them with a loud bang. "What the hell is all this? What is this ticket to England? Why you did not tell me?"

The hesitation in her voice told him that she knew she was in the wrong. "I kept trying to tell you but the moment was never right. I would almost get to the point and then the phone would go or someone would call or you'd begin talking of this or that . . . in the end I let it go, till the ticket arrived . . ."

"Till you had a fait accompli for me. I see."

"Oh, Avtar, don't. The last time I suggested such a thing, you were so unpleasant. I was *afraid* to talk to you about it!"

"But not too afraid to go ahead and send for the ticket. What is it you are going to England *for*? You say your grandfather has made you this legacy——were you even afraid to tell me that much?——and the executors want to know what to do on your behalf? Then tell them! Tell them to sell. There is no need to go all that way just for that. If you had talked to me at once, and not hidden things from me in this secretive way——as if I were no one to you at all, least of all your husband——I would have advised you what you should do."

Melanie sat down slowly on the end of a divan. "I

might not sell." Her voice was low, unemotional, very carefully pitched. She was trying, and he could see it, not to provoke him. "I might decide to let. I think perhaps the house shouldn't go out of the family. It's been in Purvis hands a long time, at least the site has . . ."

"Then he should have left it to someone who was there to live in it! But since he has left it to you, you can tell these executors to find a tenant. They will take your instructions by letter, I suppose? You need not stand over them."

Her explanations were not adequate; there was more behind this. He knew it. Melanie always did give an odd, disconcerting impression of having a secret mental life, of being propelled by motives known only to herself and quite possibly incomprehensible to others. He had been drawn to her originally almost because of that. He had seen at a glance, in her face and eyes, that she was complex, an amalgam of two quite different personalities: one straightforward and very practical; the other questing, hungry, and . . . yes, self-sufficient was the phrase. Further acquaintance had proved this estimate right, and he had found in that duality an excitement for which he had no words. But unfortunately, the self-sufficiency, which was above all the source of the excitement, also aroused in him an illogical desire to overcome it. He did not want Melanie to be able to do without him, even though he knew that the moment she lost that ability, she would cease to be Melanie and cease to be exciting.

At the moment, the urge towards conquest was almost paramount. The only thing inhibiting it was Melanie's painfully careful and low-toned speech. She was like an opponent who refuses to draw his sword. While she looked and sounded like that, he could not attack. He drew a long breath, smoothed the fury off his face by an act of will, and let himself sink gently onto the settee. "You have been upset by your grandfather's death, Melanie. You must not think I don't understand. But where is the sense in going to Gavin's Cliff now? He won't be there."

"You wouldn't," said Melanie, still quietly, but with a bitterness which she obviously could not control, "agree to my going when he *was* there. I can't put that right, ever. But can't you understand that as well as wanting to see Gran, I wanted and still want to see my home again?"

"This is your home! Here, with me. *This* is your home!"

"It's one home. But the place where I was born is home, as well."

"Oh?" said Avtar angrily. "It is a *place* you are so attached to? There is no person mixed up in this at all? No living person?"

"No, there is not! Why will you never *listen* to me?"

Staring at her, he saw that she was contemplating his face as though she would like to throw something at it. He actually saw her glance flicker over the several portable objects in the room: a cut-glass fruit bowl, a pierced Benares brass dish, a six-inch-high sandalwood elephant. He threw his head back, daring her to do it. She abandoned missiles in favour of words, but probably—as he realised a few anguished moments later—because they were more effective weapons.

"If you could see yourself," said Melanie, "sitting there with your face an expressionless mask." He realised that it probably was; an air of inscrutable hauteur worked well on recalcitrant patients and pert nurses; it was a technique he now used instinctively when involved in an argument. But

121

Melanie knew him too well. "It doesn't impress me. It just means that you're not going to listen to a word I say, that all you can see is your own preconceived, *conventional* ideas, and if what I tell you doesn't accord with them, you'll ignore me or say I'm lying. How dare you? You just take it for granted that a woman's home is where her husband is, because someone said that in your hearing when you were little and you've never taken the trouble to question it or ask if it's true . . . and you can't get it out of your head that if a woman wants to be somewhere else, it must be because of some man or other, because you think women only live through men . . ."

"Don't talk nonsense! If you don't know me better than that by now—"

"I do *not* know you better than that! You're proving my point all the time. You won't believe I want to go home because it's my *home*. Well, you can just start believing it! And if you dare say Robin's name, I'll scream out loud! You know bloody well it isn't true; why don't you admit it? *Why?* I thought," said Melanie, "that you liked Somerset and Gran. Why have you turned against them?"

"Somerset is a place like any other! A nice place, but there are millions of nice places. As for your grandfather, he was an old man and I showed him respect."

"Yes. He said once that you were so respectful that he couldn't get a straight answer out of you."

"He might not have liked my straight answers. He was a clever man but I think not good for you. I would not have said that, only you force me to it. That book, the *Computer*, it is full of ideas that are all very well in print or in a debating society, but not to live by. It's no way to live, doubting everything, overturning everything, believing in nothing.

He encouraged people—he encouraged you—to experiment with their lives. I have thought at times: For Melanie I am just an experiment—"

"But that's not true!"

"—and so is living here with me in India an experiment. But for me it is not an experiment, it is a marriage. And for my family too; they love you, they have made you part of them. You have a place here."

"I *know* that. You imagine all this! Oh God, will you never see the point? All this is just *words*. I'm homesick and I'm desperate for the sounds and sights and smells of Gavin's Cliff and I'd swim round Africa to get there! Can't you understand?"

"Yes, I understand." He felt horribly tired. *If Melanie goes to England* . . . His mind was following that trail to its darkness-shrouded and unhappy end, without his volition. "For that very reason," he said heavily, "it is best that you don't go. If you stay here, after a while, this terrible feeling of homesickness will leave you. You will forget."

"But I don't want to forget!" Melanie almost shrieked at him. "I'm not so . . . I'm not so ungrateful! It would be throwing away one of the most precious things in my life! What's wrong with you that you can't see that? Oh God, you're jealous, aren't you, but it isn't Robin. It never was Robin. He was only a blind. It's Gran and Gavin's Cliff you're so afraid of, isn't it?"

And it was, of course. The quarrel about Robin had rung false at the very beginning, even to Avtar. It was as though a pearl diver had surfaced with a triumphant expression and a disintegrating boot. Not Robin. Gran. If Melanie once went to England—his mind had reached that hateful conclusion now—she might never return. The magnetic tug of her origins, even though Gran himself was now gone, might prove too strong. Aided, reinforced by the fact that in choosing Avtar and coming to India, she had done a remarkable thing in the first place....

"Melanie," he said. "I am sorry for your grandfather's death. And sorry that you think I am jealous—was jealous—of him. Perhaps it's true. But believe me, you will get over your distress far faster if you stay here. You must stay here. This is your home. Everything I have is yours . . ."

"But what good is that if you keep me from what is mine?" Melanie demanded. "Avtar. I am going to England."

"You're not!" He came to his feet, almost as if he would seize her and hold her back by force. She took a step away, retreating towards the door.

"I fly to England on Monday week. When that flight leaves from Delhi, at eleven P.M. on that day, I shall be on it. You can't stop me."

"I can if I choose!"

"Just what do you mean by that?"

"I can . . . and if I have to, I will . . . impound your passport! You can't get to England without it!"

"Thank you," said Melanie, shaky and contemptuous, and whirled away from him and ran.

◇

Outside in the hallway, Leela stood motionless, clutching her broom, her dark eyes wide. She must have heard most of it. In the doorway of the kitchen was Bheji, her eyes full of tears. Melanie sped past them, ignoring them both. She ran for the stairs and the bedroom. Avtar came after her but she reached sanctuary just in time and bolted the door in his face. While he pounded on the door and shouted for admittance, and then, changing tactics, attempted to coax her into opening it, she tore open the cupboard which faced the end of her bed, seized the box that held the private documents, and tumbled its contents higgledy-piggledy on the bed.

Her passport was there, with her vaccination certificates inside it. She stood clasping it, scanning the room for a hiding place. Outside, Bheji's voice was joined to Avtar's, calling her name. Under the mattress? Inside the mattress cover? On top of the pelmet?

"Avtar, go away," said Bheji's voice on the landing. "Go to surgery. It must be time for you to go. When you come home all this will be put right. Surinder"—she hadn't heard Surinder come home; he must have arrived during the quarrel—"this is not your affair, go back to your studies. Avtar, you do as I say now."

Trembling in mid-floor, Melanie heard the feet on the landing retreat. A moment later she heard Avtar's car start up, heard it roar as he drove furiously away. She sat down on her bed and thought hard. Then she pushed the passport and certificates into her handbag where the airline ticket already was, stepped out of her slippers and into a pair of court shoes, and quietly left the room.

Bheji was waiting in the hall.

"I'm just going out. Not far and not for long. Bheji, it's all right."

"Avtar wouldn't . . . he has his father's temper. They both are the same. They would *say* things. But they are good men, fair men . . ."

"I know," said Melanie. Bheji's unhappy eyes hurt her. "It's quite all right." Briefly and warmly, Melanie hugged her mother-in-law. Then before Bheji could speak again, she slipped away, out to the front garden and into the road. She hoped a rickshaw would come quickly. If it didn't, she would commandeer Surinder's bicycle. Delay, she could not endure.

There was no need. A cycle rickshaw swerved across the road, springing apparently from the ether. Its proprietor planted a sinewy sandalled foot in the dusty road at her side. "Rickshaw, Memsahib, han?"

Melanie stepped in, settling herself and her bulging handbag on the slippery, sunwarmed leather of the high perch seat. "Bank of India!" she said grimly.

◌

When she came back, the car was in the drive again. Avtar must have changed his mind, left his patients to his partner, and come back. She marched up the stairs. He was sitting in the bedroom, turning over the tumbled contents of the document box, which she had left as they were on the bed.

It was the worst, the most destructive moment they had ever known.

"I wanted to see if it was here," he said. "Your passport. Not to steal it from you. Just to see if you . . . you thought I would. Did you think so?"

"I didn't know. I couldn't take the risk."

"I know I can't stop you from going to England," Avtar said. There was pain in his eyes, in his voice; she could have pitied him except that he had frightened her too much. "At the crudest level," he said, "passports can be replaced. I am not such a fool, nor, despite the things I say when I am angry, such a knave. But I am asking you, Melanie, for your sake and mine, not to go."

"I have to go. Now more than ever."

"Very well." He picked up the papers in handfuls and stuffed them back into the box. "I shan't ask where your passport is now. But it is perfectly safe from me, I promise you." He shut the box and put it away and then threw him-

126

self down on his own divan. He closed his eyes, and appeared to go to sleep.

~

"I've set the alarm for half-past five," said Melanie. She checked once more that she had set the clock correctly, and put it down on the bedside table. She did not look at him. He did not think that either of them had looked straight at the other once during the last ten days.

Nothing, throughout that ten days, had been normal. For all that time they had been formal and withdrawn from each other, like strangers obliged to share a railway carriage. Except that strangers in a railway carriage were usually genuinely indifferent to each other, while Avtar was bitterly aware that under his silences and studied small talk seethed such rage and wretchedness that if he once let it out, it might blow him and Melanie apart for ever.

He sat cross-legged on his divan, writing a note for his partner, who must look after his patients tomorrow while Avtar was taking Melanie to Delhi Airport. He scribbled mechanically while the furious monologue continued within him.

Melanie is going to England. (If this patient's condition is not satisfactory, check if he has kept to diet. If he has not, get angry. With this man, it works.) With Melanie it didn't work; she didn't understand it or him. Almighty God, didn't she *know* he didn't want her to go to England only because he loved her and was afraid to lose her? If she went away now, like this, how likely was it that she would ever come back? Did she intend to come back? Was that what her silence, her distance, was concealing? He shouldn't have lost his temper over the passport (Mrs. Ramanand will be needing help to fill in the form), but Melanie should have known he didn't mean it, should have known that love and fear were talking, shouldn't have gone away into this remoteness . . .

He looked up and found that she was kneeling by her suitcase to do up its clasps, and was watching him across it. There must be a similar maelstrom of feeling within her. She couldn't *want* them to part like this. In three years they had built up so much. But she was not going to reach out to him. He would have to do it. Even though she was going away against his will, even though she had wholly failed to recognise his signals of affection for what they were.

Very well. He slammed his notebook shut and put it and the pen aside decisively, as one who has made up his mind. But he couldn't reach out with words. He couldn't say "it is love and fear talking" because he did not want to tell her what it was he feared. Instead, he held out a hand to her. She came to him without speaking, but willingly.

Half an hour later he lay on his stomach, face buried in his arms, and wished he was a child again so that he could cry. Anger was a potent force, apparently. For the first time in his life his body had refused to answer his call. It had rebelled on his behalf against the outrage of being asked to woo someone who ought instead to be apologising to him. And Melanie knew it too, he thought savagely, ears alert to her movements. She was reacting as she always did to emotional stress. When he turned despairingly away from her, she had sprung from the divan with a muffled exclamation and was now leaning over the washbasin, choking.

They were parting tomorrow. Into his sweating arms, he said: "I'm sorry."

"It's all right." He heard water running into the basin, and the splash of it as she washed her face. For a wonder, the taps were actually working. "I expect it's the heat," said Melanie.

～

When he roused to the blare of the alarm clock, Melanie was already up, combing her hair with the help of the small light above the wall mirror. He did not think that she had slept at all.

He watched her, worrying because her reflected face was so pale, her eyes so sunken. He hoped, with a touch of exasperation, that she would manage the journey today. That had been a sharp attack of biliousness, last night. He had some antitravel-sickness pills which she could take at breakfast. He had better, he supposed, make sure that she did.

～

They ate breakfast silently. When the meal was over they said their farewells.

Surinder was debonair. "Have a nice trip, Bhabi, and come back soon."

Bheji, knowing more than Surinder did, cried openly, and as she hugged Melanie goodbye, whispered: "Don't be long!" and took care that Avtar did not hear.

The car journey was lengthy and they spoke to each other very little as they traversed the long straight road between the fields and the silver-trunked eucalyptus trees that grew along both verges, so that the road was streaked across with alternate sunlight and shadow.

When they came this way in the opposite direction, three years ago, Melanie had been full of exclamations. She had remarked on the sun rising distended and orange out of an early morning haze. "It looks hot even before you feel it. Nothing like a foggy sun in England. It's a completely

129

different shade of orange." She had marvelled at a village with thatched, mud-walled houses, where a girl was grinding corn between grindstones; she had laughed when a black and white pig ran from among the huts and narrowly escaped their wheels. On this journey she vouchsafed only one remark without being spoken to first. As they passed over a particularly rough stretch of road and dust blew in at the windows, she said: "If only it would rain."

In Delhi there was a visit to be made to the airline offices to confirm the flight and then a drive across the city to spend the intervening hours with the cousins who had been their hosts when Melanie first came to India. On the way, one of the reckless rickshaw drivers in which Delhi abounded—men who regarded the cacophanous mixture of business, lorries, cars, bullock and pony carts, bicycles, and other rickshaws as a challenge to be overcome, and the darting pedestrians as quarry to be chased—forced Avtar to swerve into the path of an oncoming oxcart. Melanie cried out as he swerved again and scraped between the cart and the side of a rumbling bus. The nearest horned head went by six inches from the car. Melanie had gone white. "If anything happens *now*!" she said passionately.

Later, as they stood getting their bearings in the seething airport entrance hall, he remembered that incident, and he did not know what to say to her. He felt as though she had already left him.

And there was no time now for the difficult kind of talking which was needed to stitch up such a wound. There was only time for platitudes.

"You'll contact me when you've arrived safely? Both in London and in Somerset?"

"Yes, of course. You'll write to me at Gavin's Cliff?"

"Yes. Give my regards to all your family. You're staying a night with Jane in London?"

"Yes. She's organising a car for me to drive to Somerset."

"Drive carefully."

"I'd better check in now."

"I'll be here till the flight leaves." *There's still a moment to say it in. I could say: Are you coming back? Promise? But even if she did promise, it's only words. She might say them so as to get away without a scene. I can't do that. I can't say it.* "I'll meet you when you come back. Er . . . have you any idea . . . *when*, exactly?"

"Two weeks, three, a month. I'll write or telephone. If I can get through!" She gave him a smile, bringing to mind the day when he had tried to telephone India from London to talk to his mother about their engagement, and after three hours of trying failed to make contact. He returned the smile. They kissed, kindly enough. But as she moved away, following the porter through the crowd towards the barrier, she turned into a stranger, a Western stranger in Western slacks and shirt and short jacket, someone who had come from another world and was now returning to it. He almost panicked, almost ran after her to haul her back. He held himself still, fists clenched inside his trouser pockets. Then she was absorbed into the privileged mass of travellers beyond the barrier and it was too late.

She was on her way back to Gavin's Cliff, to the world she had come from and perhaps should never have left. What hope had it ever had, their marriage? He saw himself dispassionately: a man not too conventional, not too deeply rooted in any culture or set of beliefs, but not much given to questioning them, either. What future could he expect with Melanie, who never stopped asking questions and who was

131

descended from and under the spell of Professor William Purvis—who regarded all creeds as analagous to sets of instructions in ALGOL or FORTRAN and whose cynical definition of a prophet—any prophet—was "a man with enough charisma to convince other people that his own prejudices are a message from the Almighty?"

On the face of it, he thought grimly, none.

It made no difference. He still loved and wanted her; the fear that she no longer loved and wanted him made him feel as though his stomach were weighted with lead. There ought to be a way through to a future somehow, he told himself, still standing in the entrance hall and staring uselessly at the barrier through which Melanie had passed. There ought to be a way.

Part Two

SOMERSET

Stopover: London

She did not expect to be met at Heathrow. But when she pushed her trolley through the green channel with her head full of queries about current taxi rates in England, Jane was there, standing out from the crowd as always. Jane's fine old-gold hair showed no sign yet of fading, and it was as usual cut and set as if for the purpose of advertising its hairdresser. The translucent glow of Jane's skin would assuredly have had Aunt Prem asking the brand names of her cosmetics, and her unexpectedly dark eyes were rendered still larger and deeper by her discreet pearly eye shadow. Jane, Melanie knew, would not have been seen dead in a ditch without her eye shadow. She wore a pale

135

green, belted, showerproof coat, and she could see over the heads of the crowd because Jane, though dryad-slender, was five foot eight and a half in stockinged feet and today her heels were three inches high. She advanced, waving, and took the trolley away from Melanie.

"Jane, how very nice of you . . ."

"It's lovely to see you. Are you completely exhausted? I know what those night flights are like. You just doze off and then someone arrives with a tray of plastic chicken and wakes you up to eat it. I had a few days holiday due to me still, so I took one today. You gave me your flight number, if you remember. You look pale. Were you airsick?"

"No. Avtar gave me some pills. But I couldn't sleep much and Delhi Airport is a sort of obstacle course of formalities."

"You'll be home and having a rest in bed in no time."

"Did you organise my car hire all right?" Melanie asked, as Jane's red mini slid out of the airport environs and took the route for south London. "If not, I can easily . . ."

"Don't be silly. It's waiting for you outside my flat. I got you a Marina. Nonautomatic. You never used to drive automatics, as far as I remember."

"No, you're quite right. I forgot to remind you about that. Thank you."

"Your telegram did say the bare minimum," Jane admitted, overtaking a lorry with a surge of smooth acceleration and slotting herself neatly back into lane in front of it. After Delhi, the traffic of England was as orderly as a marching regiment. "Tell me, what's it all about? Is it to do with your grandfather? Melanie, I was sorry to hear about that. You were so attached to him. Robin thought it might be to do with Professor Purvis."

136

"Robin?" Melanie jerked round from languid contemplation of the tidy traffic and the cool grey sky.

"Well, yes." Jane gave her a sidelong glance, as if gauging the effect of her news. "Robin Selwood. I've seen quite a lot of him lately. You introduced us once, if you recall, and then I ran into him again at a party."

"Oh, well, good luck to you." Melanie lowered the window a fraction to let in some of the soft, damp air. "Yes, I'm here because of my grandfather. He left me his house. I have to inspect it and decide what to do with it."

"Left you his house? Lucky you. And that's all, is it? I mean . . . there's nothing wrong at the Indian end, is there?"

She meant no impertinence. Jane was constitutionally inquisitive but it was only kindheartedness armed with a geiger counter. People in trouble always found Jane ready with offers of handkerchiefs, painkillers, the address of a reliable solicitor, or whatever else seemed appropriate for the crisis in hand.

But Melanie did not want to speak of things so near and so private. "It's nothing like that. Just family business, that's all. Purely family business."

❧

She had met Jane in France, on a coach tour of the chateaux of the Loire. At first sight, Melanie had not liked Jane at all.

The fact that it was a coach trip underlined the differences between them. Melanie had been talked into it by a friend who had then inconsiderately caught influenza, leaving Melanie with the choice of going alone or having a tedious argument with the tour operator about a refund. Although she did not care much for package holidays, she decided that the first alternative would be at least less wasteful. Jane, on the other hand, loved package tours. She spent much of her working life arranging travel for a globetrotting employer, and it was heaven, she said, sheer heaven, to sit back and let someone else arrange travel for her. She was alone, she told Melanie when they found themselves booked into the same twin-bedded room because they were the only two singletons on the trip, because she was between romances. "And a nice rest it is too," said Jane in the slightly too-penetrating voice which had already proved capable of turning heads at the far end of the coach. "Oh, lord," thought Melanie. "Have I got to put up with this for ten whole days? I *can't!*"

In more or less obligatory company, the two of them attended wine tastings (at which Jane commented knowledgeably and audibly on the bouquet), looked at pictures and furniture in a succession of chateaux (where Jane enthusiastically compared the styles of Louis XVI with those of Louis XV), wandered in the regimented gardens of Villandry (where Jane marvelled in ringing tones at the quaintness of making ornamental patterns out of massed vegetables), and took photographs of Richard the Lionheart's tomb in the calm and lofty Abbey of Fontrevault (where Jane aired her knowledge of Richard's life and death, complete with dates) until Melanie began to wonder if the act of throttling Miss Hanworth could possibly be classed as justifiable homicide. Jane, Melanie decided, was brittle, artificial, shallow, and a show-off. This holiday couldn't end soon enough.

But on the last of the ten days the coach, on its homeward run through Normandy, stopped for mid-morning coffee at a roadside cafe opposite a war cemetery, and there was time for a walk. As she and Melanie strolled side by side among the graves, Jane was quiet. Until, stopping beside a headstone to the memory of a Corporal Gordon McGregor, who had been born in Montreal in 1926 and killed in action in Normandy in 1945, she suddenly said: "He was so young. He was only nineteen. So many of them were *so young*." Melanie, turning to her, saw the tears in her eyes before Jane sharply turned her head away.

Back in the coach, Jane produced a mirror from her handbag, examined the minute mascara smudges which were the result of her unexpected uprush of emotion, and began repair work, muttering apologetically: "Sorry about that. But when I saw those dates . . . there were so many, all much the same . . . it just *hit* me."

"I know. It made me feel the same. Good lord, don't apologise!" said Melanie, and tried to imagine being snatched out of reach of Ambersford, exposed to perils which might keep her from ever getting back; tried to imagine living and dying like Corporal Gordon McGregor.

She felt diminished, because it was Jane who had seen the pity and horror of it, while Melanie had needed to have it pointed out to her. She felt ashamed now of all the savage things she had thought about Jane, and sorry she had ever thought her shallow. When they parted at Victoria Coach Station at the end of the tour they exchanged telephone numbers, and when Jane rang up a week later, Melanie was pleased to hear her voice.

∽

Jane's Streatham flat was tiny, but organised for maximum convenience within the minimum of space. There was no spare room, but the sitting room had a superb convertible bed-settee and one wall was filled by a teak-veneered set of storage units which Melanie promptly recognised as Hallowens merchandise. It was not cheap.

The units, as Jane proudly demonstrated, included a let-down table top which, when dropped, revealed a cavity laden with condiments, glassware, and plates. "Robin got it for me with his Hallowens discount. It saves any amount of space."

"That was kind of him," said Melanie, relaxing her back against the upholstery of the bed-settee. The inviting prospect of a bath and a long sleep in Jane's bed lay ahead, but for the moment she was relieved simply to be no longer travelling, on the ground instead of thirty thousand feet up over the Middle East, wondering whether they would encounter any more air pockets. Jane, having made coffee, now got out cups and saucers. "Sugar?"

"Yes, please." The coffee would be welcome as a stimulant. Although she was not yet ready to sleep, she knew that she was very tired and from more than the journey. The memory of her last glimpse of Avtar on the far side of the barrier at Delhi nagged at her. That farewell look had asked for her pity. She kept remembering it and the pity kept on almost appearing, only to be immediately drowned in indignation. He had no right to behave like a tyrant and then ask for compassion. Nor had he any right to fill her with conflict when she was facing so much conflict already. Ahead of her lay Gavin's Cliff. She needed her home, needed recharging with it as if for her it was a power source. But it would be a home with a difference now, for Gran would not be there. At Gavin's Cliff she would have to face the reality of Gran's death. Avtar was making her fight on two fronts simultaneously. She sipped hot coffee, grateful for its stimulation, and asked without a great deal of interest whether Robin was still with Hallowens.

"Yes, though he's thinking of going freelance. He'd like his own studio. I'm encouraging it," said Jane with a faintly proprietory air. "I feel it's something he really wants to do. He's so able."

"I know," said Melanie. She wondered, but hesitated to ask, whether anything was likely to come of the friendship. Jane and Robin must be about the same age, which was now the late thirties. Jane should marry soon if she were ever to marry at all; by most people's standards she had left it too late already. Something in her voice when she spoke of Robin suggested a wish for permanence. She might well have been searching for it for a long time. Jane always said her love affairs ended because she wanted them to, but Avtar, on the one occasion when he had met her, had remarked: "I think she's lonely."

"By the way," said Jane, "do you recognise the window curtains? Robin got those for me too."

Melanie looked round. The curtains were crimson with a pattern of white dots and misty swirls flowing over them. It was one of her own designs, the one she considered her best. *Stardrift*, she had called it. She had conceived it on a background of black or midnight blue, but Robin had produced it in other colours as well. This one had the white stars and nebulae thrown on deep red instead. In another version the white had been changed to black and set on a somewhat menacing backdrop of billowy flame and murky yellow like firelit smoke, and had been instantly pounced upon by a film company making an updated version of *Dr. Faust*. *Stardrift* had been a success, in fact. The sight of it now caused an ache under Melanie's breastbone. She had created it so easily, as though it were nothing and a thousand others waited to be drawn from the same source at will. She had been a different person then. She picked up her coffee cup again. Jane was saying: "If you want to send a telegram to India, I have a telephone here."

Yes, she would have to send a telegram to Avtar. She'd promised, and anyway she'd do it even without a promise.

～

She had a bath and slept all afternoon. When she woke they had tea and went down to try out Melanie's hired Marina. "I want to make sure you're happy with it before you drive all that way," said Jane. When they came back after a satisfactory road test, it was nearly dark. As they climbed the stairs, they saw a light under Jane's front door.

"But I turned the switch off myself. Have you got burglars?" Melanie said sharply, halting on the top step.

"No, I don't think so." The landing was lit, but not well, and it was hard to see Jane's face. Her voice sounded slightly embarrassed. "It's . . . well, I think . . . oh damnation," said Jane, inserting her key in the lock, and marched into the flat saying: "Robin, is that you?"

And Robin Selwood rose like a genie from Jane's best armchair to greet them.

～

So Robin had a key to Jane's flat. Well, splendid, it was none of her business. Shaking hands with Robin, Melanie wondered with considerable irritation why he should suppose that her reappearance in England was any of *his*. Jane must have told him when she was expected, so this visit was probably not coincidence.

Robin's handshake was brisk and strong, very Western. In India, the only person Melanie had met with a similar handshake was Rehal. Indians did not usually shake hands at all and when they did, the grasp was often limp, as if they preferred not to acknowledge the physical contact. Robin's grip would have come as a pleasure, if only it had belonged to somebody else.

"This *is* a surprise," she said with a certain amount of irony.

"An agreeable surprise, I hope," said Robin, and the characteristic levelness of his voice kept her from knowing whether he had detected the irony or not. Jane and Melanie shed their coats and tossed them over chairbacks, and they all sat down. "You never sent Hallowens any more designs," said Robin, when they had finished asking one another how they were and saying very well, thank you. "We were disappointed. I was anxious to see you, to ask about them."

"I haven't done much designing recently," Melanie said. "I've been so busy with other things. What have you been concentrating on lately, yourself?"

"I've been planning to go back to freelance work," Robin said. "I don't do all that much designing where I am. I choose and modify other people's work. It's less satisfying, even though it's more secure."

"It's so important to feel satisfied by your work," said Jane. She glanced at the untidily strewn coats, got up and collected them. "Would either of you like a drink? Robin, you know where everything is. Would you see to it while I fetch some snacks? You can give me a whisky and dry ginger."

"What'll you have, Melanie?" Robin slid to his knees in front of the wall unit. He looked the same as ever, she thought. There was the familiar deadpan face and crinkly brown hair, the calm light eyes which never showed what he was thinking and so often fooled people into the belief that he wasn't thinking at all, the ever-dapper clothes. Robin was both extremely masculine and extremely fastidious. "You used to like White Ladies," he said.

143

"I still do."

"Can you get them in India?" He backed out with his hands full of glasses and a couple of bottles jammed under his elbows. "Or is the place dry?"

"Very but not that way. You can get alcohol. But it's mostly whisky or beer and it isn't socially commonplace as it is here. I drink orange juice or cola mostly out there because of the heat."

"How hot is it, actually?" Jane came in with bowls of peanuts and crisps. "Tell us about India, Melanie."

"In a few words, like that? I can't." She thought of the size of the subcontinent, its colossal interweaving of religions and languages and even of centuries. It was a place where adjacent fields might be harvested respectively by a scythe and a combine harvester, where a limousine might creep along a road behind an elephant . . . where a girl in her twenties could be condemned, could condemn herself, to lifelong negation "because it is the custom." She tried to tell them about Arwin's marriage and Balwant's widowhood, not very successfully, for it was impossible to convey the overwhelming weight of those centuries of custom to people who had not experienced it. They were comfortingly scandalised on Balwant's behalf but completely unable to see why she had not simply walked out on Asha without a backward glance. Melanie did not mention Avtar.

"It sounds as though you're glad to be home for a while," Robin said at the end. "Did you have a good journey? Jane met you all right?"

"Yes. Why, did she tell you she was going to?"

"I told her to," said Robin, placidly consuming whisky and water.

"*You* told her to?"

"Take no notice of him," said Jane. "I was coming anyway. Have some peanuts."

"Thanks. I was relieved to see you, anyhow," Melanie told her. "I'd been wondering how I'd get into the flat if you were at work. Would you have left a key next door and a note for me in the letterbox, or what?"

"A key with next door? God forbid," said Jane without animosity. "That woman was done for shoplifting two months ago and when I had her in here for drinks on my birthday—that was before the shoplifting episode—I lost three spoons which I have since seen in her kitchen. I've a good mind to steal them back again. She's a kleptomaniac!"

Melanie laughed. Robin said: "Why the doting expression, Melanie? You're gazing at Jane like a teacher at a pupil who's just grasped the theory of relativity."

"I think"—she searched in her mind for the reason why that remark should have given her such a salty enjoyment—"that it was the nice, casual bitchiness of saying *she's a kleptomaniac* like that. It doesn't happen in India, or not among the women. They'll either be nasty and mean it or else be very sweet and mean that too. After a while you find you are missing the sharp edge that's just for fun."

On Robin's hand, closed round his whisky glass, the knuckles suddenly gleamed. "You've been in India too damn long," he said. "And if you use the present continuous out of place again, Melanie, or put *only* at the end of a phrase when it ought to be in the middle, or use that sing-song accent at me just once more, I shall throw this glass of White Horse, expensive as it is, straight at your head. You even *sound* Indian now."

There was the familiar time lag while Melanie worked out that under the even voice he was in one of his instant tempers. And then they were in the middle of an instant squabble, of the sort which had studded the whole of their stormy engagement. "Well, *you* haven't altered one iota, Robin! You should hear yourself. Laying down the law—you complained once that my grandfather did that, but you're ten times worse—and you've still got that nasty trick of losing your temper with a straight face and a flat voice . . ."

"At least it isn't a singsong voice."

"Good heavens, you two!" Jane tried to pacify them. "You only met ten minutes ago and you're fighting already. Stop it. Robin, give Melanie another White Lady and *drink* that whisky. It is expensive, as you so rightly remark, and I won't have it splashed all over my guests or my carpet."

She was half teasing, half reproving, reminding him that he was her partner, her cohost. But Melanie, in a careless moment, had quoted from the last, fatal quarrel of their engagement and now she saw that he was recalling, as she was, how they had sat side by side, but not touching, on the sofa in Robin's flat and finally, disastrously, clashed over where they should live when they were married.

"I don't mean live all the way down in Somerset, Robin. I know your work is here. But we don't have to be right in London, surely."

"I *must* live in London, I tell you. I can't think or create or keep up to date if I'm rusticating in the country."

"You can't call somewhere like Surrey rusticating. Oh, Robin, look how creative Gran is, and he *does* live in the west country, right in it."

"He thinks he's creative," snapped Robin, who disliked being reminded either of Melanie's grandfather or his home. On his one visit there, an appallingly wet weekend, he had stepped out of the car in front of Gavin's Cliff straight into a six-inch-deep morass of red decayed sandstone, and as it oozed over the uppers of his smartly polished best brown shoes, all hope of Robin learning to love Gavin's Cliff drowned with them. "He's negative," Robin said. "Turned away from life. Oh yes, he is. What else do you call all that agnosticism and anticommitment of his? I can understand him not agreeing with my political views; what I can't stomach is the way he seems to think I shouldn't have any, and lays the law down to me about it! Rusticating's done him no good. He's only half-alive and what's more, so are you."

"You only quarrelled with him because you didn't like Gavin's Cliff in a downpour," said Melanie. "You didn't even try to like either of them. I'm beginning to think, Robin, that you don't like me, as well. Or want me or need me. You need someone quite different." She was distant, on her dignity.

"I might say the same of you." Robin was on his. "Frankly, Melanie, unless you can grow up and become less limited in your outlook, less hooked on just one kind of place and one way of life . . ."

And so it had gone on, with the two of them hurling themselves against the principal struts in each other's personalities, as though for each of them, survival depended on the other's destruction, until Melanie ran crying from the flat, leapt into her car, and drove away to Gavin's Cliff and Gran, arriving there pell-mell and desperate at dawn.

Jane did not know of the quarrel. But she sensed that their thoughts were private to the two of them. Melanie caught sight of her friend's expression and recognised the hurt, I've-been-shut-out look. It was too much, far, far too much. The journey. Avtar. Balwant and Rehal. Now this. Oh, come soon, the moment when she would be free of them all and on the road to Ambersford. Her exhaustion was back, and increasing every moment, turning into a malaise. What if she were ill and could not drive to Ambersford in the morning after all? She waved the second White Lady away.

"I don't want to be antisocial, but it's been a long journey and I've an early start to make tomorrow. Jane, can I help you put together something to eat now? Then perhaps I could rest on your bed and switch to the convertible later. . . ."

"Of course you're having my bed for the night!" Concern replaced distress on Jane's face. "What time are you starting tomorrow? Are you going straight to Gavin's Cliff?"

"No, I'm staying with my cousins and Uncle Daniel, in Ambersford. I wrote to them. I want to set out well before five. I've a travelling alarm clock so I need not disturb you."

"Why so early?" enquired Robin. "I've eaten, by the way, Jane. I didn't want to impose on you when you had a guest. I'll be off in a moment. It's not such a long run, Melanie. You can take the motorway to Bristol and then turn south. It's motorway all the way to Bridgwater."

"I'm taking my old route through Guildford."

"Good God, why? The motorway knocks hours off the journey and . . ."

"I don't like the motorway. I'm going the way I prefer, the way I've always used, and I'm leaving at the time that always suited me best too."

"You sentimental pilgrim! Really, Melanie!"

"For God's sake, the pair of you!" Jane sounded really cross. "Robin, leave her alone. If she wants to go to Somerset riding a bicycle backwards all the way, I can't see what business it is of yours. Melanie, you don't look well to me. Why don't you just go to bed and I'll bring you some food on a tray."

"I'll be going." Robin stood up. "I only dropped in to

say hallo and try to get a little business for Hallowens. If you do produce any more work, Melanie, let me have sight of it. Take care tomorrow on your unnecessarily long and arduous journey, now."

He grinned as he said it. Melanie smiled and stood up too to shake hands once again. Jane saw him out. They spoke together in the hall for a moment, out of sight. There was the sound of a kiss and she heard Jane laugh. It was all right. Robin had retreated from the perilous verge of old memories and was back where he now belonged. Good. She had no spare energy for worrying about Robin.

She had no spare energy for anything, she thought, and yet despite her weariness, and despite the soothing supper in bed which Jane provided, she found it hard to sleep that night. The thunder of enormous engines still throbbed within her head and India seemed only just out of sight.

She lay in the cool London darkness and thought of India, of the hot sky and the pervasive dust. Her second-best hairbrush which she used when travelling, and with which she had tidied her hair on arrival, was filthy now with the red dust of Delhi. She thought of Avtar, of the quarrel and the unsuccessful effort at reconciliation the night before she set out. She knew quite well what that failure meant. In Avtar's eyes, still, she was committing a crime in wanting to see her home again.

She turned over, trying to quiet her mind. Tomorrow she would be in Ambersford. The thought of that was like a talisman with which to keep wretched memories at bay, a defence against demons. Even though Gran would not be there, it was that. She should think of Ambersford and her family there and let the past rest for the time being. She needed a space for thought. She wished she had not looked back at the airport. Damn that final . . . that . . . *underhand* expression of pathos. She sat up and put on the light, surveying her white face and hot eyes in Jane's mirror. What was the use of loving anyone if they did this to you? Or what was the use—putting it more accurately—of trying to love? She clicked the light off and threw herself down on the pillow again, knowing that she could no longer pretend to herself that the thought of Avtar roused in her anything other than a bitter anger.

He had meddled with something he did not understand, and he didn't even seem to *know* that he didn't understand it. He'd put his hand into a wasps' nest. Very well, let him get stung. At least, she thought, I have choice. Thousands of millions of women have no choice. They're trapped—by children, economics, the simple fact of having nowhere else to go. I have a profession and I have Gavin's Cliff. If I don't want to see Avtar or India ever again, I need not.

Breakfast in Basingstoke

In the lapse of time since she had last done the drive from London to Ambersford, Melanie had forgotten how uninviting the world could be at four A.M. in a cold climate. When her travelling alarm clock had roused her in the morning, Jane's bed seemed extraordinarily snug, and the prospect of the hundred and eighty-four miles of damp grey road ahead extraordinarily cheerless. A large number of people would certainly think she was crazy. Robin Selwood was not in a minority.

Jane, yawning, plodding about the kitchen as she semiconsciously assembled tea and toast, was clearly in agreement.

"You're out of your mind. You realise that, I hope? Why four in the morning, even if you're not using the motorway?"

"I didn't mean you to get up," said Melanie. "I said I'd see to myself." Jane, wrapped in an old pink housecoat and minus her eyeshadow and blusher, looked very tired. Her beautiful face seemed naked, less alive.

"Nonsense," she said. "Would you like an egg?"

"No, thank you." The malaise of yesterday had passed but Melanie still did not feel entirely well. She was certainly not hungry. She would breakfast properly on the way, at a more reasonable hour. She hoped the Basingstoke cafe was still there. "Can I make coffee?" she asked. "I want to fill a flask. I've brought one."

By quarter to five she was ready. Jane, overcoat tossed round her shoulders, helped to manhandle the luggage down the stairs and into the car. "You know the way to the main road? Left at the end of the street. I hope Gavin's Cliff is in good order." She wiped condensation off the rear window and came round to the driver's window as Melanie settled behind the wheel. "Are you all right for petrol?"

"Yes, thank you." Melanie sometimes felt that Jane would have made a good mother.

"Well, you're off, then. You'll be in touch?"

"Yes, of course."

"Well, goodbye."

The car drew away. At the end of the road, Melanie saw in the mirror that Jane was waving a vigorous farewell. She raised a hand in what she hoped was a visible salute before she turned the corner and was at last alone with the car, and on the road to Ambersford.

She had longed for this. She had thought of it continuously during the agonised homesickness of the last few weeks in Chandigarh. Now it was a relief, a rising joy which even the aching loss of Gran or the weight of unresolved conflict could not restrain. The steady pulse of the westbound engine, the willing accelerator under her foot; the solitude; the freedom of driving alone—together they were like the quenching of a giant thirst.

So was the ritual choice of route.

It would be possible—Robin was right—to get there much more quickly by motorway. But when Melanie and her father had first worked out their route from Croydon, they had done it with an eye for charm along the way. Motorways they considered dull, and useful only if you were in a hurry. If Melanie's father did not share her passion for Ambersford, at least he was in accord with her on the subject of making drives pleasant. Poring over the map, testing their route detail by detail over successive journeys, they had drawn closer than at any other time. Now, for Melanie, the drive to Ambersford was part of the enchantment.

It was still dark as the Marina slid out of London. The roads were wet, reflecting the street lamps on their gleaming surfaces. It was a raw morning, not raining now and not freezing, but damp in the way which penetrated crevices and ate into one's bones. Melanie rejoiced in it at first, and opened the window the better to revel in being cold and wet after three years of near-dehydration. By Epsom, however, she had had enough of it and turned the heater on, winding up the windows at the same time. No point in arriving at Ambersford with pneumonia, after all.

An object of the route was to go south and get well

clear of London before veering westwards, which was why it went by way of Guildford. There was fog on the Guildford bypass, but as she emerged on top of the long Hog's Back which stretched between Guildford and Farnham, running along the crest of a ridge, the air was clear and a dual carriageway extended ahead with hardly a soul upon it. Melanie put her foot blissfully down and let the car stretch out.

The Hog's Back was a vital landmark in the route. Up to Guildford one was still in home territory, and within the boundaries of an ordinary afternoon's spin. Once out on the ridge, an invisible frontier was crossed. At that point the mind changed gear, ready for the long haul ahead. At that point you began, in more than a geographical sense, to leave London behind.

The large, confusing roundabout outside Farnham came at the end of the Hog's Back. She missed the Basingstoke road the first time and had to go round again. Her memory was rusty. Then she was on her way once more, making for Basingstoke by way of Odiham. She passed through Odiham at six o'clock, slackening speed in order to look affectionately round her. Odiham was a country town of ancient pattern: church, pub, broad main street, neat small shops and houses of varying pattern and age. Few people were about yet, except for a milkman and a couple of agricultural workers on bicycles. A place of similar dimensions in India would be quite different. There would be people abroad long before this hour, making use of the cool early morning. Women would be grinding flour or cooking chapattis over outdoor fires; children would be running to and fro, dogs prowling for scraps, cattle wandering. And even though the Indian village might have been inhabited for as long as Odiham— and Odiham had been founded long before the Conquest by a tribal chieftain called Odi—it would still retain a curious air of impermanence, as though it were even yet something of an encampment. Melanie wondered why. Economics, perhaps, or lack of local stone to make buildings that looked as though they were there to stay. Or perhaps it was climatic. The monsoon in India could be drenching, but it was at least transient. In England, dwellings had to be sturdy and weatherproof if the dwellers therein were to survive; rain could last for months on end.

After Odiham came another complicated road junction and again she missed her way, overshooting the sign for the ordinary A30 and landing on the motorway after all. But she was headed for Basingstoke just the same and wouldn't be on it for long. It was only half-past six. She had made excellent time.

⌒

Basingstoke had undergone a good deal of redevelopment since she had seen it last, and for a while she was afraid that the cafe might indeed have vanished. Then she saw its electric blue sign standing cheerfully out of the row of shuttered shops on either side, and with a sense of homecoming slowed down to search for a parking place. She wondered if the cafe would have changed inside.

But it was exactly as she remembered it: warm, steamy, companionable. A shift must just have changed at one of the nearby factories, for the place was nearly full, and behind the counter with its tall polished urns the staff were busy. She found a table with only one other occupant, a man consuming poached egg on toast in a self-contained manner. She put her coat on the chair by way of staking a claim, and went to the counter.

It was self-service for tea and coffee and things like

155

biscuits, but for hot food you only gave the order at the counter, and when it was ready a waitress would bring it to you. She ordered fried egg, bacon and sausage, debated over the choice of tea or coffee, settled for tea because it was wetter and she felt thirsty, and carried her cup back to the table. She settled down with elbows on the formica table-top, blew the steam off the tea, and drank.

The tea was muddy brown in colour and the first mouthful tasted like nothing so much as concentrated wash-ing-up water. Melanie put the cup down hurriedly. It was scarcely believable that this turgid liquid could go by the same name as the fragrant and refreshing cardomum-scented beverage which one drank every day in Chandigarh. Anyone who called this dreadful product tea, thought Melanie in-dignantly, ought to be had up for contravening some law or other. Wasn't there something in Britain called the Trade Descriptions Act?

But her thirst was real and she was shivery. Some of the morning's damp chill had found its way under her skin. She raised the cup and sipped again. It couldn't really be as bad as she imagined.

It could. It was worse. This time the cup went back into the saucer with a panicky clatter as greenish black spots of nausea jigged before her eyes and her back teeth flooded.

"Are you all right?" asked a voice politely, from the other side of the spots.

Focusing with difficulty, she found that the self-contained man was eyeing her with concern, a forkful of toast and egg halfway to his mouth. He was a youngish family man by the look of him, late twenties, perhaps, with a responsible face. Oh, dear. If a complete stranger engrossed in his own life had noticed something wrong with her, then she must look nearly as bad as she felt. "I'm sorry," she said unsteadily. "I'm tired. I've had a long journey. And I must say," she added, trying to rouse herself into normality by sheer willpower, "that the tea is rather nasty."

A square, reddish hand reached across the table and twitched the cup away. "You're right. Real army brew, that is. What you want is a good black coffee. Stay there." He rose and went to the counter.

But it was impossible to stay there. Melanie cast a desperate eye round the cafe, located a door marked Ladies, and ran. The next few moments were disagreeable but brought their own relief. She found a sink and rinsed her mouth, half leaning against the wall and privately cursing her unreliable digestive system. Of all the times to choose to play her up. Halfway through a journey between hemispheres. She braced herself for the effort, and went back into the cafe.

Her companion was back at the table already and a black coffee was at her place. Her benefactor surveyed her with sympathy but without comment, except to say: "Drink that." Melanie examined the coffee dubiously but the aroma which rose from it was surprisingly inviting. She sipped timidly and found that her palate was working again. She gave him a shaky smile. "Thank you."

"Sure you're only tired? Not ill? Have you far to go?"

"I'm driving to Somerset." She had an unreasonable urge to tell him all about it, ask for advice about Avtar and Gavin's Cliff and how to reconcile these two opposing forces. She checked it. One couldn't pour out one's life story to chance-met strangers in Basingstoke cafes, least of all when the stranger looked as though he had worries enough of his own—a mortgage, probably, or childrens' school reports that weren't all they should be. He had that kind of face.

"Better take it easy the rest of the way," he said. "You haven't been driving all night, have you?"

157

"No, I just made a very early start. And I had an air journey yesterday."

"Oh? Where from?"

"India. I live there normally. And I do think they make tea better there than here!"

He laughed. "That's a hell of a distance." His eyes took in the ring on her left hand, and then as much of the rest of her as he could see behind the table. He was obviously wondering why she lived in India, what had brought her here in such haste, and where her husband had got to. But the light remark about the tea had warned him off and in all probability he was glad to accept the prohibition. "You want to take care of yourself," he said, as he straightened the knife and fork on his empty plate and prepared to leave.

"The coffee?" said Melanie hesitantly. "It was very kind of you but . . ."

"Don't be silly. My pleasure. I hope it did you some good. Goodbye, and safe journey." He slid a tip under his plate and moved casually away to the cash desk, having done his duty by the whey-faced traveller. The waitress arrived with Melanie's own food. Melanie, revived by the coffee but not quite to that extent, looked at it in alarm. She supposed she should eat something if she could but . . . she compromised on eating the sausage and a piece of toast and nibbling at half a piece of bacon. She left the egg. There did not seem to be any untoward reactions to the rest, but the egg would be too much of a challenge to fate.

Back in the car, she sat still for a while, wondering whether she should drive on straightaway or not. Curiously, the attack seemed to have passed completely. Nerves, she supposed. If so, driving would be good for her, not the opposite. To Melanie, her car—which meant any car she happened to be driving at the time—was an extension of herself, was home. To be at home was good for nervous upsets. Forget about being ill. Concentrate instead on the next stage of the journey. She had got to find the B3400 to Andover.

The local authorities had always had a curiously secretive attitude to the B3400. There were signs in plenty, large and obtrusive, urging the facilities of the motorway or the delights of the A30. But the lesser road via Whitchurch could be discovered only by those who were observant and determined to the point of dedication. Once, Melanie could have found it without the help of signposts, but the developments which had almost hidden the cafe from her had changed other landmarks too. But she was rewarded at length, at a junction which she did not recognise, by a shy little sign which admitted that the B3400 existed, was in this direction, and led ultimately to Andover. She turned onto it.

It was one of her favourite stretches of the route. The B3400 was a gentle, mildly sinuous road which ran among fields and woods and under low bridges—one almost never encountered lorries on it—and past places with very English and sometimes faintly ecclesiastical names like Longparish and Hurstbourne Priors. At this hour and season it was virtually empty and brought her to Andover almost as soon as the motorway could. Round the ring road and back to the A30, and on to Amesbury and Stonehenge. At Stonehenge she drank the coffee from her flask but did not get out of the car to see if the monument was open, because it was too cold. The wind blowing across the undulating miles of Salisbury Plain made the car quiver as she sat inside it in the car park. She did not mind. For Melanie it was enough to be here, in England, alone, and on the road to Ambersford.

It began to rain as she descended the long hills at the

far side of Salisbury Plain. The road sign which told motorists that they were now entering the County of Somerset leapt suddenly out at her from blowing sheets of water. Had it not been such an obviously demented thing to do, she would have stopped the car and got out and danced in the downpour. She was in Somerset, Somerset, and it was raining, raining, *raining*. As each stage of this pilgrimage was completed across the slowly changing land between London and Gavin's Cliff, she was taking on more of her own self, moving more deeply into her own place. The County of Somerset sign, the blowing rain, were for Melanie the fulfillment of steps in a rite.

Somerset was a big county. Ambersford was on the other side of it, as near to Devon as made very little difference. But she should be there by lunchtime. Her belly muscles tightened, excited. The rain eased as she came into Glastonbury, and the tower-crowned Tor stood outlined against a silver sky. She filled up the petrol tank in Glastonbury, and as she stepped out to wipe the windscreen, she smelt for the first time the characteristic smell of the west country, the mingled scents of earth and leaves and air soft with continual moisture. The attendant who served her had a mellow west country accent. Nearly home, now.

Bridgwater brought her into home territory, the Somerset equivalent of Guildford. The land was rising now towards the moors, and in the ploughed fields the raw earth was almost crimson. She had forgotten how very red the earth of this place could be. If she had stayed away much longer, how much more would she have lost?

Then she was through the last village before Ambersford and to her right, beyond flat marsh and pastureland, was a steel grey line which was the sea. Ahead, three miles off, was the darkly wooded outline of Heverton Point. On the left, but nearer, were the ruins of Ambersford Castle on their hill, which had been a headland in the days of William the Conqueror, before the sea went back and left the marshlands behind it. Beyond the castle was the steep butt end of Ravensridge; far away in the background was a rumour of faint purple-brown, the first ramparts of Exmoor. Melanie, anguished, thankful, shaken beyond bearing, pulled off the road and stopped.

What was it, why was it, this potent love of place? In a world so well endowed with lovely landscapes, why was she bonded to these hills and no others? They stood and were; they had no words to say and no demands to make; they needed neither love nor service. But they were a pattern burnt into her brain, and when she raised her head to look at them it seemed that her early life was a pattern burnt in turn into their slopes. On those distant moors she had been lost in mist and had had to drop the reins and let the horse take her home; on Ravensridge, during one of those summer holidays with Gran, she had walked with her very first boyfriend. Down in that valley she had helped to retrieve a herd of straying cattle after a tractor accident had broken down their fence; over there . . .

Whatever the cause, this place possessed her. Sitting there, arms resting on the steering wheel, she felt tension relax within her, tension which had been tightening and tightening through all these years of absence. It was like a silence after intolerable noise, a deep, three-dimensional kind of silence capable of blanketing out all the turmoil of her mind, the echoes of quarrelling voices, the ranting of angry thoughts, the whimpers of guilt and grief. She sat and let this unexpected, blessed peace take her over. No need, any more, to think and struggle. No ability to think or struggle, even.

Almost, she dropped asleep behind the wheel. She roused herself sharply, and reached for the ignition key. Only one more mile.

There was a left-hand turn up a short, straight hill and then the road bent left again and dipped into Ambersford High Street. The *Ambersford Arms* (fourteenth century and the village's classier rival to the *Sheaf of Wheat* at the other end) was at the start of the street. The *Arms* had original green fourteenth-century glass in the hotel bar windows and four-poster beds in its more expensive rooms. The *Sheaf* had hilarious beer mats, horse brasses everywhere, and a juke box. On down Ambersford High Street, avoiding those pedestrians who were sensibly walking in the road instead of on the cobbles. High Street looked as though it meant to take you into the side of Castle Hill, but the road bent sharp right at the last moment into The Narrows, between the hill and the churchyard wall. In the holiday season The Narrows were a menace, often jammed immovable for twenty minutes at a time because two motor coaches had met in the middle and neither could back until their drivers had leant out of their windows and with frantic gestures induced the cars behind to back as well. But today traffic was going through unhindered, and Melanie emerged a few moments later at the top of Hill Street. The *Sheaf of Wheat* lay ahead, on her left, and beyond it was her old home, Roadend. To her right was the entrance to a lane. She turned into it.

Along the lane, sunk between high, hedge-crowned banks, curving round the church, one more bend and there it was: the house where Frances and Roy lived with Roy's parents; Melanie's last halt before Gavin's Cliff itself. A low wall of pink stone first, with a neat garden on the other side. Aunt Lucy was an enthusiastic gardener with a penchant for gnomes and bird baths. A length of higher wall with a double gate in it, behind which was the stableyard. Behind that again, and visible because they were partway up a hill, were the orchard and kitchen garden cared for chiefly by Roy. He had once urged expansion into the market garden business but nothing had come of it. Melanie pulled up in front of the house itself, at the end of the stableyard wall. The front door had a horsey appearance, because it was made like a loosebox door, with the upper and lower halves opening independently. The top half just now was fastened open. Melanie sounded the hooter.

From within the house came an outburst of barking. Then the lower door shook under a sudden impact and a Siamese cat scrabbled up to balance on top of it. Slanting blue eyes in a seal brown mask regarded the car with suspicion. The cat dived to the ground and bounded across the lane into the garden of a small cottage opposite. A large striped tomcat loped round the corner of the cottage to meet it. Simultaneously, the other half of the Purvis front door was flung open and a young woman with curly brown hair in a tangle like an agitated furze bush, and a hairy river of dogs flowing round her legs, dashed out. It might have been an ecstatic response to Melanie's arrival—but it was not. As Melanie got out of the car she was almost overshot by her Cousin Frances, except that as Frances swerved round the car, the two of them came face to face.

"Melanie! But how lovely . . . down, Madge! Shut up, Jason! We didn't think you'd be here till teatime . . . *Roy!* Melanie's here! Oh, hell, that bloody tom's after Roxana already. Excuse me, Melanie."

Melanie, patting canine heads and pushing canine paws off her stomach, was left standing where she was while Frances sprinted across the lane and vanished into the

163

cottage garden. From behind the hedge came angry spitting. Frances could be heard clapping her hands and shouting "Shoo!" The tomcat shot out of the gate and fled down the road. The dogs left Melanie to pursue it for a few token yards, but returned quickly to the more entrancing pastime of trying to wash the new arrival's face. Frances reappeared, clutching an indignant and struggling Roxana. "Sorry about that, but she's in season and we don't want hybrid kittens. There's a Siamese stud up at the Millers' place at Stancross and that's where she's going as soon as we can get there with her. It's wonderful to see you. How are you?"

"Quite well, thank you." It seemed, now, to be true.

"Well, come on in. Roy'll bring your stuff in. Oh, Roy, can you see to Melanie's luggage? Dad's out hunting, Melanie. He'll be back for supper . . . ow! You horrible cat! Don't you dare stick your claws in me . . . oh, lord, she's getting away. . . ."

Melanie stooped just in time and retrieved the sinuously resisting Roxana. Roy appeared, broad shouldered, from the door and said: "We'll have to shake hands later!" and went to tackle the luggage. Melanie found herself laughing. She had forgotten that it was possible for a home to be quite so dominated by four-footed creatures. In India, she knew a few people who kept one small dog, but that was all. She had seen the outlines of Ravensridge and Heverton Point today, but had she not seen them, had she been brought here in darkness or impenetrable fog, not knowing her destination, she would have known by the animals that she was home.

A Sense of Bereavement

She was swept into the house on an eddy of greetings. Placid, broad-built Aunt Lucy came from the kitchen, relieved her of Roxana, and then embraced her with great warmth and perfect composure. Lucy Purvis was not an excitable woman. Roy bore her luggage upstairs. Frances, leading her up after him, flung open the door of a room decorated in pale yellow: butter-coloured curtains, primrose carpet with a shaggy pile, primrose bedspread with rosebuds scattered all over it. A very feminine room, reminiscent of Frances as she had been before she married into the down-to-earth horse, dog, and Siamese cat world of Roy and Daniel Purvis. "The phone's in the hall if you want to send telegrams or anything," said

Frances, "and there's hot water if you want a bath. I've put my hairdrier in here for you in case you need it. Lunch won't be for another hour."

She had made good use of Jane's bath, but the novelty of sitting in deep, hot water and being cool enough in the first place to enjoy it hadn't worn off. She accepted the invitation. She also used the telephone. She had better, she supposed. She sent the telegram, a brief and factual one, announcing her safe arrival in Ambersford.

The bathroom was gleamingly well kept and smelt of air freshener. Frances and Lucy Purvis were both good housewives. Melanie twisted burnished taps to mix the hot and cold together and was somewhat surprised when the water which resulted was not in accordance with its pristine surroundings. It looked as though the taps had been accidentally connected to a vat of whisky. After the amber liquid had flowed for a few moments, the tap said *gollop* and a chunk of fibrous peat leapt out of it into the bath. Melanie, who had been getting undressed, wrapped a dressing gown round her and went to the door.

Her cousin was coming out of the bedroom opposite with an armful of linen. "Frances, what in the world's the matter with the bathwater?"

"Oh God, I should have warned you. That's Old Harry. It's been wet all year and he's overflowing into the water supply. Only the washing water," Frances added hastily. "The drinking supply's all right. There's a fight going on between the West of England Coastal Counties Water Authority and the North Exmoor and Darr Valley River Board about whose responsibility it is to put it right. It's all because of a new reservoir up at Amberscombe. It's not all that well placed. I think they may have to drain Old Harry. He's a pest."

"Good lord. I thought I'd left water supply problems behind me."

"Well, you haven't. But the colour doesn't come off on you and if you use some of my bath oil it won't mark the bath either. Don't worry about it."

"I'm not worried," Melanie said. "At least there is water. It's rationed half the time in India. Dry taps for hours nearly every day. I'm glad Old Harry's still got a personality." Avtar had laughed at her when she spoke of the bog up beyond Stancross as "he," but Old Harry had possessed his name and his masculine gender ever since 1884 when Harold Miller, grandfather of the present Mr. Miller, had fallen in and drowned one October on his way home from Bampton Pony Fair. The bog was part of local folklore now. It would be a shame, in a way, if Old Harry had to go. "He's making me feel at home," Melanie said. "Frances, I am glad to be back. Everything's just the same as I remembered . . . I looked into the kitchen just now and there it all was, flag-stones on the floor and the black beams with hooks on them, where they used to hang hams to cure in the old days. Just like the kitchen at Roadend used to be." She noticed her cousin's expression, and laughed. "Though I know you won't agree with me that your kitchen's wonderful."

"My kitchen," said Frances with feeling, "is awful. You know quite well what I think of it!"

∽

Frances had never shared either her cousin or her mother-in-law's views on the beauty of the Ambersford kitchen. To Frances, a medieval fireplace built for the purpose of roasting oxen was not a piece of preserved history where hands contemporary with Henry V might have turned the spit; it was merely a picturesque nuisance, an awkward alcove which

167

somebody had once thought a handy place in which to put the modern electric stove. If you moved carelessly while cooking, you were liable to bang your head.

Come to that, you were liable to bang your head almost anywhere in the room because Lucy *would* use old ham hooks for hanging up onions and potatoes in nets. Frances had once actually bought a set of stacking baskets, but Lucy just said: "What a good idea," and went on imperturbably slinging nets from the ceiling. If you avoided the onion and potato booby traps, you might still trip on the uneven floor. It was all very well for Melanie to wax nostalgic and senti-mental at the sight of the place, Frances considered, putting pork chops onto warmed plates and pushing a serving spoon into the peas, but Melanie didn't have to cook in it. At least, kitchens might, one supposed, be even more primitive in India, but Avtar apparently had servants and anyhow, Melanie presumably didn't have to feed an endless stream of summer visitors who came for riding holidays, winter visitors who came for hunting holidays, and all-the-year-round visitors who came to try out prospective equine pur-chases.

She checked that the salt was on the table, told her daughter Molly, who was home from school for lunch, not to swing her legs like that and to stop staring at her Aunt Melanie, and slid into her own seat. "Does England feel very strange after India, Melanie? The climate must feel cold."

"Such a sad homecoming for you," Lucy Purvis agreed, passing potatoes. "I wish you had come before, under happier circumstances. Such a shame your husband couldn't come with you. You must be missing him so much."

෴

The last subjects which Melanie wished to discuss just now were India and Avtar. She had felt as though the atmosphere of home were a comforting padding on a wound. She wanted the comfort to continue, not to probe the sore place again until a measure of healing had taken place.

"It couldn't be helped," she said, and made a powerful effort in order not to sound brusque. "A doctor has a very busy life and his patients are very dependent on him. I'm most anxious to get to Gavin's Cliff as soon as I can." The change of subject *was* abrupt but she couldn't prevent it. "Who has the keys just now?"

"The solicitors," said Frances. "Only today is early closing for them. Whitehangers doesn't have a key any more. They had some sort of argument with Gran and they gave him back their key-for-emergencies."

Melanie nodded. "I'll have to wait till tomorrow, then." She searched her mind for some other painless topic of conversation. "Which pack is Uncle Daniel out with today?"

"The Devon & Somerset. He's got two clients with him; they'll be staying till the morning and then going home," said Roy. "But one of them will be buying his mount and taking it with him, we hope. Business is quite good, though we've a quiet two weeks ahead. The house will be full after that, right up to Christmas."

"And right through Christmas," said Frances. "We lay on a kind of Yuletide house party for clients who want to come for one of the Boxing Day meets." Yes, and have to cater for them. Frances dreamed at night, quite often, of labour-saving fitted kitchens with wall-mounted cupboards, wipe-clean ceramic tiling, and, for preference, back doors which didn't open direct into a stableyard. In this house the kitchen door did, and furthermore, it was left open whenever the weather was warm. Once when William Purvis was staying with them, he had gone into the kitchen in search of Daniel and come face to face with a horse. "Oh, Crusader's dead clever. He can undo his box bolts with his teeth," was all that Daniel Purvis said in answer to his father's outraged strictures on hygiene. Frances had been entirely on Professor Purvis's side.

"Fran, stop dreaming. I've asked you twice for more carrots," said Roy impatiently. He reached out a massive hand and forearm for the dish as she passed it to him. Roy was Lucy Purvis's son in looks, with her flaxen hair and heavy build, but he didn't have her equable temperament. "How," he asked, as he helped himself, "do you think Melanie's looking, Fran?"

"Oh," said Frances, glancing at her cousin and quelling the word which rose instantly into her mind: *foreign.*

～

It hadn't been apparent when Melanie first appeared in her travel-creased trousers and sweater, but now that she had bathed and changed it showed. Not crudely or obviously; her clean fawn-coloured slacks and yellow pullover could have been duplicated in half the wardrobes of Ambersford, and the lily of the valley talc of which she smelt was obtainable at the chemists in High Street. But the way she held herself inside those unremarkable clothes, the movements of her hands as she talked, the high gloss of her newly washed dark hair and the coil in which she wore it, the intonation of her voice—which in the midst of Somerset voices was like silver against weathered oak—all these added up to something unfamiliar to the point of being exotic. Eight-year-old Molly had been struck speechless by it, and it was the reason why she was now persistently staring at the stranger.

Roy was aware of it too; he was passing Melanie things with an air of old-fashioned courtesy regrettably lacking when only his family were at table. The only people who seemed quite unconscious of it were Lucy Purvis, tranquilly eating, and Melanie herself.

"I think Melanie looks very well," said Frances.

Melanie said: "I can't tell how I look. What I'm feeling is a mixture. I'm glad to be home for a while but so very sad about Gran. I want to know about Gran. What exactly happened?"

Roy explained for her how Gran had felt ill one evening when they were watching television after he had had dinner with them, how he had collapsed in his chair, how they had called an ambulance and gone with him to Heverton Hospital, all to no avail. Lucy said: "Daniel took on about it a lot next day. But there, it was a quick way to go, and he was eighty."

"Yes, that's about it," Roy agreed. "We were all upset, but you have to be prepared for it, with someone that age."

None of them sounded unduly distressed. Melanie controlled a shiver. The enveloping comfort of home could not protect her from this, for Gran was part of home. She needed and wanted to talk about him, but she would prefer more sympathetic ears. "Well, it's a sad subject for a mealtime," she said. "Tell me the local news."

∽

"None of the shops has changed hands, though Finch in the grocery is retiring soon," Frances said.

"And Amanda Viney still regularly drives the bell-ringers mad," Aunt Lucy added. "But two new gift shops have started up and another restaurant . . . oh, and there's someone quite new in that cottage opposite Roadend, where you had a neighbour once who was funny in the head, Melanie. An old man had it after that and he died a year ago, and there's a fellow there now who works for a milking machine company in Heverton. He's a rep." A smile crossed her broad face. "Prescott, his name is. From the Midlands. A little pink, chubby man."

"And he's already made a name for himself in a way that hasn't much to do with milking machines," Roy said.

"Roy!" Frances warned. Her husband snorted. "Come off it, Fran. Molly's got to live in the world as it is when she grows up. Melanie, all Ambersford is saying that chubby Walter Prescott is the father of Sheila Miller's baby. Fran told you about that, I believe. He's got this light-coloured Maxi car and it's been seen up there pretty often. They've only got a small milking herd at Stancross, after all. Maybe they met when he was on a business call, but if all the visits he seems to have made since were just business, we'd all be very surprised. Good luck to 'em, I say. Time Sheila broke away from that father of hers. Beats me why she's put up with him so long."

"Molly," said Frances, "you've finished your lunch. Go upstairs and brush your hair. I'll come up presently and plait it for you."

"You fuss too much," said Roy, as his daughter reluctantly left the room. "The point is, Melanie, that Sheila's dad doesn't want her to leave the farm because she does all the housework and a good bit of the farmwork too—and he needn't pay her, the old miser. If you ask me, he doesn't care how many accidental babies Sheila has, as long as she stays. He's a bit twisted."

"Is it the Millers who own this Siamese stud you're taking Roxana to?" Melanie asked.

Roy laughed. "Yes. If you ask me, Sheila got the animal to annoy her old man. A Siamese cat's just the sort of thing old Miller would despise—highly bred, pernickety, and independent. Roxana ought to go up there today. I'll run her up after lunch, I think. I've an errand out that way anyhow."

"Oh? Where to?" Frances asked. To Melanie's surprise, Lucy immediately cut across her daughter-in-law with a loud enquiry as to whether anyone wanted any more lemon sponge, and Roy banged down his knife and fork on his plate. "Oh, for heaven's sake, Fran! I want to look at some second-hand saddlery in Dulverton. I'm not a little boy who has to tell Mummy where he is every moment of the day!"

"I'm sorry," said Frances. She caught Melanie's expression and added more sharply: "I just asked out of interest!"

"Well, don't." Roy turned his shoulder to her. "Melanie, do you want to ride while you're here? If so, we've some good horses in the yard. I imagine you'll want a quiet afternoon and in the morning you'll be going to the Cliff, but maybe tomorrow after lunch . . ."

"Yes, I'd like that. Actually, this afternoon I want to call on Ivor Winnaford."

"You can't," said Roy. "He's away on a painting trip. As a matter of fact, I thought he was supposed to be back by now, but I passed his house this morning and his car wasn't in the drive. Look, about these horses. We can offer you a choice of—"

"I'm going up to plait Molly's hair," said Frances. She got up. Roy did not look round. She left the room and went slowly up the stairs. She did not go into Molly's room but into the bathroom instead, where she locked the door and sat down on the stool and put her face into her hands. She stayed like that, not moving, for a long time.

∽

She couldn't call on Ivor Winnaford, but there was another call that Melanie could make.

Ambersford had two churchyards. The older one surrounded the church and was enclosed within the churchyard walls. This one had long been full. To reach the other you crossed the lane behind the church and went through a gate and along a path of red earth and pebbles, overhung in summer by meadowsweet and foxgloves, and presently you came to a second cemetery lying on the slopes of Ravensridge. This cemetery still had a wide area of unused turf. Here, close under one of the yew trees which encircled the enclosure, Melanie knelt regardless of the renewed rain, one of Frances's mackintoshes belted round her and a scarf tied round her head. In front of her, Ravensridge soared up: tree-clad lower slopes, grass and heather at the skyline. Behind her, the clock of St. Oswald's was striking three. And beside her was Gran's grave.

The headstone was not yet up, but Roy had told her what kind of wording was planned. It was to be simple. It would give Gran's full name, William James Purvis, his dates of birth and death, and a text: For So He Giveth His Beloved Sleep. Melanie did not quite approve of the text, which was much too tranquil for anyone as stormily alive as Gran had been, but Daniel had chosen it, and Daniel was Gran's son. It was difficult to associate those words with Gran, and difficult, for similar reasons, to realise that all that was mortal of Gran was here under the earth in this quiet graveyard, within a few feet of her.

In fact, quite impossible. Melanie stood up, shaking her head. Whatever memorials William Purvis had left behind him, that rectangle of green marble chips was the least of them.

◠

Uncle Daniel arrived home at quarter-past five, clattering into the yard with his clients on horseback. Melanie ran out to greet him. He slipped from the saddle and took her hands. "So you're here. Welcome back." He scanned her face, as though trying to read in it the difference which three years of marriage and India might have made to her, but for the moment said no more. At supper the clients joined them and the talk was all of the day's sport. But when the meal was over, he said: "I want to talk to Melanie for a bit on our own. She and I'll go over to the *Arms* ahead of the rest of you, if you don't mind. You'd like to come, would you, Melanie? We usually drop into the pub of an evening, same as always. Fran and Lu take turns to stop with Molly."

Sitting opposite her at a table in a corner of the *Ambersford Arms* hotel bar, he said: "That's better!"

"I was waiting for you to come back," Melanie said. "I wanted to see you very much. I wanted to talk about Gran."

"Oh aye. And all the rest of them just said, well, poor old man but it was time he went, or words to that effect? They don't mean any harm, Melanie, but Fran and Lu aren't his blood relations and Roy just about liked him, but nothing more. You very cut up about it?"

"Yes."

"I know. Eighty or not, you feel it just the same if someone matters to you. He was always there, like. We were a lot different, him and me, because I take after my mother and my father wur always a mystery to her . . . he was a

175

mystery to Lu, as well. How he used to go to for me over the way I talk. It comes natural to me somehow, but he hated it. But there, he's left a gap as far I'm concerned, there's no denying it."

Melanie gave him a tremulous smile. "I feel better, for hearing you say that."

The hotel bar was restful. There was no sense of hurry here. Rain sighed gently on the narrow, leaded windows with their flawed medieval glass; a log fire crackled in the fire basket in the middle of yet another of the gigantic hearths so common in Ambersford. Above the fireplace, the head of a twelve-pointer stag surveyed the patrons with enigmatic glass eyes. Melanie herself did not like hunting, but she could not imagine the bar of the *Arms* without its presiding trophy, any more than she could imagine Uncle Daniel without his stable full of hunters. It was a thing on which they had long since agreed to differ. She sipped a sour and refreshing draught cider, the very taste of which was almost the exclusive property of the west country. At the back of her mind she was wondering what Bheji or Arwin would make of this place. To them, the concept of an establishment dedicated to the sale and consumption of alcohol, to which people in need of relaxation might casually repair, was hardly thinkable. But for Daniel Purvis, the *Arms* was virtually an extension of his sitting room and he stepped into it on most evenings of the week, hardly noticing that he did so.

Bheji and Arwin, she could think about without pain. But she wasn't going to be able to escape the subject of Avtar, not during this private talk with her uncle. Daniel was bound to ask after him. To her relief, he made it easy. "That's enough of the looking back just for now," he said. "Let's take a look at you instead, Melanie. You're too thin. Need some of our good cream to put the flesh back on you. What's the trouble? Climate? Homesickness?"

"Both, I think. I don't eat very well."

"Don't your husband mind? Or don't he notice?"

"He's terribly overworked. A doctor's day is never done," said Melanie, and smiled.

Daniel nodded. "Get on with your in-laws all right?"

"Oh, *yes.*"

"That's a mercy. Wouldn't be a bad thing, I sometimes think, if Roy and Fran didn't live with us. Seemed logical at the time. Roy's a partner in the business and the house is big enough, Lord knows. But it b'ain't working out ideal. Now, Roy's interested in the market gardening and that, and he's talked of setting up on his own. I'm for the idea, but Fran don't seem to like it. Yet I don't think she likes being with us either. Don't know why not. She's not worried over money and Lu gives her a free hand to decorate the place any way she likes, but there's *something.* Molly senses it. Makes her awkward. Shame they only had the one, maybe. Don't know why they stopped at Molly. Space enough for a dozen if they like."

Melanie thought of the crosscurrents at the lunch table and shook her head, more to express unwillingness to comment than lack of comment to make. Her cousin Roy had struck her as bullying in his manner and Frances looked exhausted. Other people had their troubles as well as Melanie —that was clear. She was sorry. She looked at her uncle and was glad that he at least was the same as ever. She noticed that the thick brown fingers linked round his beer tankard were attached to fully operational hands and arms. "How's your fractured arm? The one you got when you were thrown into a hedge in the summer."

"Sound enough now. I got rid of the mare, though. At

177

a loss. She wur a bad buy. Cussed animal, she was. Nearly as cussed as humans, some creatures are. Though," said Uncle Daniel, taking a pipe out of his pocket and lighting up, "to be fair to the humbler creation, I never met one as cussed as old Miller up at Stancross. Heard about the scandal round Sheila Miller, have 'ee? Well, you see that fellow who's just come into the bar?"

"The short plump one? That isn't Miller."

"No," Daniel agreed, "that's Walter Prescott. Heard of 'un?"

"The milking machine man? Sheila Miller's . . . ?"

"That's him." Daniel puffed on his pipe and his tea-coloured eyes danced. For a moment she saw his father in him. "Amazing, b'ain't it? Imagine him being the one. Don't look like young Lochinvar, do 'ee?"

"Who is it he's talking to? In the tartan jacket."

"Oh, that's a River Board bloke." The amusement in her uncle's face broadened. "No one important . . . assistant to an assistant engineer or something, he is. But the lanky hawk-nosed fellow at the other end of the bar is a Coastal Counties Water Authority inspector from the Heverton office. Him and the River Board fellow drink in here a lot, but as far away from each other as they can manage, allowing that the bar b'ain't that long, these days."

"The brown bath water?"

"You don't take long to catch on," said Uncle Daniel approvingly. He cocked his head. "Not that they're discussing bath water now. Should of kept my big mouth shut. Seems my melodious rumble's a bit too loud. Listen."

Melaine listened, keeping her gaze on the cloudy amber surface of the cider. The word "Lochinvar" floated past the crackle of the fire, and a burst of laughter followed it. The barmaid gave Prescott his Guinness, and his money went on the counter with more than a suspicion of a bang. "Joke's okay till it goes on too long," he said. The accent was distinctively Nottingham. The top of his head, which was bald, had gone pink, like his face.

"Oh, heck," said Uncle Daniel. Something approximating to regret had appeared after all on his wind-roughened features. "He's getting stroppy. Had enough, I reckon. Up to a few weeks back, none of 'em would lay off it for a minute. Then it quieted down and now I've set 'em off again. He's a good-natured chap too."

The tartan-jacketed man from the River Board spoke, too quietly to be heard in their corner but with a pitch and timing which suggested a pseudoapology with a sting in it. There was more laughter. In the middle of the group, a man whom Melanie now recognised as the proprietor of the Ambersford Garage turned and winked at Daniel.

"After a bit," said Prescott audibly, presenting his back to the Purvises, "it gets boring. Understand?"

From the other end of the bar, the Water Authority joined in. "Come on now. No offence meant. It's mostly sour grapes with this lot, you know that, Walter. What're you drinking?"

"I'm all right with what I've got. Thanks," said Walter Prescott.

A farmer standing alongside the garage proprietor murmured something pacific. The tartan-jacketed man, however, possessed a mischievous temperament. "The thing is," he said, turning to Prescott with a confidential air, "what we're a'dying to know is, what's she called it? Not a whisper there's been about that. Is she calling it Walter? It's a boy, b'ain't it?"

"Oh, lord," said Daniel, plunging his nose into his beer.

Prescott, however, was displaying unexpected resourcefulness. "I wouldn't know what she's called it," he said. "But

179

it's nothing to what the neighbourhood will be calling you, and him at the end there, if you don't settle your differences and get our water back to normal. What I washed in this morning was more like wood varnish than water. So how about that, hey?"

Heartfelt agreement rose from the rest of the group, led by the Ambersford Garage and seconded by the farmer. The tartan-clad River Board engineer said defensively: " 'Tisn't the Board's affair at all. The Water Authority's in charge of supplies to users and—"

"Rivers," said the hawk-nosed representative of the Coastal Counties Water Authority, "and the streams and bogs that give rise to them are the Board's affair. And since it's that bog that's causing the trouble—"

"That's a questionable argument," said the garage proprietor. "Once that there water gets polluted and, by God, polluted it is, it's the Water Authority's job to get it unpolluted. And we'd like to know . . ."

Half a dozen voices passionately expressed the belief that someone ought to grab the Board and the Authority by the scruffs of their necks and bang their heads together until they did something constructive and stopped scrapping like kids in a bloody playground. In the midst of it, Prescott gulped down his pint, wiped his mouth, and left, unregarded. At the bar, the combatants got down to steady, practised, and on the whole good-humoured wrangling. Prescott and his putative baby were forgotten.

"Clever little bugger," said Daniel. "More to him than meets the eye. Which there'd have to be, to get past Old Man Miller. Well, Melanie, you'll be at Gavin's Cliff tomorrow. Reckon it must feel like the end of a long, long pilgrimage."

A Ghost of One's Own

Melanie would rather have gone alone to the solicitors and Gavin's Cliff next day but Frances offered to accompany her and Roy endorsed it. Frances was in the passenger seat of the Marina, therefore, when Melanie set out on the final stage of her journey.

It was not a long stage. Two miles of winding road to Heverton, during which Melanie annoyed herself by slowing up for the bends like a stranger instead of driving into them flat out as the locals did, knowing they were nowhere near as steep as they looked. A brief call on Barnes and Chaldicott; a few words exchanged with Vincent Barnes, who was elderly and had known Gran well, and was full of regrets for his passing and pleasure at Melanie's return. On down Heverton High Street, its pavements edged with pollarded plane trees and its shops standing back behind paved forecourts where in summer stood racks of postcards and souvenirs, and small tables for the consumption of coffee and ice cream, Continental fashion. Here Melanie slowed down again, deliberately this time, for the pure pleasure of looking. She halted at a pedestrian crossing so that a woman pushing twins in a double pram could use it. She took the opportunity of gazing round her, noticing that the Creamery was still in business although the shop selling jewellery made out of local stones had disappeared. Frances waved to the woman. "Who's that?" Melanie asked, as she let in the clutch again.

"Mrs. Viney . . . no, I mean *young* Mrs. Viney. Amanda Viney's daughter-in-law. Amanda Viney was against the marriage at first, but since the twins came along it's been different. Only trouble is, the parents can't keep Granny's nose out of the cradles."

At the end of High Street was a left-hand turn onto the harbour road. The smell of the sea and the sound of gulls came in through the window. The promenade and the sea wall on the right were almost deserted now, and the hotels which lined the road on the left were mostly closed. Past the harbour and its grey curve of wall, past the *Fishing Boat,* and past, with disdain, a notice which said No Through Road. Round the base of Heverton Point, behind the lifeboat house on its concrete plinth jutting from the midst of the rattling shingle. And then, as the dead end of the road came into sight, Melanie swung the car to the left, onto an unmade track. Above them the trees closed in. The leaves were changing already from their dark, late-summer green to the first of the gold and red which in a week or two would make the Point look as though it were on fire. *I shall stay to see that, whatever happens,* Melanie silently told herself, and brought down the gear to meet the changing gradient.

"Appalling track this is," said Frances. "And a railing or two wouldn't do much harm, either."

To the right, the hill fell steeply towards a sea whose shining wrinkles were further below with each successive glimpse through the tree trunks. On the other side, the hill towered up, trees emerging from the soil at a startlingly acute angle. Once they passed under an archway made of a perilously leaning pine. Presently, rhododendrons began, a dark green wall on either side. In May and June, scarlet flowers would flare along the way, but today the bushes were as funereal as the yew trees in Ambersford Churchyard. Then there was light ahead. They drove out into the open space in front of Gavin's Cliff and stopped.

It was the first time in her life that Melanie had come to this house and not found Gran there awaiting her. It hurt.

∽

Gavin's Cliff was not a beautiful house. Of the Tudor farmhouse which had stood here once, nothing was left, unless you counted the few contents which had been saved: Gavin's portrait, the lifebelt collections, and one or two items of furniture. The house which had replaced it was plain and sturdy, as became a house which must overlook a rocky shore and stand with a cliff at its back. It was built of grey stone dressed only on the sides where it met other stone, and the roof was of grey slate. The inside was utilitarian, with small fireplaces and innumerable built-in cupboards. The kitchen had a certain functional beauty (it was the one bit of Gavin's Cliff which Frances really appreciated). Gran was an excellent cook; he had exasperated both his wives by continual intrusions into what they considered to be their personal domain. He had turned his kitchen into a culinary palace, with all the formica, ceramics, stainless steel storage and gadgetry that Frances's heart could desire.

For the rest, the house had a parlour overlooking the fields which swept down to the cove and were now owned by Whitehangers, a room which had been a dining room till Gran moved a desk and a lot of wall units in there and turned it into his den, and four bedrooms, two of them attic rooms with dormer windows and wildly sloping ceilings. A bathroom had been made out of what had originally been a fifth bedroom. From outside, Melanie observed that the dormer windows were heavily overshadowed with ivy and that ivy now hid considerable areas of the grey stone walls. Three years ago, the ivy hadn't been as thick as this. It was romantic to look at but it was probably a structural hazard. She must say to Gran . . .

Gran wasn't here. Gran would never be here again. If Melanie wanted ivy moved—or collapsing pine trees cut down—Melanie must take the decision and foot the bill. She pulled on the handbrake with a rough jerk and threw open her door. "No good sitting here. Let's go in."

The front door of Gavin's Cliff had a small pointed porch and was set in the side of the house, facing the track. Gran, when expecting callers, usually left it open. It seemed odd to be unlocking it. Inside they stood still, uncertainly.

"It doesn't smell damp, anyway," said Melanie. Her voice was too loud, finding echoes even though the house was fully carpeted. She gazed round the hall: barometer, hall stand with Gran's old all-weather raincoat hanging on it, the stag's head which was almost obligatory as a hall decoration in this part of the world. "What shall we do first?"

"What about a cup of tea?" said Frances with a practical

air. "I've brought the makings, and Mr. Barnes said the water and electricity were on." She set competently off towards the kitchen. Melanie, still hesitant, began to follow her and then on impulse turned into the parlour instead. It was exactly as she recalled it, a long room with a bay window at the end, leading the eye towards the sea. There, unchanged, were the sheepskin rug, and Ivor's *Light and Water,* and the grandfather clock and the rosewood table in the window bay, and the three-piece suite upholstered in ivory-toned cotton with green and blue flowers straggling over it. Melanie stood listening to the silence. One was always keenly aware of the silence here, and yet it was never complete. You could hear the sea in the distance and the wind in the pines. And, surely . . . there was a sound missing. She turned to gaze accusingly at the grandfather clock. It had stopped. She repaired the omission, setting the hands at twenty-five to eleven. She heard, with satisfaction, the deep slow tick of the clock begin.

"Melanie!" Frances called from the kitchen, "where are you?"

"Coming."

"The point is," said Frances as they sat together at the kitchen table, "what exactly have you got to do here? Look over the house and decide what to do with it as a house, I know. But what about the contents? And there's the car. That's yours as well. We brought it back and locked it in the garage here because it was in the way at home. It's ready for use."

"I know . . . the things, as apart from the house, will be the most complicated. There are all the papers in Gran's den, and all his clothes and his books and the lifebelts and his souvenirs of his travels. . . ."

"It'll take a long time," said Melanie slowly. "Frances, I think I should stay up here while I do it. I'm crowding you at home anyway. You've clients to look after. If I have to work here all day, I may as well sleep here."

"Here? On your own?"

"Yes, why not? It's not that isolated. Whitehangers is just along the track."

"The Professor fell out with the Heatons. I told you."

"He may have done, but I haven't. I'll go and call on Mary Heaton when I get a moment. What was it about, do you know?"

Frances shook her head. "Never mind that. Look, Melanie, you're not crowding us. We've plenty of room."

"But I want to stay here," said Melanie. It was more than that, she thought. She needed to stay here. Only in solitude, at the Cliff, could she take possession of it, resolve the ties that she and it had had with Gran. And only in solitude, in a place such as the Cliff, could she face the task of thinking about her future.

"Well," Frances was saying dubiously, "you'd better have one of the dogs with you. That is, if you really mean it. I know this place is pretty safe—the only way in is via the track and it's a long walk from either direction—but the sound of those pines would give me the heebee-jeebies."

A curious metallic whirring and clonking made them both jump. Frances, in the act of pouring second cups of tea, almost dropped the teapot. "Good God, what's that?"

"It's only the grandfather clock clearing its throat to strike. I wound it up. There it goes. Quarter to eleven."

"I never liked that clock," said Frances.

❧

186

To be alone.

A yearning for solitude was not, to say the least of it, an Indian characteristic. If you sat alone in the house in Chandigarh, people were apt to come in search of you and good-naturedly offer to keep you company. It had been good to drive down from London alone and maddening to have bodily weakness interfere with it. It would be good to have Gavin's Cliff to herself tonight. And it was good to be on the hillside across the valley from Ravensridge, with Ambersford lying in the Darr Valley between them, alone except for her equine escort, Falcon, whom Uncle Daniel had introduced to her as a "nice little horse."

The *little* was an affectionate diminutive. Daniel Purvis loved the equine species. He had been heard to call an eighteen-hand Shire a nice little horse, even. Falcon was over sixteen hands tall, long-legged, deep chestnut in colour, with a blond mane and tail and the head carriage of an aristocrat. He was little neither in body nor in personality. After the thin, resigned ponies of the East, he was sunrise and revelation.

He snorted, impatient at being asked to stand still. She had halted here because it was a favourite place of hers, affording a view of the Darr Valley from its inland end where the moors rose up and Darr had its springs, to where the river passed between Castle Hill and the end of Ravensridge and began its last meander across the marshes to the sea. Immediately in front of it, across the valley, was the steep side of the Ridge itself, its trees now bronzing with the fall.

The vista from where she and Falcon stood was actually better than from anywhere on top of the Ridge, which was why, in the Iron Age, the local tribes had had a lookout post up here. Falcon was standing now on what was still recognisable as the banked earthwork round the lookout. Melanie had often wondered what kind of people its constructors were, and whether she might have ancestors among them. It was possible.

There were places, plenty of them, in India where you could feel the past. It was strongly about you in the crypt of the Taj Mahal where Shah Jehan lay beside his queen, and she had visited the gardens and palaces of other departed Moghul rulers and in her mind had seen the lamps which once swung by the long shallow lily pools, and heard the sitars to which girls in sparkling skirts and veils had danced. But she had had no sense of kinship with them; her imagination or her psychic sense, whichever it was, had made her watch them, not become them. Sitting here in Falcon's saddle, listening to the wind in the upland grass, she could enter into the being of those Iron Age people as she had never entered into the people by the lily pools. To do that, perhaps, one needed one's own ghosts.

Falcon snorted again, and Melanie realised that she was cold. The Ridge was clear-cut and dark with promised rain, and to the north, the sea was as hard as pewter, with Wales a sharply delineated warning. Never mind. Her stout mac and hard hat, further loans from Frances, would protect her. But they should perhaps move on. She urged Falcon forward, out of the earthwork ring and on to the pink, stony track along the crest of the hill towards Amberscombe and the moors.

Half an hour later she had passed above Amberscombe and Stancross Farm and was on the first heathery slopes of the moor proper. From here one could see far across the grain of Exmoor. For it had a grain. Its long smooth hills lay parallel to each other like the orderly rollers of a vast and petrified tide. She drew up once again, looking to her left. "Ugh!" said Melanie, with force.

On her left, the edge so close that Falcon's hooves were already in spongy ground, was Old Harry. He had spread; no past memory recalled him extending as far as this. Now he occupied an enlarged area on the flattened top of a rise, his grasses threateningly green and his reed-tufts warningly rank. Further in, his surface rippled faintly in the wind. Old Harry was not, strictly speaking, a dangerous bog. Harold Miller had drowned there because he was drunk at the time, not because the marsh was lethal. It was too wet for that and lacked suction. People who fell in— Daniel Purvis had been in twice, getting thrown while hunting—usually climbed out again soaked and filthy but otherwise uninjured. But swollen to this extent . . . Melanie's eye travelled to where a peat stream flowed out, tumbling over the lip of the slope and down into the next valley, running in a deep channel in the heather. The stream was much bigger and noisier than usual; here no doubt was the cause of the peat that was getting into the reservoir. If the whole bog were to spread right to the lip and spill over all the way along it, there would be a fine flood down that hillside. There was a road below, which the stream crossed in a watersplash. That road would certainly be put out of use for a while. It was high time someone took action. Winter wouldn't be drier than summer, and Old Harry was like a loaded gun, ready to go off at the sightest nudge on the trigger. Maybe a few more quarrels in the *Ambersford Arms* would do some good.

She rode in a circle round the bog, enjoying the exhilaration of the height and the space and the blustery moorland wind. Returning towards Ambersford on a different path, she came once more within sight of Stancross Farm.

Since this was the home of Sheila Miller and the inadvertent offspring whose paternity had so enlivened the *Arms* the previous evening, this too aroused her interest. "Shall we go down and see if Sheila'a about?" she asked Falcon's quirking chestnut ears. "I wonder if she'd remember me? No. I've hardly set eyes on her since we were at school and she might think I was being nosy. She'd probably be right too. And her father might be about and I definitely don't want to see *him*."

She had encountered Mr. Miller occasionally, when playing with Sheila at the farm as a child. The farmhouse was an ungracious place and Edward Miller an ungracious man and Melanie's recollections of them were tangled together as though the man and his home were facets of each other. She had a pictorial memory of the farm's interior: gloomy hallway with a shotgun hanging on the wall and a pair of mud-caked gumboots standing beneath it, steamy kitchen with an unfriendly dog which growled at visitors, living room full of cornery furniture with a moth-eaten stuffed parrot and the kind of wallpaper that didn't show the dirt. Edward Miller, on his brief and uncommunicative appearances, had left an extraordinarily similar impression: gaunt, cornery bones, feet clad in muddy boots, a tendency to growl at visitors, and a shirt that wouldn't show the dirt. He had eaten tea with them once or twice, tea being prepared by the pale and prematurely responsible scrap that was Sheila. He hadn't been actually rude, but he was the kind of man who couldn't ask for another cup of tea in anything but a surly voice. Melanie had found him both depressing and alarming. The thought of him still was.

Even as a child, Sheila had spoken disparagingly of her father. Why, Melanie wondered, didn't she just leave? She must have had opportunities, or could, with a little resourcefulness, have made them. Trotting along the track above the farmhouse, Melanie observed that a car was leaving the yard, gingerly negotiating the one-in-five lane that led from it down to Amberscombe. A light-coloured car. Walter Prescott, perhaps, going home after an earnest conversation with Sheila on milking shed hygiene or standby generators.

Just as well they hadn't called. "We might have interrupted something," she said to Falcon. She patted him and he pricked hopeful ears and pulled on the bridle. A spatter of rain blew against her back. The track ahead levelled out invitingly. "I bet you can't race the rain," she said to him, and let him go.

One did not forget how to ride. She sat down hard and he reached out with long forelegs and the ground flowed past beneath him. There was nothing else in the world like this. An aerobatic pilot, giving himself up to the spin and roll of his aircraft, might experience some of it—but not all, for an aircraft could not think for itself. Falcon could. He could choose his path and carry his rider with him. There was no speed that felt as fast as this, and no freedom as free.

It was one of the things she had never been able to explain to Avtar.

❧

Gavin's Cliff was different, the second time she entered it. She paused on the threshold while Jason, the black-muzzled boxer dog who was to be her guardian, pressed against her legs. Why was it different? Then she heard the steady tick of the grandfather clock and knew that it had brought the house to life. With Jason snuffling at her heels, she walked with confidence into her home.

Her home?

Not quite, not yet. This morning, though she and Frances had investigated nearly every corner of the house, there was one room she had avoided. For if the essence which had been Gran still lingered anywhere, it would be here, and she must face the moment of confrontation alone. There were things to which one did not want witnesses. The curious muffling of emotion, the almost physical sense of being swaddled—which had descended on her as she drove into Ambersford two days ago, and which was still so marked that it was actually beginning to puzzle and even worry her—had not extended to her grief for Gran then, and did not extend to it now. This was Gran's own place, and in it he was still stronger than any other influence. She had to brace herself to walk to the door of Gran's den and throw it open.

She stood in the doorway and put on the light, not at first venturing to enter. The other rooms in the house had been Gran's to use; this one was part of him. The dark leather armchairs were his idea of ideal seating; the books which lined two walls were his auxiliary memory. His stereo and his records and cassettes were here; the music which was also part of the furnishing of his mind. Most of it was classical and much of it of a rarified kind which Melanie had always found beyond her. This was the point at which he outstripped her and went away into a kind of intellectual stratosphere where she could not breathe.

She moved forward, slowly. The reading lamp was in its place on his desk and the typewriter was pushed back against the wall. One of his pipes lay on the desk along with a tin of tobacco and a paperknife. She tiptoed to the desk and touched the things on it. Then she sank into the nearest of the leather armchairs, and the tears which she had known would come as soon as she entered this room rose up in her. He had not been in the churchyard at Ambersford, but she had found him now.

◦

The sounds of grief brought Jason pit-patting from the kitchen to push his head worriedly against her hand. "It's all right, Jason, it's all right." She looked blurrily at the fireplace and the surrounding wall, hung with its historic lifebelts. This room was like a record of the past of Heverton coast, a distillation of the world in which the Purvis family had grown and been shaped. It was a world, she thought, which had no interface at all with Avtar's.

She studied the lifebelts. The oldest came from a ship called *Highlander* and a plaque above it gave the date as 25th October 1859. On that day, the coasts of England had been lashed by a Force Twelve hurricane which sank a hundred and thirty-three vessels in British waters, and took eight hundred lives. Four hundred and fifty men had drowned outside Liverpool that day when the *Royal Charter*, bringing miners home from the Australian goldfields, was driven onto rocks and sank. But no one on the *Highlander* had died. The men of Heverton, with the Purvises of Gavin's Cliff to lead them, had brought twenty-eight sailors to safety from their foundered cargo boat, notwithstanding hundred-mile-an-hour gusts, and seas like prowling mountains.

Cape Agulhas hung next to *Highlander,* dated ten years later, a case of a ship going off course and onto the rocks known as the Fangs because her captain and crew had been having a bottle party. Then came the *Maria Valdez,* the *Lynx,* the *Silveranne* . . . last of all was *Java Head,* the trawler whose destruction in Gavin's Cove Melanie herself had witnessed. She knew them all by heart.

Gran's own souvenirs were on the opposite wall, arranged round the portrait of Gavin Purvis. Gavin, arrogant and sensual, stared back at her from a remarkable frieze consisting of an Australian boomerang, a No-Mask with an expression of murderous ferocity, a seashell necklace, a canoe prow, a round shield . . . and a shrunken head, possibly plastic, but gruesome all the same. Melanie pulled herself out of the chair and advanced grimly on the No-Mask and the head.

If she were to use this room in the future, even for a little while, those repulsive objects must go. They might be valuable and certainly couldn't be disposed of until she had made sure, but remain in this room they should not. It was her first truly possessive act in this house, the moment when she took seisin of her inheritance. She unhooked both from the wall and carried them up to one of the attic rooms. The place was already a gloryhole full of bits of discarded furniture. She dumped head and mask in a corner and withdrew, brushing her palms together.

Back in the den, later, after she and Jason had had supper, a brief examination of the desk and the filing cabinet beside it gave her further warning of the work which lay ahead. Both were stuffed with papers. There was a substratum of properly organised filing—letters, conference papers, copies of articles—with a floating population of unallocated documents on top. In a basket on the cabinet were some papers clipped together in bundles, which in conjunction with a wastebin full of torn-up material suggested that some kind of filing blitz had been in progress when death intervened. It would be for her to finish, perhaps with Ivor's help when he returned.

It was not late yet. She could begin tonight.

But she was too tired. Suddenly she was as exhausted as if her limbs had turned to straw. Tomorrow would do.

She had that morning made up a bed for herself in one of the spare rooms (she could not use Gran's room, not yet, and instead had arranged the sorted piles of his clothes on the bed there, ready for the Salvation Army). Yawning, sleepy as if she had had tranquillisers in her last cup of tea instead of sugar, Melanie collected Jason's blanket and, with the dog at her heels, made her way upstairs.

∽

She woke once in the night. The moon was out, picking up the retina of Jason's eyes as he lay, also wakeful, by the bedside. The pines outside tossed in a rising wind and cast groping shadows on the carpet. Melanie sat up, convinced beyond all reason and sense that Gran was in the house. She even knew where. He was at the foot of the stairs, standing in the patch of moonlight which came through the hall window, gazing up at the stairs, his hand on the banister as if about to climb. If she were to go on to the landing and look down, she would see him.

Even the most beloved dead would not be welcome, if they returned.

She switched on the bedside lamp and lay listening to the creaks of the house as the wind increased. Jason, aware that something was wrong with the human being he dimly understood he was there to protect, clambered on to the bed and pushed his nose against her. She caressed him, glad of his solid warmth. Very slowly, the haunting impression faded. With its going, Gran had wholly left Gavin's Cliff. They had said farewell to each other now, and henceforth the Cliff was altogether hers. She turned out the light again, and fell asleep.

X Factor

Frances Purvis, seated in the white Allegro which her father-in-law described as their "dignified transport" (the rest consisted of two horse trailers, a businesslike Range Rover, and a very old van), traversed, without enthusiasm, the track from Heverton to Gavin's Cliff.

It was a wide track and the trees grew close enough together to form an effective barrier against the seaward drop, but Frances still detested it. That Melanie should wilfully choose to stay up here alone was, in Frances's opinion, final proof that Melanie was eccentric. If her extraordinary marriage and departure for the other side of the world hadn't proved it already, Frances thought with irritation.

But none of this absolved her from the duty of watching over Melanie's welfare while her cousin was nominally staying with them. Frances had therefore equipped herself, by way of excuse for the visit, with a bottle of milk plus a towel which Melanie had left behind, and was on her way to see if Melanie had safely weathered her first night in self-imposed isolation.

There were signs of occupation about the house. Jason was snuffling about in a drift of leaves, and Frances, getting out of the car, discovered that the kitchen door was open. "Where's Melanie, then?" she said to the dog, and went inside.

The kitchen table was laid for breakfast. On the stove, an egg reposed in a saucepan of steaming water. The hot-plate under it, however, had been turned off. The door to the hall stood wide. She called Melanie's name and stood with head cocked for a reply. There was no answer in words. But from the upper regions of the house came a sound both disagreeable and homely. Frances raced up the stairs, three at a time, and arrived pell-mell in the bathroom. "Melanie!"

Melanie raised a green-flushed face from the washbasin to which she was clinging. Tendrils of black hair stuck to her damp forehead. "Hello. You didn't say you were coming this morning."

"It's a good job I did come . . . what's wrong with you?"

Melanie sat down cautiously on the edge of the bath, not too far from the basin. "God knows. I was late waking up. I pottered about and let Jason out. Then I started making breakfast and all of a sudden . . . *this*!" said Melanie in an anguished voice, and launched herself once more at the basin.

With that spasm over, her face lost some of its green tinge. She perched on the rim of the bath again and said apologetically: "Sorry."

"For what? It isn't your fault." Frances wrung out a face flannel in cold water and handed it to her. Melanie wiped her face. Frances sat down on the toilet seat. "Now," she said in a down-to-earth voice, "you tell me. How long is it since you last had a period?"

～

"Don't be absurd," said Melanie after a pause. "My Fallopian tubes were damaged when I was a child. I can't conceive. You know that."

"That," said Frances, unimpressed, "is what they told young Mrs. Viney."

"Told young Mrs. . . ?"

"I waved to her in Heverton yesterday, remember? Pushing twins in a pram. She thought her Fallopian tubes didn't work, either. That's why Amanda Viney made such a to-do about the marriage. Well, young Alice Viney went to the doctor thinking she'd got appendicitis. She said afterwards that when the doctor had examined her, he nearly fell off his chair laughing."

"Maybe this is appendicitis," said Melanie. She prodded her stomach experimentally.

"Tummyache? Fever?"

"No."

"I see. You didn't answer my question. How long?"

"Oh, I don't know. Some while." Melanie calculated on her fingers. "About mid-August, I think."

"*Mid-August!*" Frances squealed. "Are you telling me . . . ? Melanie, this is the *twelfth of October*! The . . . twelfth . . . of . . . October. You haven't seen anything for nearly two months and you haven't *noticed*?"

"Of course I've noticed. But it doesn't mean anything,

not with me. I went seven weeks when I first arrived in India, because everything was so strange. I thought it was the shock of hearing about Gran. I thought I'd come on when I got here."

"And have you?"

"No. Look, we needn't go on sitting in this bathroom. I feel all right now. I do get bilious turns, you know. I had one driving down, but it passed off. I couldn't face my breakfast in that cafe in Basingstoke—you know the one. But when I was back in the car, I felt perfectly well again."

"That settles it as far as I'm concerned," said Frances, following her cousin down the stairs. "I was like that with Molly. Sick one moment and perfectly all right—in fact starving hungry—the next. Does your stomach feel different at all? In any way?"

In the kitchen, sitting down while Frances filled a kettle, Melanie once more prodded her middle. "It feels tight, like a drum. I thought it was the stodgy English food."

"Heaven grant me patience. Evidence to left of her, evidence to right of her . . . Melanie, I'm going to get Dr. Channing out from Ambersford to have a look at you. If you're not pregnant, you're ill. But I'd take my bet on pregnancy. You may not know it," said Frances, turning to stare at her, "but that's the way you look. Even your hair is shining."

❧

"Frances, there's no need to worry about me. I shall be quite all right."

"If only you'd come back to Ambersford, just for a few days, till you've adjusted to the idea."

"But I'd only have to keep on coming up here. I've all

those papers to see to. The den's more like a giant wastepaper basket than a room. Dr. Channing said I could stay if I wanted to."

Surprisingly, he had. "What's all this about you staying up here alone? Mrs. Purvis tells me she and her family are more than willing to have you with them."

"They are, but I prefer it up here."

"Yes? Well, I can understand that," Channing said. He did not elaborate on what, precisely, he understood; Melanie had an odd sensation of having communicated with him by telepathy. It was as though she had told him without words of the curious quarrel at the lunch table and the hurtful absence of grief in Roy and Frances. He was a stranger to her, but he had in fact been in practice in Ambersford for some years. Probably he knew Frances's household well. He was a tubby man with receding hair and an unexpectedly light, dry voice which contained a trace of Yorkshire. And he had plenty of experience, no doubt, both in diagnosing pregnancy and estimating patients' states of mind.

"But it would be much more sensible to be with your family. In these circumstances . . ." Frances protested now.

"We don't know for certain that there are any circumstances. We shan't be sure till the test results come from Heverton Hospital," said Melanie, knowing it for a specious argument but hoping that Frances wouldn't.

"Nonsense. Channing thinks you're pregnant and if he thinks so, then you are. Melanie . . ."

"For God's sake, Frances! I need to be alone. I want to think."

Frances's blue eyes were first puzzled, and then sharp. "Melanie, are you saying you don't want this baby? Won't Avtar be pleased?"

"Yes, of course he will." *Frances, go away!* "It's just that it's . . . good God, it's such a shock. I never dreamed . . ."

"If it's been a shock, that's all the more reason for you to come back to Ambersford."

"Well, I'm not coming." Melanie abandoned argument for outright defiance.

"I don't know what to do." Frances was irresolute. "I ought to stay with you for a bit, I know I ought. But I've got to be back to make lunch and this afternoon I'm collecting Roxana from Stancross . . . Roy was going at the weekend but Molly wanted to go with him and he said no, he was seeing a pony over at Exford on the same trip and the business talk would bore her, and she started to sulk and finally I said I'd get Roxana today and then for some reason they both got annoyed . . . everything's so *awkward*."

"It isn't in the least awkward. For heaven's sake, Frances, I'm all *right*! I'll phone you in the evening and in the morning as well to put your mind at rest if you want. But for now you can go home with a perfectly clear conscience."

It was with considerable relief that she saw Frances at last drive off down the track, taking her indefinable air of minor domestic strife with her. Left alone, Melanie went into the hall, collected Gran's ancient raincoat which she had left there on its hook in case she needed it herself, and called to Jason. Then she set out for the shore.

༄

Gavin's Cove was ill-named. It was less a cove than an indentation in the shore to the west of Heverton Point, at a place where the cliffs fell back to make an easy slope where fields could lie. Further west, the steepness reappeared and

201

after a mile or so jutted into another headland, Gannet's Head, where there was a Coastguard station and a green and white, lantern-topped lighthouse.

Melanie walked quickly down the sunken path towards the sea, between the raw, ploughed fields which in summer would be full of oats or barley. At the cove, she crossed a ridge of heavy shingle before reaching the small shingle and the narrow stretch of wet sand which was left when the tide was out. It was out now, though on its way up. Plumes of spray hung over the Fangs and boiled round the feet of the two headlands. The wind was strong and cold and the sky unfriendly.

It was much too cold to stand still. She whistled to Jason and turned towards Gannet's Head, throwing pieces of driftwood ahead for the dog to fetch. Between throws, she thrust her chilled hands into the pockets of the old coat and bent her head into the westerly.

A baby.

Funny. The man in the Basingstoke cafe had probably guessed at it. He had looked at her so concernedly and twice told her to take care of herself. Frances seemed to have suspected it almost at once. She herself had had no suspicion. Yet it had happened. Dr. Channing had congratulated her. At the word *congratulations,* realisation had come like a solid punch in the solar plexus.

She looked up at the slope of the ploughland above her, to Gavin's Cliff, sturdy and beloved, gazing down at her from its rock-walled perch. If she went back to India, she might never see it again.

She thought: I'm face to face with it now. I have to decide. But I *can't* decide. I can't *think* . . .

Today's revelations had at least explained the swaddled state of her emotions, the queer loss of feeling which for three days now had muffled her memory of Avtar and its accompanying anger and wretchedness. It was not just due to the ambience of home, though that perhaps was part of it. Pregnancy had a hand in it as well. She had heard of this effect before. Avtar, talking of his work, had mentioned it sometimes. "So nice to see that young woman calming down; she used to be so nervy." "He says his wife keeps going to bed early and falling asleep at once, but I told him don't worry, pregnancy is a first-class soporific." Her state of mind was another indication that Frances and Dr. Channing were right.

But it was a symptom she couldn't afford. She couldn't put up with being tranquillised now. She had a choice to make and how could she make it if all the issues were blurred like this, if Avtar and India were going to drop away over her mental horizon like this? And they had dropped away. She stopped short on the beach, a piece of wood in her hand, ignoring Jason's appealing woof. With a rush of panic and then of guilt, she was realising just how far they had receded.

At this moment, to look back on Avtar and India was like looking back on a shipboard romance, an interlude separate from real life and vanishing into the past as soon as real life was resumed. Avtar had visited the Cliff only once, briefly. He had left no memory of himself here. If he had, it might have helped. She looked round her once again, and nothing in the things she saw—the sea or the headlands, the lighthouse or the ploughed fields or the grey house itself—spoke his name.

Yet he *was* real. Whatever her distorted emotions might say, that was a fact. He was a real man and India was a real place. She had parted from him at Delhi Airport only last Monday and she had glanced back at the last moment and seen that anguished expression on his face. He existed, and so did his feelings. She threw the bit of wood for Jason and paced on. Here at the Cliff she had broken free of Avtar. Here she had a home, could no doubt put together a future if she liked, could afford to let Avtar and his feelings slip out of her mind because here they couldn't get at her. But if she went back, she would be immersed, in five minutes, in the conflicts which his love created—the old demand, expressed sometimes subtly, sometimes overtly—that she should abandon her past and become wholly Avtar's, wholly Indian. She had loved Avtar at the beginning. The thought departed into the past tense as smoothly and depressingly as air departs from a pierced tyre. That persistent demand, which he had begun to make almost from the day they landed in Delhi, had been destroying love a little at a time ever since. Clear away, with a huge effort of will, the pink cotton wool from her mind, and she could see that, of that love, only a fragment was left and that composed mainly of habit. One got used to a person, the sheer detailed knowledge of one another which living together produced, created a link.

Only, there was now a new factor to deal with.

A baby.

Her baby but Avtar's too. And also real. She needed advice. But who was there to advise her?

❧

Diwali, the autumn Festival of Lights, was in gregarious and admittedly somewhat gluttonous progress. The house at Chandigarh was as packed as it had been for Arwin's wedding. On this occasion there was a hard core of guests who would stay until late and in some cases all night, and a drifting population who would sample three or four parties in the course of the festival. Several had even left parties of their own in order to do so. A good Diwali party, once the food was circulating and the laughter was under way, could continue under its own momentum or in caretaker hands for hours while its sponsors dropped in on the neighbours. The houses, festooned in strings of lights, as Arwin's had been for her wedding, beckoned visitors.

Bheji, emerging from her kitchen with a laden tray of sweetmeats, surveyed her crammed sitting room with satisfaction. Arwin, following her with a tray of fruit drinks, said: "I think we have never had such a crowded party, Mummy." Beautiful and assured in one of her trousseau saris, turquoise with a gold border, Arwin had come with Saranjit to make a short call, and resumed her old helpful ways as she always did the moment she was across the doorstep. "Only," said Arwin, "it is such a pity Melanie is not here."

"Yes," said Bheji, saddened at the reminder, "it is."

Crowded the sitting room unquestionably was. The seating had run out long ago and half the guests were now sitting cross-legged or curled on the floor. In a corner, she on a stool and he on the carpet, sat Nirmal, smiling shyly, and beside her the boy to whom she was now officially engaged, visiting from Delhi for the occasion. Nirmal's father was in the middle of the floor singing a Punjabi folksong while Saranjit's father, who had succeeded in claiming an armchair, beat time on one of its fat arms. Surinder and Saranjit were by the window, eyeing the glow of a barbecue in the garden opposite and probably planning, if Bheji knew either of them, to gatecrash the party over there. Aunt Asha and Balwant were on the sofa, being amused by the comic bits in the folksong. Balwant's laughter sounded a little determined; however, she was managing. A good, reliable girl was Balwant, and in a way it was a pity . . .

But Avtar was standing beside Asha, occasionally exchanging a word with her, and about Avtar's bleak unsmiling face there was something which was a good deal more than a pity.

"Oh dear," Arwin murmured. "Avtar looks so miserable."

"So I see," said her mother, and, sweetmeat tray borne high, stepped over the pile of footwear in the doorway, the feet of a number of floor-sitting guests, and made straight for her son just as the folksong ended.

"You must try this pista barfi, Avtar. Would you believe, Arwin made it herself. Going to so much trouble when the rest of us just buy it. What a splendid party we are having. But I am surprised to see you staying so long, you must have had so many invitations . . ."

"I'm not in the right sort of mood for invitations," said Avtar. He obediently took a piece of barfi.

"No? Well, well, that I can understand. But Melanie will be so sad that she missed this Diwali, one of the best we have ever had, isn't it? You must write her all about it. Have you written yet?"

"I . . . no, I keep meaning to but then something comes up . . ."

Another folksong had started. The new singer had a loud voice and the noise he was making was good camouflage. Words spoken low into someone's ear would be heard by the recipient but not by anyone else. "It hardly matters what you put in the letter," said Bheji quietly and instructively. "Just friendly chit-chat, any kind of news, that will do. Say anything, son. But say *something*."

❧

Ivor Winnaford, retired professor of history and part-time artist, friend of William Purvis recently deceased, pushed back his armchair from the sputtering driftwood fire in the hotel lounge, and paced to the window. There was nothing to be seen but cloud, racing in low from the west, so that the hotel was wrapped in flowing fog.

"What's the forecast?" he said over his shoulder as a fellow guest came in.

"Dubious. Wind moderating tonight, likely to worsen again before tomorrow night. We stand a chance of getting off in the morning but not a good one."

"I was a fool to risk it, in October."

"Why? We're comfortable enough here. I don't mind being marooned." His acquaintance took Ivor's vacated chair and poked the fire philosophically. "Granted, you artists can't paint and we naturalists can't go bird watching, but the bar's well stocked and the food's superb. If we do sail tomorrow, it'll be a ghastly trip. You've nothing special to get back for, have you?"

Ivor Winnaford said: "No, nothing special." But did not sound too sure of it.

Distress Signals

Melanie woke at daybreak to the sound of rain on her windows. She lay cautiously still for a while in case she was again attacked by nausea, but nothing happened. Jason whined to be let out so she rose with care, donned a dressing gown, and took him downstairs. Cold, damp air rushed into the kitchen as she opened the back door. The wind had eased but the sky promised no let-up in the rain. Shivering, she put on the wall heater, set the kettle to boil, and switched on Gran's portable radio, which stood on a shelf above the refrigerator. It announced lugubriously that the Force Four winds now prevailing in the area of Lundy, Bristol Channel, and the Irish Sea would be Force Seven by nightfall, veering northwest, with heavy rain and poor visibility. Melanie turned to another station.

". . . most cultures take it for granted," said a smooth, male, and obviously political voice, presumably defending a controversial government policy to do with immigration, "that the female partner in a marriage should live in her husband's country of residence. This has always been accepted as the norm and . . ."

Oh, what do you know about it? thought Melanie, and was instantly overtaken by the sickness which had failed to materialise earlier. By the time it was over, the kettle was belching steam all over the kitchen and Jason was now whining to be let in. She attended to both of them, turned off the radio, sat down at the table in front of the pot of tea she did not yet want, and put her head in her hands.

Yesterday, she had not been able to think it through. She had in fact given up trying to think at all. She had come back from her walk and spent the afternoon pumping the tyres of Gran's Ford and taking it into town for more petrol and to shop for provisions. After that, she had taken the Marina back to the hirer's Heverton depot, returned to the Cliff by taxi, and sorted out some more of Gran's belongings. But think she must, and soon.

Consider the alternatives. If there had been no baby, she would have had little difficulty in remaining in England, if she so chose. She could have gone back to work, either returning to London to seek a post and keeping the Cliff for holidays, or else staying here and working as a freelance. Either way, rooms could be let in the Cliff for holidaymakers. That would have helped with income.

A baby narrowed the possibilities considerably. It would

be hard to undertake a full-time job and take care of a child as well. That left freelancing, and the amount she could earn from that, which would now have to support two, would be uncertain even with the help of Gavin's Cliff.

Yet other women managed. They always had. Women whose husbands had died or left them, women who had run away, women who never had any husbands in the first place. She could manage as well. If she wanted to.

Did she want to? Did she want never to see Avtar again? Sitting up, looking round the familiar kitchen and through its window to the pine trees which bordered the yard and overhung the track, she thought that it was less a case of never wanting to see Avtar again than of most emphatically *not* wanting to spend the rest of her life in India and never see Gavin's Cliff again. And going back would mean that. Or else it would mean years of fighting against Avtar, contesting with him, in an ever-reappearing quarrel. Once, the thought of never seeing Avtar again would have been like the thought of dying. Now, she could contemplate it. She forced a passage through the mental haze produced by her physical condition and looked at him close up, but the old love and longing were not there. Something akin to dislike, even dread, was there instead.

Oh yes, life without Avtar could be contemplated.

Only, there *was* the baby, and babies had fathers. Her baby might even look like Avtar.

He, and Bheji and Arwin and Surinder too, would expect her to go back under these circumstances, no matter what she might have done in others. And even from beyond the curve of the earth they might yet be capable of making their opinions felt. But . . .

"I can't!" said Melanie aloud. She thought of buying the ticket, packing, getting on the plane, committing herself to that future in which her home, Ambersford, Gavin's Cliff, would have no part. She did not think that she could do it.

The nausea had left her. Restless, she collected toast and tea and carried them into the parlour. She put on the electric fire and ate her breakfast from the rosewood table. She gazed out of the bow window, thinking that in India she had yearned for coolness and rain and there was no denying that Somerset was doing her proud. The world outside was chilly and saturated, the yard a morass, and the rhododendrons mournfully dripping. Intermittent rain squalls blanked out the sea and when the Channel was visible, it was steel grey, streaked with the manes of white horses. A cargo ship, bound probably for Cardiff, wallowed unpleasantly in the midst of them. The wind, as the radio had foretold, was rising again.

Her thoughts had reached a full stop, just short of a final decision. There was no chance of going out. Jason had settled down on the hearthrug, curled into a brown crescent of sleepiness. Melanie took the breakfast things back to the kitchen and washed up, glanced in a desultory fashion at some more of Gran's massed paperwork, collected a couple of paperback thrillers from the bookshelves in the den, and went back to bed.

꒰

She got up to make herself some lunch and over it, suffered a reaction.

The way she was behaving was disgraceful. Avtar had been right; she had treated him and India like an experiment. An experiment which had now failed: Oh dear, what a pity, empty the test tubes down the sink, sterilise them ready for the next project, and file the notes in the archives. You couldn't treat people like that. What *about* Avtar, for God's sake? What would *he* feel? She knew the answer to that for she had seen it at the airport. And what about Bheji, who loved her?

But—round and round the weary argument went—what was the use of dutifully going back, if it meant spending years in a tug-of-war, herself as the rope between Avtar and Gavin's Cliff? If it meant years of being angry? What good would that do any of them?

The muffled feeling, which was probably by its nature intermittent, had lifted, leaving her unprotected in a welter of emotions, not one of which seemed to be compatible with any other. It was like being in the midst of a crescendo of discordant noises. It was unbearable. And on that thought, as though a preset switch in her mind had clicked by itself to another position, she ceased having to bear it. The conflict stopped, laid aside for the time being. Something like this had happened the day after she broke with Robin, she recalled. She had been here at the Cliff with Gran, fretting, repining, and then in the middle of all that, irrelevantly and also insistently, she had had an idea for a design and spent the rest of that day doing it. She cleared away the lunch things, and marched purposefully up the stairs.

૦

She had stowed her suitcase in the landing cupboard, and a few things were still in them. Her second-best hairbrush, still full of red Delhi dust, was there, along with a pair of lightweight sandals, useless at Gavin's Cliff in October. And there too were a block of graph paper, several sheets of cartridge paper, paints, fibretips, geometrical aids, and a squirrel collection of postcards, bits of fabric, doodles on scrap paper, and experimental colourways in a small, scruffy notebook. Melanie's designing tools were part of her. Had she been bound for the South Pole, she would have packed them automatically. She had brought them with her from India. She took them down to the parlour.

After all, if she were even thinking of resuming life as a fabric designer, she ought to get her hand in again. This time, the idea which she half developed in Arwin's Sangeet decoration seemed to be coming to fulfillment. She saw, at last, the possibilities of the arch as a device. Framed in arches, incompatible or contrasting elements could be brought together. Her pencil tested possibilities. Moghul arches alternating with Norman or Gothic. The lattice . . . an English landscape through it? Hot, vivid colours like orange and peacock and sun gold, contrasting with mist grey and water green . . .

At three, she fetched coffee and sandwiches and the portable radio and rested, listening to another news bulletin. There was a report on the deteriorating weather, of a gale rising faster than anticipated, of shipping in trouble. A cargo ship and an oil tanker had been in collision near Bideford. RAF helicopters had been called to the scene.

Rain blew against the windows and the wind buffeted the cliff with a blunted sound like soft thunder. Poor devils, out there in the Channel in their damaged vessels. She altered a sketch, frowning, wondering if it would work up. She would need a healthy portfolio if she were to launch a new career in England.

Was her choice made, then? But what of the child, half hers and half Avtar's? For the first time she let the word *abortion* shape itself. It lasted half a second and then a steel shutter came down between her womb and it. She was astonished at the strength of her own resistance, the urgency with which her forces closed round the threatened life to defend it. The vague outline, which had been all she could visualise of the baby until now, came into focus. Though

213

only an inch long as yet, it was her daughter or her son. And she would safeguard it with all she was and all she had.

It didn't help. And the decision was not yet made.

‿

In England it was three-thirty. In Chandigarh it was evening and the last postal collection would have gone. But that, thought Balwant nervously, wouldn't matter. Once the letter was in the mailbox it would be beyond recall, safe from interference either from Asha or from her own timidity. And this was a golden chance to get it there. Asha had gone to visit a neighbour, leaving Balwant behind because Balwant had volunteered to make a chicken curry now that the maidservant had gone home. She had skinned and jointed the chicken at high speed to leave herself time to write the letter, and she had done the writing at high speed too, so as *not* to leave herself time to think. It was ready to post. Of course, it meant leaving the curry to bubble in its pot all by itself for a few minutes.

Never mind the curry. If she were to go through with this, she must contemplate its meaning fully and not take refuge in trivialities. She wished she were more like Melanie, who had decided what to do and had done it, in the face of all opposition. It was difficult to imagine being Melanie.

She sealed the letter quickly, before hesitation could get the better of her. She picked up her shawl and turned down the gas. It would take five minutes to get to the post, and five minutes back.

Her hand almost twitched the letter back as it went through the slot, but it was too late. Her fingers had already let go. She went home slowly. It was all right, perhaps, for Melanie to do such a thing. Her world was different. But for Balwant? What consequences would there be for her,

214

now that she had done what she had done? Now that the letter was irretrievably on its way, she would have given all that she had to get it back.

The smell of the curry greeted her as she entered the kitchen. She was glad to have an accustomed task to do. When Asha returned half an hour later, she found Balwant very busy about the stove, adding spices, frowning as though this simple task were oddly difficult, but deft in her movement and composed as usual. "You are a good girl, Balwant," said Bheji Asha approvingly.

∽

It was still a long time till nightfall, but under the heavy sky which now covered the west of England darkness seemed imminent. Daniel Purvis stood uneasily in his kitchen doorway, studying the livid clouds over Ravensridge. "I don't like the look of it, Lu. I've four ponies in the river meadow up the valley and the river could spate. Look at that there rain. I'd best take the trailers and get up there. Drat Roy, where's he got to? He's got one of them. Don't Fran know where he's gone?"

"He went over to Exford to see that pony you thought of buying," said Lucy. "He's been held up, I expect. He's thorough when he looks an animal over."

"I suppose that's a virtue," Daniel said. "Where's my heavy mac, Lu? I'll just have to make two trips, that's all. Damnation."

∽

In Gannet's Head Coastguard Station and Maritime Sub-Rescue Centre, Senior Coastguard George Petersham, who had been following a small vessel through a pair of binoculars, lowered them sharply. "She's in trouble. No way on her and drifting sideways, inshore. That wind's enough to blow the QE2 off course if she lost her power. Get hold of Swansea."

With a sizzle of static, the radio forestalled him. "Mayday relay. This is Swansea Maritime Rescue Centre. Mayday signal received from vessel *Fairlight,* position—"

"Swansea MRC, this is Gannet's Head. We've got her in the glasses. Repeat, we have the *Fairlight* in the glasses. Details please. Over."

"Engine failure, attempts to rectify unsuccessful. She's reported drifting out of control, direction of drift taking her into the coast west of Heverton. She has three crew members and twelve passengers aboard."

Smoothly, a well-rehearsed routine began to roll. A telephone rang in the North Devon Infirmary and the medical staff prepared to receive up to fifteen cases of shock, exposure, and possible injury. Another telephone rang in a Devon RAF station, with a request for a helicopter scramble, and a Sea King helicopter with the capacity to winch fifteen people aboard in a single airlift took off into the threatening sky. In the Heverton area, in one house after another, the men of the Lifeboat Crew, and the volunteers who formed the Auxiliary Coastguard Force, banged down receivers, grabbed boots and oilskins, and abandoned hearths and TV sets to rendezvous in Heverton. The doors of the Lifeboat House opened and the lifeboat rolled out.

The rain grew heavier.

❧

At Stancross Farm, Sheila Miller prepared early high tea, eyed her father covertly, and hoped to heaven that he wouldn't let the bad weather interfere with his plan to go to a Farmers Union meeting in Dulverton tonight. If he decided to stay at home, her intended visitor would need a good excuse for calling. Blasted weather. But there, her dad was as obstinate as they came; he'd get a kick out of going to the meeting regardless, and come back making comments about the soft old bastards who'd stayed home by the fire. In all probability, she was worrying for nothing. But lord, what a gale. That wind wasn't the Force Seven the radio had prophesied at breakfast time. Nearer Force Nine by the sound of it, and going past the farmhouse it sounded like an express train. Pity the poor men who were at sea in this. Must be hell sometimes, being a sailor.

&

George Petersham glared at the VHF equipment through which Maritime Channel 16 had just conveyed such unwelcome news and said: "Bloody hell!" His subordinate officer ended a call to the infirmary and said: "What was that?"

"That was the helicopter that was coming to us. It's been diverted to that collision off Bideford. One of the machines they had out there has had to return to base with winch trouble. Half an hour before they can get another chopper in the air for us and that ship's almost on the Fangs *now*! The lifeboat and the land party will have to do it, that's all. Lunatics, they must be on that ship. Chartered vessel, that's what she is, bringing a party of naturalists and what-have-you off Lundy. Madness, trying to sail in this . . ."

"They probably left in the morning when the forecast wasn't so bad," said his subordinate mildly.

"They've eyes in their heads, haven't they? They'd only to *look* at that sky this morning . . . we need reception arrangements in Heverton, then. There's the *Fishing Boat*, or maybe Whitehangers would . . ."

217

"Gavin's Cliff is occupied now. The granddaughter's home. My wife met Frances Purvis in Heverton yesterday."

"Gavin's Cliff?" said Mr. Petersham. "Now, that would be a help, for a change. If the lady's a proper Purvis, that is. Met her once, I think. Hope she hasn't altered. Been abroad, hasn't she? What's the number?"

～

And on the moors above Amberscombe, blackly and stealthily, lapping at his peatsoil verges and then welling smoothly over them, Old Harry overflowed.

～

At Gavin's Cliff, the grandfather clock whirred and clicked its way into the four o'clock chimes and then was drowned in a single, shattering crack of thunder. The lightning flash came simultaneously. Melanie, who had been sitting on the hearthrug with her drawings, looked up, startled. Little could be seen beyond the window. The heavy sky was almost black. She stood up to put her papers on the table and the corner of her eye caught another glimpse of lightning. *Scarlet* lightning? She ran to the window, in time to see a vivid red flare fall back towards Gavin's Cove. Just as, out in the hall, the telephone urgently began to jangle.

She slammed the door between the phone and the still loudly commenting clock, snatched up the receiver, paused to let another crack of thunder go by, and said: "Heverton two two oh."

"Gavin's Cliff?" The voice on the other end had a bass Devonian accent, overlaid with the clipped note of official-dom.

"Yes. Mrs. Melanie Avtarsingh speaking."

"This is Gannet's Head Coastguard Station. We have a

ship with engine failure drifting onto the Fangs, and the helicopter is delayed. Auxiliaries with rescue equipment, plus our own Landrover, are on their way and Heverton lifeboat is putting out. If we fetch everyone ashore at the cove, can we bring them initially to you? We can take them to Heverton later."

Behind the officialdom was a trace of doubt, as if she were a stranger. Once, anyone snatched from the Fangs would have been deposited at the Cliff without a by-your-leave, Purvis cooperation being taken for granted. "Of course they can come here!" Melanie almost barked. "Warm blankets and hot coffee will be ready. How many are on board and what kind of vessel is she?"

"She's a chartered trawler called *Fairlight.* Twenty-nine tons, bringing twelve artists and naturalists back to Heverton from Lundy. Thought they'd make it before the weather clamped, and didn't, and had engine trouble on top of that. Three crewmen, twelve passengers, cargo is fish and empty calor gas cylinders and so on. Nothing explosive and no pollutants. We're ringing Whitehangers and they'll be along to help. We'll be with you shortly. Many thanks."

He hung up, the clean break of a man in a crisis. Melanie stood by the phone, arranging her ideas. Other people's disasters, she noticed in dry parenthesis, were an effective way of forgetting one's own. For the foreseeable future, her own confusion would have to wait. What, she asked herself, wanted doing first?

But she knew, of course. Memories of that childhood occasion when Gran had masterminded reception arrangements for a shipwreck, stories of other wrecks in other years, and simple common sense came together like a miraculously solved jigsaw. Blankets. The cupboards of Gavin's Cliff were full of them, always had been. Put them to warm in the parlour. Towels too. She put her designs out of the way on Gran's desk in the study and shut Jason in there because he was following her about and twice she had almost tripped over him. She raced upstairs, threw the piled clothes off Gran's bed, and made up the bed at top speed. She dragged a camp bed out of the attic and cast blankets over that too. Glancing from the window, she saw that the Heverton lifeboat was already in position, with a searchlight on the *Fairlight,* which moved sluggishly in the beam like some wounded creature. It was already among the rocks. The lifeboat was standing off, unable to get nearer. Rescue would need to be quick. Once on the Fangs, a ship in heavy seas would be hammered to bits in a frighteningly short time.

The thunder and the lightning had ceased. But the wind in the pines was now roaring so that the house was wrapped in noise, and the rain continued unremittingly to fall. She was in the kitchen, putting out coffee, tinned soup, eggs and bacon, and cursing because she had not nearly enough, when headlights swept the yard. She opened the back door and out of a Landrover, holdall in one hand and a large plastic carrier in the other, climbed a small, flat-backed woman in an anorak, followed by a tall shape in oilskins.

"Mary! Bill Heaton! Quick, come inside!"

"Gannet's Head said you'd need a hand." Mary Heaton had small, wind-roughened features which, however, were split by a broad smile as she ducked through the rain into the lighted kitchen to drop her burdens on the table. "Melanie, my dear. We're so glad to see you, though we wish the circumstances were nicer. There's eggs there, bacon, sausages, frozen chips, and baked beans, and the *Fishing Boat*'ll send more up if we need it."

"Right glad you're here," said Bill Heaton, inserting his

six foot four through the door in the wake of his wife. Whatever Gran's quarrel had been with the Heatons, they were obviously not extending it to Melanie. "We'd have been over long since, but there's a landslide on the track beyond the farm and we've been trying to shift 'un. Coastguard'll have to come up by way of Heverton, Melanie. There's an ambulance on its way too. Seems one of the crewmen's hurt."

"We heard your news, dear," Mary said to Melanie, tumbling tins and packets out of the carrier. "You're feeling quite fit, are you, to cope with all this? Your Aunt Lucy telephoned me last night and told me all about it."

"Good God. Gran always said this place had more efficient jungle drums than any African tribe ever invented. Do you always keep that much bacon handy?" Melanie asked.

"Our four boys are at sea just now," said Bill Heaton in his slow voice. "Two of them'll be home any day, though. We stock up beforehand. They eat like wolves."

"Wait till you have four, Melanie," Mary said, chuckling. "And maybe you will now. Well, what wonderful news it is. How all the doctors can be wrong. A child cements a marriage, there's no doubt about it. . . ."

"I think," said Melanie, "that I can hear another engine."

◠

Time began to go faster, like a speeded-up film. Advancing headlights heralded the arrival of the ambulance, which drew up behind the Heatons' vehicle. Then came the Gannet's Head Landrover. Bill Heaton went out and spoke to the driver of the Landrover, ran to his own transport, and climbed in. Both vehicles bumped away, heading for the path to the Cove. Mary said: "You haven't put any sheets down, dear."

"Sheets?"

"My dear girl, the carpets! This house is going to be full of dripping wet people oozing seawater and mud and stamping about in huge boots. Is there any spare linen we can use? Or newspapers?"

Spreading newspaper along the hall and in the parlour, Melanie remembered the Sangeet and marvelled that two occasions so wildly unlike should have this one feature in common. A marriage-tide full of vivid silks and music and perfume; a sea disaster full of danger and Force Nine winds and hot coffee—yet an essential part of both was to protect the floor from the feet of the participants. Strange.

The carpets were hardly covered before headlights blazed outside once more, rods of rain glittering in the beam. Melanie opened the door again and a coastguard stepped in. Behind him was the ambulance, with activity round it. "First batch here in a moment. Ambulance is taking a man with a fractured leg to Heverton Hospital. It'll be back, just in case. If it can get back." He eyed Melanie grimly. "You're Professor Purvis's granddaughter? Met you before, somewhere. You want some forestry work done up here, my lass. There's a tree coming down on that track any minute, lower down. And you'll get a pine through the roof up here one of these days if you're not careful."

"Now, that's not fair, George Petersham," said Mary. "Melanie's hardly back from abroad and she's not had time to get her breath. I hope the tree stays up a bit longer but it's no one's fault except the Professor's and he's dead. What's happening in the cove?"

"She's on the rocks but she's jammed level and close to the Point. Anyone fairly able-bodied'll be able to scramble ashore with a rope or two to help them. Assuming they *are* able-bodied, that is." Mr. Petersham was a man in whom competence and aggression were about evenly mingled. "Three of 'em are over sixty, if you please. Some folk are clean barmy. Lundy's three miles long by half a mile with four-hundred-foot cliffs all round it and next to nothing on it but sheep and birds and high winds, and still twelve nutcases want to go painting and bird watching on it in what's practically winter. If they all come out alive, it'll be a miracle. See you."

He plunged back into the weather. "Such a rude man, but he means well," said Mary.

"It was at a lifeboatmen's ball that he met me," said Melanie. "I remember him vividly. He trod on my feet."

They laughed. Then Mary said: "I think our first batch is arriving."

"Coffee's boiling," said Melanie.

❧

The house became full of movement and urgency, pervaded by a curious mixture of smells: seawater and coffee, wet clothes and brandy (she had raided the parlour sideboard for that). The kitchen floor became slippery. There was a pool by the table where she had caught at the arm of an elderly man as he stumbled through, and the thick knitted jersey sleeve protruding from his mac squeezed like a sponge in her hand. The parlour was an amalgam of hospital, changing room, and cafe. Wet clothes and boots were piling up in the hall, thrown out as their wearers discarded them. A sturdy, dogged figure, Mrs. Devine from the *Fishing Boat*, trudged across the yard and banged on the kitchen door, to present a basket of extra supplies and inform them that the tree across the track had duly come down. "Couldn't get my

223

van up and the ambulance can't get back neither. Seems you'd best feed them all up yur as best 'ee can. Stay and help if 'ee want."

"We'd be thankful," said Mary. "Have a hot drink yourself, you must be soaking. What a night!"

The smell of frying eggs and bacon now became dominant. The Gannet's Head vehicle appeared with a second batch of rescued people. The first across the threshold was being supported by a coastguard. He was another elderly man, with a plump face now shrunken with cold, and he shook with uncontrollable shivers. "He ought to be taken down to the ambulance," said the coastguard. "We'd have driven him down the track and transferred him; it's waiting there at the other side of that flaming tree. But no, he insists on coming here. Got right stroppy he did, when we tried to persuade him. You got a warm bed for him?"

"Nothing wrong with me. Just cold. 'Lo, Melanie," said the elderly man, mumbling through lips almost too chilled to move.

"Dear heaven," said Melanie. "Ivor!"

∽

"Ivor, aren't you getting a bit old for this sort of thing?"

"What sort of thing?" said Ivor. His face was nowhere near its usual agreeable pink, but a warm bath had given him back at least a trace of colour, and he had ceased to shiver. Two plump paws outside the blankets of Gran's bed were curled round a mug of soup. "Shipwreck wasn't on the official itinerary. The hardest thing I thought I'd have to do was climb the path from the landing on Lundy to the top of the island. It was a grand trip till the last few days." He added dismally: "I've lost all the paintings I did, with the *Fairlight*."

224

"Thank God that's all you lost!" She thought of what it must have been like on the drifting ship: the cold rain playing like a hundred hosepipes on the shuddering deck; the seas coming aboard like demolition balls of black water. Melanie was a bad sailor, but she and Gran had twice made the crossing to Lundy from Ilfracombe, and once in rough weather. She could imagine all too well what the last hours of the *Fairlight* had been like. She said: "The ambulance doctor says you're to stay in bed tomorrow. Either that or let yourself be taken to hospital, since there's no one at your own home to look after you. Why wouldn't you go to hospital?"

"Pointless. I wasn't hurt. They've got really ill people there to look after."

"If the helicopter had arrived in time, you'd have been in North Devon Infirmary whether you liked it or not."

"Well, I'm not. I'm here." Ivor sounded positively smug. "The helicopter did come in the end, didn't it? I heard it."

"Yes, it took the last three or four off. But the captain and the mate are here. They insisted, like you. Said they wanted to be where most of the others were. The mate came ashore clinging to his accordion, if you please. He's promised to entertain everyone in the parlour later. Do you want anything more solid after that soup?"

"Does this officious ambulance doctor of yours say I can have it?"

"He didn't say you couldn't. You're really hungry?" Melanie's voice was thankful at these signs of normality. "I'll get you something," she said.

At the foot of the stairs she found Captain Trelawney of the *Fairlight*, Jim Hawkins the mate, and Mary Heaton clustered round the telephone. The captain, blanketenswathed, was hanging up. "The line could have been down in this storm but we're in luck, she's not," he said. He was a Cornishman, short and dark, with alert brown eyes. When he came into the Cliff he had been drawn and silent with misery, but his face had lightened now. "I just rang the infirmary," he said to Melanie. "And then I rang Heverton Hospital. They're all comfortable, my crewman as well. Simple fracture of the tibia. He'll be laid up a good while but he's not in danger now. The rest are just thawing out nicely. And the old fellow upstairs, how's he?"

"Also thawing out," said Melanie. "And wants solid food."

"So they're all safe," said Mary and fled, hands to her face, as her mouth twisted out of control.

In the kitchen, Mrs. Devine patted Mary's uncharacteristically bent shoulders while Melanie put two teaspoonsful of brandy into a hot coffee and handed it to her. "Mary, it's all right. It's all over. Drink this, now."

"You don't know what it's like," said Mary between sobs. "I've four boys at sea and whenever there's a storm, I think, suppose they're in it? I wish to God just one, just one of them, hadn't gone to sea. It's in their blood; they look like their farming dad but they take after my dad inside— and he was a sailor and he was drowned off Bideford Bar when I was ten. I'd have done anything, if only one of them had wanted to farm instead. I'm sorry, I can't help it, it's the relief. Everyone's safe. I never thought they would be. My father used to say: A storm always claims a life. I'm sorry, I can't stop crying, I can't *help* it!"

❧

Edward Miller stamped on the brake with fear-induced violence and stopped his van just in time, on the edge of what had been a watersplash and was now a leaping torrent. In his headlights, sticks and debris went swirling by on a surging jet black surface, and he could hear stones from the hillside grating in the depths. He looked up, and through the rain and the gloom glimpsed the cataract that now poured down the heather-covered hill beside him. Old Harry, of course. Them stupid sods in the Board and the Authority had left it too long, just like everyone had been telling them for weeks.

He was late for his union meeting already and now there was this. No getting the van through that; be turned clean over, he would. Bloody lucky he'd stopped in time. And the water was rising. He hastily reversed away from it. No way round that would get him to Dulverton in time now. The alternative route would put five more miles on the journey, and what's more, it meant a one-in-four descent he didn't fancy. His brakes were soft; he'd felt it just now. Better wash out the meeting. Wash out. Hah! That was a good one. He scowled into the murk. Well, half of them wouldn't turn up in this, anyhow. Wouldn't even try, probably. Not like him. Lazy good-for-nothings, most of them. He wouldn't be missing much, he thought, and continued morosely backing the van until he found a place wide enough to turn it.

There were too many lights on in his farmhouse, he decided, as he drove back into the Stancross yard. That would be Sheila, wasting electricity just for the hell of it. Well, he'd have those lights off in double-quick time, anyhow. Got a hefty streak of spite in her, that girl of his had, just like her mother. Not that she didn't keep the place straight—well, fairly straight—and see his meals got cooked regular, and there was no doubt that on the farm she could turn her hand to just about anything, good as a man and better than some. He was a fair man and he appreciated it. She'd get her reward one day. Pity she had maggots in her head about men. Extraordinary. He'd never had maggots in his head about women. Well, maybe once, but he'd soon got his senses back. And he hadn't gone near a woman since Liz left him. Sheila's mother had walked out on Edward Miller sixteen years before, not greatly to anyone's surprise. They had had a moderately amicable divorce, the amity being based on the fact that each of them was equally determined never to set eyes on the other again. In the case of Liz Miller, this loathing had extended beyond her husband to their daughter. Sheila carried Edward Miller's genes in her, and that was enough to make Liz more than content to leave her at Stancross.

Well, Sheila had grown up a better cook than her mother ever was. He hoped she'd be able to put a bit more supper together for him. Ten to one she'd be grooming that infernal Siamese cat or some such nonsense. . . .

He circled the van to put it in its usual parking place and then halted in astonishment. Something was parked there already. He studied the pale-toned car in his lights. So it was still going on, was it? Edward Miller switched off lights and engine, sprang out of the van, and ran head down through the rain to the back door. Faint human sounds came from the living room. He tore off his shoes, the better to pad unheard through the passage. The living room door was ajar.

There they were, in front of the fire—even in his state of outrage, Miller observed that the coal was piled on the fire more lavishly than his economical soul could bear—and—God, it was indecent—on the *floor*, on the *hearthrug*. Even as Miller watched, the two entwined bodies completed themselves, went soft, collapsed together, locked close and laughing.

He wanted to rush forward and tear them apart with his bare hands, scream obscenities, throw them bodily out of house, unclad as they were, into the downpour.

He strode into the room. They broke apart and sat up, seeing him now, two pairs of wide eyes, two faces aghast.

He began to shout about the things he wanted to do to them, the creatures he thought they were. It hurt so much, that Sheila should betray him like this. Hadn't she betrayed him enough and hadn't he forgiven her and let her keep her home here and her bastard with her? He'd given her everything—everything—and one day she'd have all he possessed as well. Why couldn't she give him this, just this one thing, her good faith, so that he could trust her? It hurt so much. It was like a swelling in his chest, stopping his breath and stretching his ribs until they cracked. He couldn't think anymore. He could hardly see. It hurt so much. . . .

Tribute to a Storm

". . . we heard the seas breaking on the Fangs before we could even see them," Ivor said, sitting up in bed, drinking tea. His hands were as yet not perfectly steady. "We were all terrified and so *cold* . . . we were bundled up in all the clothes we had, padded out like a lot of astronauts, but the wind cut through as though they were nothing. I thought if I wasn't drowned, I'd die of exposure. When we hit the rocks there was a grating noise first and then a shudder and then an almighty bang and I thought: Well, that's it, that's the end. I was on deck, holding on to the rail. I could just make out Heverton Point looming over us, but what with the gloom and the rain it looked completely remote, not likely to be any help at all. Then, out of nowhere, there was a blaze of light and a lot of shouting and the captain came and herded us all to one end of the ship. She was jammed between the rocks, I think. The waves were breaking over her but she wasn't sinking. Then a coastguard came scrambling aboard and someone pushed a rope at me and said, 'Catch hold of this,' and I thought: Well, maybe we'll live after all. Then we all started clambering over the side and across the rocks. Those coastguards are marvels with a stretcher. They took the lad with the broken leg off as though it was no trouble at all. He did it falling down a companionway when we first went adrift and the sea took to playing with us. Do you know, I wasn't sick? I think I was too frightened." He nodded towards the window, through which could be seen a magically serene sky and hushed, dripping pine trees. "Last night seems quite unreal now."

"It's left a few mementos," Melanie said, shaking down the thermometer which she had used before handing Ivor his tea. "You're still subnormal. Do you want a doctor to see you again today?"

"No, thank you. Did you get a lifebelt from the *Fairlight*?"

"I did. Captain Trelawney gave me one himself. What's more, he put it up on the wall of Gran's study for me. If you could see the mess in the kitchen and the parlour this morning, you wouldn't say that last night was unreal. Mary's coming over later to help me clear up."

"Did it turn into a party? I woke once or twice and I thought I heard the accordion going."

"It lasted till three this morning." The party had blown up like a second gale as soon as they knew that the rescued people in the two hospitals were not in danger. It had continued even after Bill Heaton had arrived to say that he and two of his farmhands and their tractor had cleared the fallen tree from the track. By then, they had investigated the matter of what else the parlour sideboard contained besides the bottle of brandy Melanie had used, and were getting high on it. Jim Hawkins had his accordion, and presently it transpired that Captain Trelawney sang a melodious bass. Even his natural grief for the *Fairlight,* which he had owned, yielded at last to the euphoria of rescue and the effects of several Scotches, and "... he started singing Al Jolson songs," said Melanie. "And it's a funny thing, but the Cornish accent suits them. Then we all started singing and then two of the naturalists got completely sozzled and had an owlish argument about whether it was or wasn't possible that a golden oriole had been seen on Lundy last summer, and one of the coastguards said he'd once been an engineer on a cargo ship called *Oriole* which nearly went down in a typhoon in the Indian Ocean, and that started everyone off swapping sea stories. Then Captain Trelawney got to his feet and insisted on making a solemn speech of thanks to the coastguards and the Auxiliaries and the Heatons and me, and we rooted Gran's camera out of the den and took pictures of the party. . . ."

Ivor, sitting plumply in the bed with Professor Purvis's best pyjama jacket stretched uncomfortably over his much larger shoulders, said: "You look worn out this morning."

"Do you wonder?" said Melanie.

It was not, and she knew it, her physical tiredness which had drawn the deep lines from nostril to mouth, which her mirror had shown her this morning. But she did not want to talk to Ivor, or to anyone, about the atmosphere which had pervaded last night's party, climaxing when they all raised their glasses and smiled into the camera successively held by Captain Trelawney, Jim Hawkins, and Bill Heaton. Sitting there among the men she had helped to succour, and those who had worked beside her, meeting their friendly and comprehensible eyes—the eyes of people whose backgrounds and mores and experience of the world were so like her own—she had for a while had a sense of oneness with them which was so intense it was almost a fusing of identities. She had recognised then, clearly and without possibility of change, that she was indivisibly part of this community, part of these people. She had woken this morning still knowing it, and aware that the child she carried was a force which quarrelled with it, and would, if she so allowed, wrench her away, and back to an alien world. She was on the edge of decision now but she did not want to face it. It was easier to draw away into exhaustion and say: I am too tired to think.

"Three o'clock," she said again. "We did break the party up then. Several people had homes or hotel reservations in Heverton, and the Devines at the *Fishing Boat* had arranged sleeping accommodations as well for anyone who wanted it. Fortunately, Bill Heaton and one of the Auxiliaries were teetotal so there was someone to drive the trucks. Everyone was gone by half-past three except for the two argumentative naturalists. They were past going anywhere and they spent the rest of the night in chairs in the parlour. I phoned for a taxi for them this morning. They went away," said Melanie, "nursing headaches. Now I'd better get you some breakfast."

She prepared it, listening to the local news as she did so. The *Fairlight* formed a major part of it. There was a

233

reference to Gavin's Cliff and to herself (described as Melanie Purvis, granddaughter of the late Professor William Purvis, as though her marriage and absence from the country had never happened) carrying on the rescue tradition for which Gavin's Cliff had always been noted. The source was probably George Petersham. After that came more storm news. The Darr had flooded and drowned miles of meadowland, though the road up the valley to Amberscombe had fortunately remained open. A motorist had narrowly escaped death when tiles ripped from a roof came down on his car. The Heverton marshes were mostly under water, and the bog known as Old Harry had overflowed, sweeping cattle away and flooding the road across the moor between Stancross and Dulverton. She took the radio upstairs with the food, thinking that it might help Ivor to pass the morning. She found him recalcitrant.

"I can perfectly well get up, Melanie. I want to help you with your grandfather's papers, and perhaps sort out what I can use for the biography. I was very angry when we were delayed leaving Lundy."

"You've got to stay in bed," said Melanie. Ivor might look like an elderly cherub but he could be as awkward as Gran if he felt so inclined. "You're suffering from shock."

She left him, grumpy but more or less acquiescent, and went to feed Jason. She was putting his dish on the floor when the telephone rang. Frances, probably. She went out to the hall. It was indeed Frances. A Frances breathless and upset. "Melanie! I thought you'd never answer!"

"Sorry," said Melanie. "I had a late night. A ship went on to the Fangs and—"

"Yes, yes, we heard, it was on the early news." Frances's voice was high-pitched, in a way which made Melanie's fingers curl convulsively round the receiver. This was not an enquiry after her well-being. "That storm, that bloody storm!" said Frances. "Oh, Melanie, it's too awful, please come, please. Roy's gone off to Heverton Hospital. Edward Miller's had a coronary."

～

Presumably there was logic of some kind in this disconnected statement, but it was hardly obvious. "Fran, what are you talking about? Yes . . . yes, of course I'll come if you want me, but what's Roy got to do with Miller and why should *Roy* go haring off to the hospital because Miller's had a heart attack . . . oh, Fran!" Melanie caught up with one possibility. "Roy's all right, isn't he? I mean, he's *at* the hospital, not in it?"

"Oh, Roy's all right!" Frances's voice ceased to be hysterical and changed to a serrated bitterness. "More's the pity. *Quite* all right. He was up at Stancross with Sheila Miller when Edward Miller walked in on them. Miller was going to a Farmers Union meeting but he couldn't get through the floods, so he turned back . . . and what he saw when he got home gave him a coronary. Oh, Melanie, don't be dense, don't you understand? Roy's the father of Sheila's baby!"

"What?" said Melanie faintly.

"Yes! He and Sheila got Miller to hospital somehow. The ambulance got through. The Darr's flooded but not as far as the road. The river meadows are under water . . . Roy didn't come home last night. He was supposed to be at Exford, looking at a pony, but when we rang the man there he said Roy had left hours before without buying, and after we'd been frantic all night Roy rang up from Heverton

235

Hospital. His father's gone there to talk to him. Melanie, it's awful, it's unbearably awful . . . I must have someone of my own, I must! Melanie, please, please come!"

"I'm on my way," said Melanie.

◡

Crisis was following crisis like a series of deformed rabbits out of a black magician's hat. She made a quick call to Mary Heaton to ensure that Ivor would not be left alone for long, and a few minutes later was in Gran's Ford, making her way down the track. Sheila's baby, fathered by *Roy?* Had that been Roy's white Allegro she had seen then, leaving Stancross when she was out on Falcon? Must have been. And all the time Walter Prescott had been taking the blame—or the kudos. Maybe insignificant little Prescott had enjoyed his short-lived masquerade as the alpha stud of the Darr Valley. Did Frances want her to do anything specific, or was her need simply for moral support?

It was impossible to drive fast on the road between Heverton and Ambersford. Here, on the low ground between the hills and the sea, the aftermath of the torrential rains could be seen. To her left, the marsh pastures were under water, blending with the sea, grey sky reflected and rippling where green grass had been. The road itself had a skin of water on it in places, through which the car must crawl.

The Purvis house in Ambersford, when at length she reached it, had a curiously pillaged air. Somewhere within it, a Siamese cat caterwauled an unregarded protest at the disruption of the household, and the front door stood wide as though everything which had any value had already been stolen.

In the kitchen, as Melanie walked in by the side entrance

236

via the stableyard, a meal of sorts was in progress. Molly, brown hair tangled round her face, was picking at a plate of stew while Lucy ate her own with too much enthusiasm and tried to make conversation about horses. Frances was not eating, but sitting slumped in an old wooden armchair in a corner. Molly raised her head at the sound of footsteps, only to turn away when she saw who it was. She laid down her knife and fork. "Eat that up, Molly," said Frances automatically.

"Can't. I thought Daddy had come back," said Molly. She pushed back her chair and ran out of the room.

"*Molly!*"

"I'll go after her." Lucy rose. "You talk to Fran, Melanie. Good thing you've come. Fran, you make a nice cup of tea, now."

Frances, from the armchair, said as Lucy went out: "If one more person tells me to have a nice cup of tea, I'll—"

"You need a strong drink if you ask me. And something to eat. Did you have any breakfast?"

"No. I can't eat. Don't blame Molly, really, if she can't either." Frances, propelling herself upwards by her hands as though her leg muscles were not working properly, came to her feet. "I'll get drinks. It's supposed to be lunchtime. Shall I make you some sandwiches?"

"No. I'll do it. You stay where you are. I know where to find things."

Melanie fetched drinks and made ham sandwiches, wanting to ask questions, hesitating to do so unless Frances led the way. Her cousin's face, she saw, had grown mysteriously older, its once soft and pretty contours newly harsh. There was no need to ask questions, as it proved. Frances watched her in silence for a few minutes, until Melanie handed her a whisky. Then she said, answering the unspoken

237

enquiries, "When I was carrying Molly, that's when he had his first little excursion. It was a girl in Heverton. I found out and we had a grand set-to, ending with me in tears apologising—I'm still wondering for what—and him promising never to do it again. But he did, of course. Funny, his parents never knew. I couldn't tell them; it would have been like saying I was a failure. But I'd never agree to have another child after Molly. I always thought: If I can't stand it anymore it'll be easier to cope alone with one child than two. Besides, I had to get back at him somehow. He wanted more, you see. But I didn't suspect about Sheila. I didn't think he knew her except by sight. She doesn't ride and everyone said it was Prescott she was going with, anyway. But he called at Stancross, it seems, two years back when his radiator sprang a leak one day. Sheila gave him some water for it and he took one look at her close up and there they were in the hayloft or whatever. Oh, he told me all about it before I rang you this morning," said Frances acidly. "Disarmingly candid, he was. He told me to see Barnes & Chaldicott about a divorce, just as if he was saying bring back a few pounds of potatoes when you go out. He went to the hospital with Sheila and he says he's going back afterwards to live at Stancross with her and her father if necessary."

"What in the world is old Miller going to say to that?" asked Melanie. "If finding out about them made him ill?"

"Oh, he won't care as long as Sheila stays there, as long as Roy doesn't take her away. Roy said he was sure of that. The old man's afraid of losing Sheila. Nothing to do with morality! Well, I'm afraid of losing Roy but it's happened. I've tried, Melanie, really I've tried. I've never fitted in in this village or this house. I'm a town girl and I don't belong here. I hate this kind of life, all these blasted dogs and horses." She held out small, roughened hands. "Time was, I was never without nail polish. What would it look like on these nails? But I have tried to fit in. I have tried, I have!"

Melanie put the sandwiches on the table. "Does Molly understand what's happening?" she asked.

"Yes. I don't think I would have done, at her age, but she's known or guessed about his other women for a long time. She's said things to me, though not where her grandparents could hear. She's even got an instinct about keeping it from them." Frances looked towards the window. "Someone's coming."

A vehicle pulled into the yard, its noisy engine proclaiming it to be the elderly Purvis van. A door slammed and Daniel Purvis came into the kitchen. He scanned their faces silently for a moment before he said: "Miller's gone." Melanie cleared her throat. Frances said: "And Roy?"

"Still there. With Sheila. Asked me to pack a case for him. They're going straight back to Stancross. I've got to go up there anyhow to fetch Roy's car and the trailer back. I'll take the case with me. One of the men can come to drive the van back."

"Of course. We must get the van and the trailer back safely. The business must be kept running," said Frances.

"There's no call for that, Fran. It does have to be kept running, you know that. It's sheer luck those clients have left. Fran, I tried with Roy but there was nothing I could do."

"Except agree to pack his case for him," said Frances.

Daniel considered her helplessly. "He may change his mind. Sheila's in a state—"

"And I'm *not?*"

"—she was fond of that old man of hers in her fashion, though maybe fonder still of the farm. Old Miller always threatened that if she ever left he'd sell up and then she'd never get it. Now, Melanie, it's no good you looking scandalised. You ought to understand that if anyone does. You're in England as much because you love Gavin's Cliff as anything. See here," said Daniel, leaning an elbow on the wide mantelpiece as if to draw support from it, "it's a hard thing to say, Fran, but if he don't change his mind it's maybe all for the best. He's been restless here for years, always wanting to go in for the market gardening and that. He'd have started up on his own long ago, only you always said you couldn't stand the life. But the truth is, you can hardly stand this life, either. You and him've never got along, now have 'ee?"

"And whose fault was that?"

"Not all his," said Daniel hardily, and Melanie saw what she had hitherto only sensed: that Frances's in-laws did not like her. "You can be pretty hard to please," said Daniel. "Redecorated this place twice over, haven't 'ee? And always questioning Roy. Where's he going, when'll he be back, who was that on the phone? Enough to get on any man's nerves, all that."

"He means it," said Frances, not to Melanie but to the fireplace, the back door, and the gods above. "My God, he means it! Roy's unfaithful with half a dozen different women and his father *still* wonders why I ask him who his phone calls are from!"

"It wur like that with you before there wur any question of other women," said Daniel. "But there. You're you and Roy's Roy and these things happen. The two of you just don't match. Melanie, if you'll make a nice pot of tea . . ."

240

Frances jumped up, banged her empty whisky glass down on the table, seized the plate of ham sandwiches, and hurled the contents at her father-in-law. He stood with sandwiches showering to the floor round him and waited for the last one to get there before saying: "Well now. No use talking anymore, is it?" and walking out of the room. They heard him go upstairs. Frances said: "This family. They stick together." She put her head down on the wooden arm of the chair and burst into tears. Melanie, feeling ineffectual, began to clear up the sandwiches. She groped for something to say and came up with a cliché. "Perhaps when Roy realises you still love him . . ."

"*Love* him? What's love got to do with it? I got over all that in the first three months. How am I going to bring Molly up alone, that's what I'm worrying about. You can't imagine what this is like, you just don't know. I've tried to avoid it, for years and years but . . . love him? I detest him. It's a rotten marriage. But to rear even one child alone is a hell of a business, and besides, Molly's his daughter. I'm glad to be rid of him—or would be if it wasn't for Molly—but she *can't* be rid of him, don't you see?"

"But you needn't be on your own. Roy's the one who's left. You could stay here."

"Here?" Frances shouted, as though Melanie were a lunatic. She raised a smudged face. "Here with Roy's parents? You've seen how much they love me. My God! Stay here, and incidentally be finally suffocated in hay and horse blankets . . . no thank you! But what I'll do I daren't think. My own parents aren't well, either of them. They can't help much. It's a nightmare and I wish I could wake up but I can't. . . ."

"Yes, I see," said Melanie. She did. One could play with ideas of abandoning all natural support and putting to sea along with one's infant in a sieve made of optimism and a tenuous talent, but what if you had no choice? What if you were forcibly thrust out onto that empty, frightening ocean?

As if Frances had picked the idea up from her mind, her cousin said suddenly: "Are you going back to India?"

There was a startled silence. "Why do you ask?" Melanie said finally.

"This and that. Your letters this last year. You sounded homesick, as if the magic had worn off. Well?"

"I'm going back," said Melanie quietly. Throughout all the time when she had been unable to think, while she doodled designs and cooked eggs and bacon for the men off the *Fairlight* and rushed to Frances's side, thought had actually been going on by itself, deep within her. Now it crystallised into cold little sentences. *This is Avtar's child too. This child will need its father.* Seeing Molly, she could have no doubt of that.

"You're wise," Frances said. "If you've got a husband to go to, you go. You're lucky." There was a flash of resentment there, the misery of a *have not* confronted by a *have*. "After all," said Frances, "life would be pretty uncomfortable for you if you stayed here, you must admit. Worse than for me, even." Clearly, she found a grim satisfaction in that.

"I don't quite follow," said Melanie.

"Oh, don't be silly," said her cousin. "Yours will be a half-caste child, after all."

She said it as though she had no awareness of giving offence. She was finding words for what she obviously considered to be an unquestionable and hallowed attitude, with which Melanie was bound to concur. This is impossible, Melanie thought. That is still Frances, the cousin I've known all my life, sitting there. She can't metamorphose into a classic, stereotype "woman in Woolworths" in a single sentence, just like that. I didn't hear her properly. "What did you say?" asked Melanie.

Her voice held a warning but Frances did not notice it. "I said it would be a half-caste child, of course. It's bound to make difficulties. I know you didn't expect it to happen when you married Avtar, but now that it has . . . whether or not you really want to go back to India, you're quite right to go if you mean to have the baby. I mean, they're neither one thing nor the other, are they? People won't accept them here."

Melanie found that she was backing stealthily away from Frances, as in India she might have backed from a beggar with leprosy. Frances, taking in her cousin's reactions at last, looked surprised. "What's the matter?"

"Matter!" Melanie swallowed. It was cruel to be angry with Frances now. "Frances, you're talking about my . . . Avtar's . . . child!"

"Yes, I know. Well, of course, since it's your own baby . . . but there's no point in being blind to facts, is there? It is, or will be, half and half."

"It is, or will be," said Melanie unsteadily, "Indian as well as English. Inheritor of two lands, two tongues, two literatures. Someone with a chance of growing up richer, more knowledgeable and less prejudiced than anyone limited to only one of each. Is that supposed to make people into something *less* than human? What's wrong with you, Frances? I never knew you were so narrow-minded."

"Narrow-minded? You've never known what other people are really like, Melanie." Frances had been bruised beyond endurance during the last few hours. Now Melanie had bruised her again. Melanie had checked her tongue but she could not command the anger in her voice, nor its blaze in her eyes. Frances, hurt by all the world, struck back. "We were all too polite to tell you, of course, but you don't think any of us liked you marrying a coloured man, did you?"

"What?"

"Oh, come on, Melanie." Frances uttered an acrid little laugh. She had forgotten that she had called Melanie here to stand by her, to be someone of her own in a world full of enemies. Melanie, by virtue of having what Frances had not, had become the enemy herself. "Did it never occur to you to wonder what your grandfather really thought about your marriage?" Frances asked. "Didn't you ever ask yourself why, precisely, he left you Gavin's Cliff? Ask Ivor. He knows all about it."

❦

The slow drive back to Heverton was an agony, maddening, frustrating. The churning mind longed for the relief of speed and was denied it. *What did your grandfather really think of your marriage?* She had lost him once already, by death. To lose him in this other way as well would not be tolerable. Frances was lying. Must be. Frances was spiteful. Odd that you could know someone all your life and not discover something as fundamental about them as that.

Ask Ivor, Frances had said. *He knows.* Knows what? Will he tell me? The car growled its low-gear way up the climbing track to Gavin's Cliff with as much rapidity as Melanie could get from it, and the squeaky protest of her brakes as she jerked to a stop outside the house at last brought Mary Heaton hurrying out to greet her. Mary seemed to be in a fluster. "There you are, Melanie! Now what in the world is going on?"

Melanie scrambled out. "You could say that the storm claimed its tribute after all. The victim was Edward Miller of

Stancross, in an oblique sort of way. But I can't explain just now. I must see Ivor."

"That's why I was looking out for you. He's downstairs in the study. I know he wasn't supposed to get up but I couldn't stop him. He would *not* listen. He's got one of the professor's dressing gowns on and he's fiddling about with the professor's papers and I didn't think you'd like it and . . ."

"Thank you," said Melanie, and made for the den.

Ivor was at Gran's desk, the chair turned sideways and a wastebin at his feet. A folder was open on his knee. The red dressing gown, with Ivor's round face topping it instead of Gran's thin one, made her heart lurch. He glanced up guiltily as she came in. "I took my temperature again and it's nearly normal. I couldn't see the point of staying in bed. What happened with Frances?"

Melanie told him, shortly, and then brushed the subject aside. "I don't want to be rude and I know you were Gran's friend. But do you really think you should have started to go through his papers when I wasn't here?"

"Don't be silly, Melanie. We know one another well enough not to stand on quite so much ceremony, I hope. Sit down, you're upset about Frances, I expect. I've been reading some of William's old conference papers. What an amazing man he was. And how extraordinary that he should suddenly appear like that in the midst of a farming and fishing family, like a volcanic island appearing out of the sea. I shall use that phrase in the biography, I think."

"I went to give Frances moral support over Roy, but I ended up quarrelling with her. You and Gran were both concerned."

"Me and William?" Ivor's pink baby-face became pinker. "What do you mean?"

She explained. The pink turned into a beetroot flush. "Oh, really. *Really,* Melanie. You expect me to know what Frances was talking about? Of course I don't. I doubt if she did, either. From what you say she must be in a very confused state of mind, and people will say anything that enters their heads when they're thrown off-balance like that. Did you come rushing back here to demand an explanation? I can't oblige, I'm afraid."

"Can't you?" said Melanie.

She sat down in one of the leather chairs and considered him, observing his embarrassment. All her life, Gran and, to a lesser extent, Ivor, had been her gurus. She had admired them, sought their good opinion. She had gone against Gran just once, because then Avtar was stronger. It seemed to her now that Avtar was still stronger, that he was reliable as granite against the two friable, crumbling images which were or had been Gran and Ivor.

Facts were sliding remorselessly together in her mind. Gran had disliked her marriage. Gran had also left her Gavin's Cliff. And according to Frances, there was a connection.

According to Frances too, Ivor knew what that connection was.

And Ivor, delayed in returning from Lundy, but landing fortuitously at Gavin's Cliff in the end, had resisted attempts to send him to hospital and had seized the first available chance of getting at Gran's papers—in fact pouncing upon them in Melanie's absence.

And twice since she came in, he had let his glance stray, momentarily, towards the wastebin at his feet. Melanie rose from her chair and she, too, pounced.

She had emptied the bin at breakfast time. The one scrunched-up ball of paper in it must therefore have been thrown there by Ivor. "What are you doing?" he asked in a horrified voice. She knew by that, before she had smoothed out the sheets enough to read them, what it was she held.

⌁

The words rose up from the creased and ill-typed carbon. Gran had been one of the two-finger breed of typist and a fairly haphazard one at that. But the letter was clear enough, despite the smears and overtypings. It was the voice of Gran and the voice—only how could she reconcile such opposites? —of betrayal. "My dear Ivor," said those deceiving tones, Gran whispering to Ivor behind her back, "thank you for your (*smudge* but the word was probably *cheering*) letter. We've done a hell of a lot of quarrelling in our time but it seems that there are some rock bottom principles on which we agree. Normally I would not attempt (*interference?* Yes) of this sort, but my grandchild is very dear to me . . ."

And then, in black and white, unequivocal wording, the thing at which Frances had hinted. ". . . the terms of my will may serve to bring her home to Gavin's Cliff. I hope so. I should like to think of her making a new start one day with a more appropriate partner, setting this escapade in its place as the youthful adventure which I sincerely believe it is. If once she comes back to the Cliff as its owner—and I shall recommend that the executors ask her to return to inspect it—I think she may find it hard to leave again. One blessing is that this ill-considered and unsuitable marriage of hers will at least not complicate matters by producing off-spring . . ."

"No wonder you were so annoyed at getting stormbound on Lundy," said Melanie. "And no wonder you were so desperately eager to stay here last night. Did you know this was here?"

"I suspected it," said Ivor. He was pale now and the cherub mouth had its corners tucked back into the nearest approach to grimness of which it was capable. "He used to take carbons automatically. He said to me, not long before he died, that he was going to clear out his papers and get rid of anything he didn't want to leave behind. He knew he was ill and it might not be all that long. But I think it came too soon for him after all. I didn't want you to see that letter, no."

"If I hadn't been so slow in getting down to work on Gran's files," said Melanie, "I'd have found it already. You shouldn't have risked Lundy in the equinox, Ivor. Not if you wanted to be sure of getting here when I did. Careless of you." She put the letter down on the desk and went to the window. She stared out at the pines, not seeing them, talking to her grandfather inside her mind.

Oh, Gran. You wicked, scheming, diabolical old man. Avtar was right to be afraid of you.

You write a book like the *Organic Computer*, preaching the power of mankind to do new things, create new patterns for living, go free of ancestral prejudices and habits. And then what do you do? You lay snares for the feet of your descendants, to entrap them in precisely the same old ancestral prejudices and habits. You talk of prophets who abuse their charisma, and then shamelessly abuse your own. Your parentally instilled programs were too much even for you in the end, weren't they?

And finally, dear, arrogant, egocentric Gran, dreaming of posthumous fame, you take carbons of even the most damning correspondence and fail to destroy it when you realise your mistake. You didn't think you'd die so soon, did you? Perhaps you didn't really think you'd ever die at all. I know you so well.

The bitter thing is that you were right. This is my home. But I carry Avtar's child and the child and Avtar will need each other. Whatever that means for me in deprivation and heartbreak.

"You agreed with him," she said, turning to Ivor. "He asked you for advice and you said he was right."

"Yes. There was one person who didn't," said Ivor, "and that was Mary Heaton. Curious, that. It was one of the few times when William and I did agree, when he came down off that intellectual pole-squat of his and reacted like a human being. But Mary was furious with him. The matter came up in conversation between William and me one day when the Heatons were here, and William told them what he'd done. Bill Heaton didn't say much, but Mary lectured him at length and after that Gavin's Cliff and Whitehangers weren't speaking."

"I see," said Melanie. *Wonderful news. A child cements a marriage.* Mary had been talking very much to the point, in the kitchen of the Cliff last night. "Gran seems to have chatted very freely," she remarked.

"He told his family, certainly, as well as me and the Heatons. Everyone except Mary, and possibly Bill, agreed with him."

"Mary believes in marriage. The value of it, I mean. Don't you believe in it, Ivor?" Ivor's wife had been dead for years, but they had by all accounts been very happy.

"Usually. But I wouldn't, for instance, compel a couple like your cousins Roy and Frances to stay together. Melanie, it isn't that either of them is better than the other, it's just that they don't belong together. When you told me Roy had left, it was no surprise to me. William and I were expecting it to happen, sooner or later. It's the same with your marriage. You've married a man, a way of life, that's alien to you.

249

I'm not talking out of racial feeling, believe me. Avtar may well be a more admirable and useful human being than you are. But you and he don't fit."

"May I ask how you think you know?"

"Things William told me, mostly. I saw some parts of your letters home. They were revealing."

"I was homesick, yes. I'd be homesick if I'd married the boy next door and he happened to take a job in Australia. I'm going back to India, Ivor."

Ivor sighed, looking at the creased carbons still in Melanie's hand. "You were always perverse. I was afraid of this."

"Oh, not on account of this." Melanie waved the papers casually. She was thankful that it was the truth. She had taken a right decision for a right reason, before ever she had listened to Frances or Ivor. The accusation of perversity would not stick, would not have her asking awkward questions of herself at three in the morning. "I want to go." That was a lie, but she managed to make it sound convincing. "And," she said, smiling into Ivor's face, "Avtar and I are expecting a baby."

The Scent of Sandalwood

Melanie afterwards remembered the following three weeks as both busy and disjointed. Ivor developed a subnormal temperature again ("No more than you deserve," said Melanie unsympathetically) and it was several days before he could leave Gavin's Cliff. On his instructions, Melanie visited his house in Ambersford and came back with clothes, shaving tackle, and a tape recorder. When Ivor at length took his leave, he took with him a bundle of letters and photographs which she had sorted out for him from Gran's study, and two hours of her own tape reminiscences. The biography would come into being, whatever had befallen Melanie's own views on her grandparent.

She received confirmation of her pregnancy and went to Dr. Channing's for a check-up. In the waiting room, she encountered Sheila Miller with what was evidently Roy's small son, sneezing. Sheila did not recognise Melanie, and Melanie therefore had ample opportunity to look at her. It was easy enough to identify the attraction which had suborned Roy and made the paternity of the infant the subject of fascinated speculation among the local males. True, the frizzy hair was dragged back from the face and tied in a bunch like so much dull blonde wire, without the least attempt at styling. True, the face itself was still as innocent of cosmetics as it had been when its owner was a washed-out waif of a schoolgirl. And true, Sheila was wearing a raincoat too long for her, open to reveal a baggy blue fishermen's knit sweater and faded corduroy trousers which were obviously years old. It made not the slightest difference. Like Arwinder, though in a completely different manner, Sheila possessed charms which were indestructible by any amount of neglect. In Sheila Miller, coarseness and beauty were mixed in equal proportions, enhancing one another. The broad lips and the wide nostrils, the excellent teeth and the strong cheekbones, the sloeberry eyes full of sleepy promise, more than accounted for Roy's indiscretions.

Looking covertly at the unknowing Sheila, Melanie suddenly thought of Gavin Purvis's portrait at the Cliff. Sheila and Roy were both his descendants. They did not precisely resemble him. Yet in spite of the physical blurring, the dilution of his genes, they were very much his kin in spirit, possessed of the same sexual arrogance, the same casualness, the same essential ruthlessness. Poor Frances had never had a chance. Imported into such an environment, she had been as much at a loss as though she had been taken to live among Eskimos or the tribes of the Amazon River. There was no need to go halfway round the world to find incompatible people.

With the pregnancy confirmed, of course, it was time to write to Avtar.

She began the letter four times and then gave up in despair, having been defeated in each case right at the start just by the salutation. "Dear Avtar" sounded somehow cold. He might be anyone—brother, colleague, mere acquaintance. "My dear Avtar" brought back instant memories of that smudgy, nasty carbon which had started off "My dear Ivor." "My darling Avtar" and "My darling" were both correct openers for a letter from a loving wife to a far-off husband; the trouble was that Melanie could not see herself as a loving wife. She was simply a wife, and a prospective mother. And for the sake of the coming child and because it was her duty, she was going back to an alien country and a man she could no longer love.

She decided to telephone him instead, went straight to the telephone without giving herself time to worry about what she should say, and was informed that there were no lines available to India. Perhaps she would like to try in a few hours' time? She banged down the receiver, knowing that the impetus was lost. For the next twenty-four hours she managed to maintain a somewhat dramatised image of herself as a righteous martyr, about to sacrifice herself to an entirely unpalatable way of life in the interests of Motherhood, capital M. She saw herself living through the years, a smiling, beautifully mannered model of behaviour, making polite small talk to Avtar and such people as Aunt Asha, caring for her offspring, making love on request with the gracious and heartless efficiency of a courtesan . . .

It occurred to her at the end of the twenty-four hours that if she couldn't manage to write a simple letter or persist in a phone call, she wasn't making a very good start. Then, since Jason was wanting his morning run, she walked down to the bottom of the track to where Gran's postbox stood—expecting postmen to trudge all the way up to the Cliff never had been reasonable—and a letter from Avtar was waiting.

On the airmail envelope his familiar handwriting looked strange. He had had occasion to write few letters to her and none, of course, from overseas. Not until now. She sat reading it in the kitchen. It was quite long, but to her relief none of it could be classified as a love letter. It talked of Diwali—"many people missed you and were enquiring when you would be back"—and of various relatives and friends—"Balwant and Aunt Asha are the same as ever"—and—"I think Surinder is studying too hard." It did not appeal to, nor attack, the emotions.

She read it in the spirit of a Monte Carlo rally entrant examining a route map. For these events and people were the features of the life she must shortly resume. Balwant and Aunt Asha represented a hazard, like icy roads in the Alps. She must be ready to master a surge of sheer fury whenever she set eyes on either of them. Surinder she must worry about, in a proper and sisterly fashion. "Arwin seems very happy and is all taken up with her new life, but I think she will write you soon." Arwin she would be glad to see again; that would be an easy stretch. Bheji too. "Bheji sends her love and wants to know when are you coming back. Please write soon about your plans."

She went into the study and sat at Gran's desk. This time, she would get that letter written.

In the end it was a conventionally loving letter, beginning "Dear Avtar," thanking him for all his news, remarking anxiously that it was indeed important that Surinder should not work himself into a condition of staleness, and then moving gently on to her own news. She glossed over Frances and Roy, did not mention Gran's perfidy at all, and described the storm and the *Fairlight* in some detail. She would be finished with the house in December, she said. She proposed to keep it in her possession but let it out in summer with the help of an agent. She was arranging to have the ivy and some dangerous pine trees dealt with. She would be back in India before Christmas. She sent her love to everyone.

And in the final paragraph she told him that the doctors who had attended her in her childhood had all been wrong, and that there was to be a child next year.

It was a poor letter, she thought. Stilted. Written like an English exercise, an examination piece. *Imagine that you are obliged to make a trip abroad and that you are writing to your family to announce the date of your return . . .*

Oh dear God, to what was she returning? To the place where Balwant was held a prisoner in custom and tradition, to Avtar who wished her to forget Gavin's Cliff forever, to endless heat, to endless yearning.

But Avtar must not realise it. She must go back as though she had never thought of doing anything else, hiding the mutilation in her spirit.

She sent the letter off. She received and answered, in an affectionate and lively vein, another letter, this time from Arwin, full of enthusiasm about Saranjit, and Nirmal's forthcoming nuptials. She also received her own family in force. One afternoon, Daniel, Lucy, Ellen and her husband from Taunton, Dick and his wife from Gloucestershire, and with them, swept along as if on a wave, a pale, taciturn Frances and a tight-lipped Molly, all arrived at Gavin's Cliff. The gathering had been organised by Uncle Daniel to discuss Frances's future and also to mend the quarrel between Frances and Melanie. Frances obviously wished, as Melanie did, that he hadn't bothered, but they cooperated. Frances was polite. Melanie was also polite, was hospitable, offered what help she could in the practical discussions and talked about going home soon, in a cheerful voice. Aunt Lucy asked if Melanie would show her how to make a real Indian curry, so they made one together and the party had it for dinner. Daniel said she didn't look too blooming and doubted if rich foods like curries were good for her.

But she knew that her strained face had no more to do with curry than with the party after the shipwreck.

On the last day of the three weeks since she had come to her decision, she sat by the parlour fire in the evening, watching the darkness fall, too depressed to make the effort to go to bed. She had spent the day listening to powered saws cutting their way through pine trunks, and the rending rustle of creeper being torn from the walls. If trees and ivy could possess minds, she thought, they would probably feel much as she did now. She listened to the quarterly chimes of the grandfather clock and watched the intermittent flash of the Gannet's Head lighthouse, recording them in her memory to take with her when the time for departure came. When, past midnight, she at last forced herself to climb the stairs, she slept heavily. And woke feeling more ill than at any time since this unexpected pregnancy began.

During the last week she had instituted, on Channing's advice, a kettle and tea tray in the bedroom. She could plug in the kettle simply by reaching an arm out of bed. A cup of tea taken in leisurely fashion before rising, Channing said, would reduce morning sickness. So far he had been right. But today trouble was on her before she was fully awake. She tumbled out of bed towards the basin which, made careless by four mornings successively free of sickness, she had left on the windowseat. It seemed a long way off. Bed, dressing table, window, wardrobe—all revolved gracefully as in an old-time waltz, and then darkened and vanished. She had just enough presence of mind to topple back onto the bed before she fainted.

She came to lying on top of the eiderdown. She was cold and more than cold; she was agonisingly lonely. The nausea had passed but the depression still lay on her like a black pall. Sitting up, fumbling to get back under the covers, she found herself longing for Bheji. If Bheji were here, she would be fussing over Melanie and taking care of her and all the other women would come to see her and tell her how many times they'd fainted when they were pregnant and what they did about it. She would be wrapped in a warm feminine fleece of folklore and protectiveness, something to be valued as the vessel of life. A *warm* fleece. This autumn morning was as damply chilly as a wet fish stall. Had she really, said Melanie to herself, wallowing in self-pity, ever complained about *heat*?

It was Jason, padding about with a click-click of claws on the linoleum at the edge of the carpet and whining, who at last compelled her to get up. She put clothes on, slacks and a heavy sweater. It was too cold for anything less. She followed him, shivering, down to the kitchen and let him out. A few minutes later he was back at the kitchen door, gazing at her with melting eyes, tail on the wag and a stick in his mouth. Melanie's head was throbbing. Fresh air might help, she thought groggily. She fetched Gran's old coat and let the dog coax her out of doors, and down the path to the cove.

In the cove, even now, signs of the storm remained. A section of the *Fairlight*'s bows was still there, cocked up between two rocks, and at the high tide mark were bits of planking and debris. People had come to retrieve waterlogged luggage and other reclaimable flotsam, but what was of no use had been left. Yet despite these signs, it was difficult now to visualise the violence of that night. The Channel this morning was lolling at ease: long, slow breakers dawdling out beyond the Fangs and the water as harmless as a pond within them. She threw the stick for Jason and let him run after it while she looked at the sea. It was not only serene, but beautiful. The sky above it was softly barred with silver and lemon, and the smooth water made a muted answer, overlaid with a sparkling patina as a light wind broke the surface.

The elements of a design were there. She had not touched her work since the day of the storm. There seemed to be no point. The sketches she had made that afternoon, she had put away. Now, for the first time since that day, her fingers wanted pencil and crayon.

She took Jason back before he was tired of his game, giving him a food bowl to assuage his disappointment. She herself did not want to eat. Her drawings and her materials she had put away again in one of the suitcases, upstairs in the landing cupboard. She went up in search of them. She dragged the case she wanted out of the dark depths, and, kneeling on the landing, she clicked up the hasps and threw back the lid.

From the interior, from the second-best hairbrush that still wanted washing, from the lightweight sandals and the lining of the case and its dusty hinges, dizzying and evocative in nostrils which for weeks now had smelt only the woods and the sea, there rose the scent of sandalwood.

∽

It pervaded India, that scent. The part of India that Melanie knew, at least. Shops were perfumed with it; Arwin's Sangeet had been aromatic with it; it was carried in the very dust of the air. It was lodged among her belongings like the spores of memory. As she sat back on her heels, the spores germinated and grew into images. She saw the domed head and broad-leaved ears of an elephant under a load of hay, with a glossy limousine crawling patiently behind. A red-hot, distended sun sank into the brown dust-haze of a plain. A girl spun a grindstone, a beggar capered, Surinder ate toast in a sunny kitchen with a textbook leaning against the cruet.

She was smitten through, without warning, by an enormous longing. For the first time since the plane had lifted her from the ground at Delhi, India was a place to be desired. A place where she had a family.

She got up, walked or stumbled to the landing window, looked out.

Like pictures cast on the screen of the sea, the images were. Other images had joined them now. Falcon's mane tossing in the wind. George Petersham marching in from the weather, his oilskins gleaming in the light from the kitchen. The flawed medieval glass in the windows of the *Ambersford Arms*. Jim Hawkins and his accordion . . .

There seemed to be no difference, any longer, in the power of these opposing symbols. It was as unendurable now to think: Will I never see India again? as once in Chandigarh it had been unendurable to think: When will I ever see Ambersford?

Oh, wonderful. She'd really done it now. You've fallen in love, have you, Melanie, she said cynically to herself, leaning on the window sill, hooked yourself like a heroin addict to two places on opposite sides of the world, two sets of people, two ways of living? Well, forget it. You can't have both. If henceforth, wherever you are, whether in India or England, you are going to yearn for the place where you're not, that's your misfortune.

259

Misfortune? Turning round, she stared at the suitcase where it lay, lid flung back, in front of the open cupboard. The sketches she had made on the day of the storm were lying in it, flat. She went over and picked up the topmost one. Had there been anyone to see her, they would have thought she moved like a sleepwalker. She stood on the landing, studying the drawing in her hand, went back to the window with it and studied it again. Then she put away the case, and moving now not like a sleepwalker, but with excited purpose in her step, she carried the sketch downstairs to Gran's study.

She spread it out on Gran's desk, turning on his Anglepoise lamp. The drawing, being only pencil, needed a good light. It was a pictorial, suitable perhaps for a hotel dining room wallpaper, for the sort of place, anyway, where people would look about them and comment on the decor. An older child might like it, too, as bedroom wallpaper. It was for paper rather than for curtaining, she thought.

It consisted of contrasting vignettes: an Indian girl with a basket on her head and an English milkmaid complete with pails. A young horseman with a turban, a hawk on his wrist, and a huntsman with hounds. An elephant carrying hay, and a horse-drawn wain. She had used linked arches to frame the vignettes, alternately Norman and Moghul.

Sometimes, with a complex design, there was a struggle before the elements ceased whirling like a mental kaleidoscope and took on the coherence of a pattern. In Melanie these jumbled images had been spinning for a long time: while she tried uselessly to work on a hot morning in Chandigarh, when she decorated Arwin's Sangeet walls, while she sketched in the Gavin's Cliff parlour and the storm built up outside. Only now had the pattern become completely still, and quiet, and identifiable.

Not opposing symbols. Facets. Part of the same thing but angled differently, throwing back reflections that looked —but were not—like contrasts. Essentially, her two homes, in India and England, were the same kind of place.

Extraordinary. But when you thought about it, true. Both possessed deep roots, continuity. It had been continuity which she had missed long ago when her father took her away from Ambersford. Not only personal continuity and personal memories, but the sense of belonging to an ancient and ancestral place. The elephant and the grindstone—part of the same world for twenty, thirty centuries and part of it still, along with combine harvesters and cars. The windows in the *Arms,* made by a man to whom Geoffrey Chaucer was "that modern poet up Lunnon way." George Petersham turning to Gavin's Cliff for help in a crisis because his grandfather would have done the same thing; Arwin crying at her wedding because her mother and her grandmother had cried at theirs.

Neither place precisely paradise, of course. It was hard to say whether Frances or Balwant represented the greater human disaster. But both places in which Melanie could be at home. She would not have thought she had to choose between them, had Avtar not insisted.

She sat staring at the design. She must not let herself be made to choose between them. Such a loss would be a bad thing not only for her but for her child. The child would belong to both far more thoroughly than Melanie herself did. It was imperative that Gavin's Cliff remain part of their lives. Can't have both? She must!

Somehow or other, Avtar must be won over. He must be coaxed, reasoned with, outwitted, or, if necessary, fought toe to toe. But the chances were, Melanie thought with rising excitement, that he would understand. For things were not as

261

they were when she had left India. The child, for whom this new venture was so necessary, would itself change the situation.

She thought about it, thought about that dark, stark Avtar who had for so long loomed in her mind like a joyless duty. *Would* he understand?

But he would understand that the child, their son, their daughter, was half-English. That was a simple, biological fact and Avtar was too intelligent to ignore facts. He also possessed integrity.

Far away from him, divided from him by thousands of miles of space and a fog compounded of rage and hormones, she had forgotten that. In a temper he had threatened to conceal her passport, but she knew now that he would never actually have done it. When he said he was looking only to see if she thought he might, he had told the truth. She heard his voice saying it and heard the note of honesty. Avtar had considerably more integrity than Gran. Briefly, during that unpleasant confrontation with Ivor, she had perceived that. She should have kept hold of it.

❧

Jane had a cold. Her voice on the phone was dispirited. "Yes, by all means," it said in a nasal monotone. "Of course you can stay a few nights with me. Any time. Which nights, particularly?"

"I leave for India on twenty-first December. It's a Friday. I want to come on the previous Sunday. I've some business to do. It'll take me a few days. Say, Sunday the sixteenth."

"You're driving up?"

"Yes. What time do you want me to arrive?"

"Oh, any time. I'll be in."

"Jane, are you all right? I mean, apart from your cold? You sound so flat."

"It's the weather and too much to do. My boss is a workaholic."

"How's Robin?"

"All right as far as I know. I haven't seen much of him lately. We're both so busy. Oh hell, there's His Nibs's buzzer. See you on the sixteenth."

Melanie rang off and stood in the hall contemplating the telephone. Then she looked at her watch and, picking up the receiver again, she once more began the long and tortuous process of placing a call to India.

Gently, naturally, unbidden, it had come at last. She was lonely, and for Avtar.

Vaya con Dios

"How did you know I was in India?" Rehal asked, not altogether amiably. He lay relaxed on one of the two charpoys which, along with a stool and an old-fashioned washstand, were all the furnishing in the little second-floor room. There was no fan and even in November such confined spaces were hot. Rehal was clad only in underpants. Avtar, fully dressed, was sweating as he sat on the stool beside him, like a doctor at a patient's bedside, except that Rehal's muscular brown body had nothing whatever the matter with it.

"A patient of mine saw you in the coffeehouse. He recognised you and the people you were with. He lives over there." Avtar gestured at the window and the flats opposite.

264

The flats had a plethora of balconies festooned with washing. The balconies were used as observation posts by the womenfolk, who gossiped across the gaps and watched with enormous interest the seething street of pedestrians and cyclists, and the activities of the neighbours.

"I billeted myself on my friends here because they *were* here," said Rehal. "A nice, busy, anonymous corner of Chandigarh, I thought. No one would find me."

"I take it," said Avtar, "that you're here because of Balwant."

"What makes you think so?"

"She told Arwin she'd written to you."

"And Arwin told you?"

"Not until I informed *her* that you'd been seen in town. I guessed aloud that Balwant was the cause and her face gave her away. After that, she was willing to talk to me in confidence. There was no other reason why you should return in secret, Rehal. Are you serious about this business?"

"I am if Balwant is. And it is *our* business. Not yours."

"I know that. Don't be a fool. I can still be concerned for Balwant. She is a member of my family."

"How is your immediate family?" enquired Rehal politely. "When is Melanie coming back?"

"At Christmas. I'm going to England to meet her. She telephoned me yesterday. She had," said Avtar cheerfully, "news for me."

◇

It had been a bad line. They had both had to shout. But enough had made its way across the wires that linked East and West. Melanie was letting the house. She was coming home. That appalling grandparent of hers *had* been trying to interfere, had in fact deliberately tried to entice his wife

265

back to Gavin's Cliff for good. And had failed. Melanie still loved him, Avtar. And (he had made her repeat it twice, unable to believe that what he was hearing was not merely a distortion of long-distance sound) she was with child.

Bheji and Leela, overhearing him as he repeated Melanie's words, had started dancing, out in the hall.

". . . in early summer," said Avtar, answering Rehal's query.

"But that *is* most splendid news!"

"Yes, it is. But we must talk about it another time. Listen to me. You will be taking Balwant to London if it . . . well, will she be happy there? Are you sure? She is a very traditional kind of girl."

"I will make her happy. I am well paid enough to see that she visits her home from time to time and that will make a difference. My editor is a nice man," said Rehal. "He even allowed me unpaid leave to come here and settle the future with her. He and his wife will ask us to dinner when we are both back there. They will help me introduce Balwant to her new life."

"You sound very sure of yourself."

"I am. Balwant will be all right as long as she isn't cut off from her roots. Even I, and I am very westernised, need them sometimes. When you were in England, didn't you once go to an exhibition of Indian art, because you were homesick? I've never heard of you setting foot in an art gallery otherwise. Keeping in touch with one's origins can make all the difference."

Avtar got up sharply, turning his back on Rehal and staring out at the river of humanity in the street. That he and Melanie had disagreed vigorously over Melanie's journey to England was common knowledge in the family. From what Arwin had said, he suspected that Melanie's deplorable example had had something to do with Balwant's unexpected fit of independence, and her letter to Rehal might well have said as much. "Rehal, are you trying to make some kind of oblique comment on my private affairs?"

He looked round. Rehal's dark eyes held perfect understanding. The guess had been accurate. "I wouldn't have the impertinence," said Rehal evenly.

"No? I wonder, Rehal, if you have thought what will it do to Asha, if you run off with Balwant?"

"I wonder," said Rehal, "if you have thought, Avtar, what it will do to Balwant, if I don't?"

∽

London was lead-coloured and unwelcoming. Melanie drove there in another hired car, having at Daniel's request left the Ford behind on extended loan to Frances. Frances, in the throes of moving back to Middlesex, was glad of it and had been properly, though still somewhat brusquely, grateful. As the claws of the city closed round her, Melanie thought that it was odd that *heartache* should be such a cliché word when it was so accurate. Only the fact that if all went well, she would in time return to Gavin's Cliff—not once, but often—made the parting bearable at all. That and a deliberately created maelstrom of last-minute activity, such as seeing the bank manager, settling final details with the house agent and the solicitor about letting the Cliff, clearing out Gran's den so that valuables could be stored and the room locked up to keep the visitors out of it. On the telephone when at last she made contact, Avtar's voice had been warm and strong. She had forgotten the sheer familiarity and security of him, as well as his integrity. She could only hope that when they met, he would understand what she wanted of him. Whenever she thought about that, she was shaken to find at the back of her mind the idea that perhaps it was a good thing that Gran, whose influence Avtar had so greatly and justifiably feared, was dead.

Jane was waiting with the fire on and the curtains snugly drawn. The flat seemed to be slightly untidy and although Jane's cold must have cleared up long ago, Melanie thought her friend's face seemed drawn, as though she were still unwell. Sipping tea, making conversation about Ambersford, she was glad that Avtar was coming to meet her and that she would not have to stay the whole week with Jane. In his last letter Avtar had said that he had the keys of Rehal's house in Southall and permission to use the place until their flight on Friday. He expected to arrive on Wednesday morning. His plane was due in at 7 A.M.; she was not to meet it as morning sickness and airports didn't mix, but he would telephone as soon as he reached Southall and would then come to collect her. Rehal, apparently, was back in India. *There may be some news about Rehal soon*, the letter had said tantalisingly. She hoped she had guessed at its nature.

"Why the absent-minded smile?" Jane asked, reaching for Melanie's cup in order to refill it.

"I was thinking about a bit of family news Avtar hinted at when he wrote. I haven't asked you what news you've got. I keep chattering on about me and Gavin's Cliff. What's been happening here?"

"Not very much. I've been working so hard lately that when I get home in the evening, it's egg on toast and a bath and then bed. I've finished with Robin, by the way. We really had nothing in common."

"Oh, dear. I'm so sorry. I'm taking some designs to Hallowens on Tuesday morning. Do I give him your regards or not?"

"Preferably not," said Jane lightly and, having seen to Melanie's cup, settled back into her chair. The light of a standard lamp fell on her face. For the first time, Melanie noticed tiny lines in Jane's skin, round the eyes and mouth.

∽

"Migraine?" Avtar said into the telephone at his home, two days after his interview with Rehal, two weeks before his flight was due to leave for London. "But she has had that on and off for years . . . I see . . . what treatment? Yes, very well, I will come. Give her nothing, only water or lemon juice if she asks for it. Keep her quiet. Darken the room. I am coming."

"Balwant," he said, hanging up and turning to Bheji, standing anxiously beside him. "The fourth attack of migraine in ten days, Asha says, and none of the remedies their doctor has suggested will work. Asha has lost confidence in him. She wants me to go. I had better, I suppose. I'll go round by the surgery to warn Ved I'll be late, and I'll pick up some drugs while I'm there."

When he reached Asha's house, before he had even rung the bell, he could hear the maidservant being harried for being too slow with hot lemon drinks and for making too much noise. At the sound of the bell Asha came to the door herself, running.

"Where is she?" Avtar asked. "Upstairs?"

In the dim room, Balwant lay on her back, a basin beside her. He drew back the curtains and she flinched away from the light. By the stiff way she held her head in one position, he knew that movement was agony. He felt the muscles of her neck and looked carefully at the pupils of her eyes. "Any stomach ache?"

"No, except that I am so sick and that makes me ache

269

here." She put a hand below her ribs. "It is just migraine, but so bad. Like an iron band and nothing eases it."

"I have something that will," Avtar said.

He opened his bag. Aunt Asha watched worriedly. He avoided her eyes.

Migraine had more than one origin. Some people had it when they ate certain foods. Some women experienced it at the wrong time of the month. Many people, men and women, suffered it when they were tired or in a state of conflict. He knew quite well to which category Balwant belonged. He had not missed the significance of that sudden attack on the day that Rehal came home, any more than Melanie had.

He did not want to get involved in this any further. He had assured himself of Rehal's honesty and determination and would have liked to close his eyes and leave the rest to fate. But professional ethics were not going to let him.

The first thing, anyhow, was to stop the pain. He turned to Asha. "From what you say on the phone, your usual doctor has not used this. Perhaps wisely, for it should not be lightly resorted to. But for once it will do no harm. Give her one of these. Not through the mouth; I recommend nothing by mouth because she won't keep it down. It's a suppository. Get it into her and sit with her until it takes effect. I estimate fifteen to twenty minues."

"What it is?" asked Asha suspiciously.

"Ergotamine tartrate. It will constrict the blood vessels and slow down that violent pulse into the head. I shall come back into this room in a quarter of an hour. Then I wish to talk to the patient alone."

Fifteen minutes later he stood by the bed again. Asha was puzzled and slightly annoyed by his insistence on being left alone with Balwant, but Asha was accustomed to yield to male authority and he had used his advantage. He saw that the tension had gone out of his patient, and the distended darkness from her eyes. She gave him a hesitant smile. "It is just like magic. The headache has all gone. I am not even sick now."

"Still, you are to eat nothing today. Water, a little tea later if you want something hot. Nothing more. And now," he said, sitting down on the side of the bed, "you had better tell me what it is that is worrying you so. You have had four attacks in ten days, so your mother-in-law says."

"But I am not worrying about anything," said Balwant in her soft voice. She did not look at him.

"I am aware," said Avtar quietly, "that Rehal is in Chandigarh. I even know where. I've seen him. So have Arwin and her husband, Saranjit. We know why he is here and so secretly. So, I think, do you. I am a doctor, Balwant. I keep my patients' counsel. Nothing that you say to me in this room will I ever repeat outside it. That is the law of my profession."

In a voice so low that he had to lean closer to hear it, she said: "He wants that we should marry. He has . . . he has arranged it."

"And you?"

No response. Balwant turned her head and gazed towards the window and the sky beyond. Avtar said: "You want to go to him but you are afraid? Why? Do you think it would be wrong?"

There was a small nod. Dr. Avtar Singh studied his patient silently.

Such situations were part of the lives of most doctors. Virtually every doctor in India was at times compelled to challenge custom and taboo in the name of health and science and compassion. And not only in India. Once in

England, when on duty in a casualty ward, he had found himself mercilessly bullying a couple of Jehovah's Witnesses who did not want their child to have the blood transfusion which would save its life after a car crash. He had hurled himself against their religious convictions as if storming a fortress, with the sanctity of human life as his war cry. He had done it with such aggression that they had been frightened, and given in.

He might not want to get involved in this matter of Balwant and Rehal. But what was sacred in human life was more than simply the physical processes of breathing and eating. Equally sacred were the processes of using life, living it, giving it. Balwant had touched the same chord of responsibility in him that the injured child had touched. He could not remain aloof now.

He said: "There is a phrase the English use, although it is not in their language. It's Spanish. The thing is that most of the English dislike speaking seriously of God. If they are in such a state of mind that they need to do so, they are happy to do it in someone's tongue. *Vaya con Dios.* That is the phrase. You speak English well, but have you come across that?"

"No," said Balwant, listless, humouring him out of sheer weakness.

"It means: Go with God." She stirred. "You understand. You need not be afraid, or guilty. Choose what you want to do. Then do it. Now I shall leave you and give your mother-in-law instructions for looking after you. I am telling her that the weather is less hot now and you should have air and exercise. I am telling her that she should send you out often on little errands by yourself and you should walk briskly, faster than she likes to walk. That should simplify whatever plans you have made—and they are your private business, not mine. Tell me nothing about them. But . . . *Vaya con Dios.*"

Balwant said: "Rehal . . ."

"Your eyes give you away if you even say his name. Did you know?" said Avtar.

Going down to Asha, he thought: I have done more than I meant to do, gone further than I intended. Was I right or wrong? Melanie will say I was right. She will be pleased with me. But how pleased am I with myself?

He had told Balwant not to be afraid, or guilty. Only time would tell whether he could justly take that advice himself.

One More River

London, and Hallowens, were geared up for Christmas.

Hallowens was a prestige store, and it did not go in for the Christmas trees with hypnotically winking lights, the polystyrene Father Christmas grottoes, or the stuffed donkeys laden with parcels which filled the windows of lesser establishments. Instead, its windows displayed a multitude of warm and glowing wares: copper pans and golden Afghan rugs, terra cotta stoneware and rosewood furniture. In the midst of it all was an eyecatcher, five feet high, made of variously coloured fluorescent rods bent into circles and intertwined. To Melanie's knowledgeable eye, Robin had had a hand in that.

His office hadn't moved; he was where he always had been, on the third floor at the end of the fabric department, with the designers' workroom beyond. He had a view of the fabric department through his glass door and saw her approach. He opened the door for her as she reached it. "Come on in. You're right on time."

She had been careful about that. She had made the appointment by letter in an impersonal, businesslike way, and made a point of punctuality because that was businesslike too. She found that she was more nervous of this meeting with Robin than she could ever have been with a stranger. He gave her a chair, and some coffee from a gadget on the windowsill. "It's good to see you again. You arrived back in London when?"

"On Sunday. Did you do that display in the left-hand window downstairs? Left-hand as one comes in, I mean. It's lovely."

"Yes, that's mine. I'm glad you approve. Well, how was Somerset? Muddy as ever?"

"Worse. Stormbound." She told him about the *Fairlight,* and then about Roy and Sheila. "I'm sorry," he said, "sincerely sorry, especially for the little girl. It's hell for kids. I was always thankful I hadn't any. But despite all these interruptions, you seem to have got some work done. Is that it, that portfolio you're balancing on your knee?"

Melanie handed it over.

"Get yourself some more coffee while I look. You want a reaction now?"

"Please."

She sat down with her coffee to wait. Robin's powers of concentration were remarkable. It was as though he gathered himself into a point and aimed himself at the task in hand. He would not raise his head until he had finished.

Curiously, it was the same attitude that Avtar had towards medical problems. She remembered those breakfast times, so many of them, when her husband sat wrestling silently with unlooked-for complications in a patient, refusing to communicate with anyone until he had found a way through.

She grew still more nervous as the silence lengthened. When he did speak, it was almost brusquely. "You've travelled," he said.

"Travelled?"

"A long way. These are light years away from *Stardrift*. Better, I'd say . . . but astonishingly different. There's a new fashion, of fabric hung flat, without folds, displaying a design or picture *as* a picture, with a related design on curtains hung in the ordinary fluted way on either side of it. There are one or two here which would lend themselves very well to that. These vignettes, perhaps—you've marked them as a wallpaper design, but paper or fabric, it makes no difference. The related design on either side could make use simply of the archway shapes . . . are you willing to undertake the extra work?"

"Yes, of course. They're saleable, then?"

"Of course they're bloody saleable. You knew that or you wouldn't be here. This one"—he picked up the design which Melanie had eventually produced from the barred sea which had sent her to root in her suitcase with such memorable results—"this will make a good curtain design and we can do it on a smaller scale for chaircovers and the like. This other one with the lattice effect I don't like personally, but plenty of people would, and this one . . ."

She had forgotten how satisfactory it could be to talk over one's work with Robin, how instantly he would see possibilities which you hadn't seen yourself. He was an expert.

Only, for some reason she was getting the impression that he was an angry expert. He pushed the sheets together, leaning back. "So. What next? You say you are willing to undertake more work on request. Fine. There are four designs here which interest me and I can suggest further ideas. But what of the future? Will you be functioning in the future and, if so, under what circumstances? What are your plans?"

"I'm hoping to settle down to being a freelance. Working from India and collecting customers there, as well . . . different designs for the Indian market. I expect to visit England from time to time, but meanwhile, things can be mailed."

"You're definitely returning to India?"

"Certainly."

"I'll be making some changes in my own life too," Robin said. "I think I told you that I was considering going back to freelance work myself. I have now made up my mind to do so." He seemed to expect some kind of comment. Melanie regarded him blankly.

"You are quite maddening," said Robin. "Don't you understand? When I say I have made up my mind, I mean I have made it up finally during the last few minutes. I propose to commission you for some future work for Hallowens, if you will accept the commission. But you will deal with my successor, not with me. Because frankly, if you're going to turn up repeatedly in this office in years to come, the strain will be too much for me."

"The strain?"

"When you wrote asking for an appointment," said Robin, "instead of simply shoving your designs into an envelope and sending them registered post, did it not occur to you that I might think, or hope, that you had more than just business in mind, that you wanted to see *me?* That, perhaps, you meant to stay in England?"

Melanie gaped at him, taking in the implications. And was staggered by them—and outraged. "Of course it didn't occur to me . . . when did I ever give you the idea I'd come back to stay?"

"In your voice when you talked of India, the time we met at Jane Hanworth's flat. You sounded thoroughly disenchanted. And you never mentioned your husband once. Small indications, but enough for imagination to feed on when it's hungry. Why did you come yourself, today?"

There was no mistaking the anger behind the familiar flat tone, but it aroused, as ever, an answering wrath in Melanie. This was intolerable. The past was behind her; after a lapse of years she might reasonably have supposed that it was safely behind Robin, as well. If she had decided after all to stay in England, still Robin would have had no part in her plans. In all her anxious deliberations at Gavin's Cliff, about how to live and rear a child without her husband, the thought of Robin as a solution had never once entered her head. "I came to sell my work," she said coldly. "Hallowens was a natural starting point. Making a sale is often easier if you talk to your customer face to face. I never dreamed you would see more in it than that."

"Obviously not. If these designs weren't so damn good, I'd tear them up and throw them at you," said Robin. "Very well, Melanie. We'll let things go your way. You've got your sale and you've got your commissions. You've used your pull, and it works."

"You *want* those designs," Melanie pointed out angrily. "I wasn't to know you still felt like this. I'm sorry, very sorry. I wouldn't have upset you in such a way for the world."

"Yes, you would. You always did go headlong for your

own interests. Ruthless, like that ancestor of yours that you and Professor Purvis kept telling me about, the one with the portrait in Gavin's Cliff. If what I felt wasn't written all over me when we met at Jane's . . . Well, if you couldn't read it, you don't know your alphabet, my dear."

It was true, of course. In coming here in person she had been out to gain whatever advantage could be had from a face to face meeting, and at least half-consciously had been out to harness, if she could, Robin's lingering feelings for her. She had indeed read them, although she hadn't been prepared to admit it either to herself at the time or to Robin now. Ruthless? Yes. With a short stab of guilt she realised that the charge was true. To build the future she wanted would not be easy; if it could be made easier by immolating Robin in the foundations, then she was prepared to immolate him. So be it. She observed, with wryness, how very short the stab of guilt had been. "I thought," she said, "that you and Jane were going to settle things."

"If by that timid euphemism *settle things* you mean get married or something indistinguishable therefrom, forget it. Jane's decorative," said Robin coolly, "and good company and very accomplished but others are all those things and younger too. Also, she isn't ruthless."

"What?"

"Oh, it's part of your appeal." He sounded exasperated. "Like calls to like, darling. Jane is merely persistent. She is now just a person who keeps on ringing me up. Are you going to tell Avtar about this interview?"

"I shall tell him that I visited Hallowens, sold some designs, and saw you in the process." She had already decided this. During their telephone conversation she had felt the mysterious link which marriage engendered gradually tighten and draw them together. Paradoxically, a sense of freedom had come with it. She would be able to talk to Avtar now. She did not think that he would misinterpret this encounter when he heard of it. If he did, if she were wrong, then all her hopes might well be void. But if so, it would be better to know. Yes, she would tell him.

"You will say simply that you sold designs to me, as I am Manager of the Design Department?" Robin asked. "That's all?"

"Yes," said Melanie. "What else can I say? It's the truth. I'm sorry."

"With your permission," said Robin, "I will take these selected designs from the file. I will give you a receipt or, rather, ask my secretary to do so. You will get a letter in due course offering terms and explaining future requirements. Leave your permanent address with my secretary. And then, would you mind going away?"

Leaving, finding her way out of Hallowens as though it were both unfamiliar to her and unpleasant, she felt sick but not on account of Avtar's offspring. She had known, always, that Robin had that cold, that nearly cruel, streak in him, but she had never seen it so clearly before. Jane kept ringing him up, did she? It was Robin who had abandoned Jane, not the other way about. Well, more fool Robin. Jane was pure gold without alloy and too good for him. Avtar, by comparison . . . was security and reliability, would never talk about anyone as Robin had talked of Jane, and would be on English soil tomorrow.

～

Jane had taken three days off in order to be at home during her guest's stay. They both woke early the following day, eyes going to the telephone the moment they went into the living room. It rang at nine o'clock, thirty seconds after

Melanie had said: "It's too soon to expect him yet. I think I'll make some tea," and gone into the kitchen. She went on filling the kettle in case the call wasn't from Avtar after all; then Jane shouted: "What was that you said about too soon?" and appeared in the doorway with the handset in one hand and the receiver held out in the other. "Already?" said Melanie, and heard the gasp of joy, of relief, in her own voice. "Give me that kettle," said Jane and, taking it from her, turned away.

A few minutes later, Melanie cradled the receiver again, and replaced the phone on its table. "He's ringing from the house we've borrowed in Southall. The plane was punctual." She wished now that she had met it after all, although Avtar's instructions on that subject had been precise and probably wise. Waiting at the airport and watching information boards in a winter dawn and in the atmosphere of nervous anticipation which characterised all arrival terminals, she would certainly have fallen prey to nausea.

But she would have missed seeing that momentary look of pain in her friend's eyes. Jane, too many times, had waited by telephones that failed to ring. "So you're collecting your things and whizzing off in a taxi?" Jane said now.

"Yes. He wants to come here but I can tell from his voice how tired he is. I'm going to him instead. Oh, Jane." She wished she did not know the reason for Jane's drawn face. It was hard to know the reason and still be unable to offer any comfort. Not that Jane would ever ask for any. She had had her hair done yesterday and she was dressed for the day in a very smart suit. "I've been using you as a hotel," Melanie said. "I do apologise."

"Whatever for? Do you really want this tea or shall we have a farewell drink? If you can manage it so early and it won't hurt the infant, that is. It's just beginning to show, did you know? My friends are always welcome, Melanie. I hope you'll come and stay with me again one day."

Twenty-four carat. No doubt about it. Robin, you idiot!

∽

So here she was, entering Southall, alone in the back of a taxi. It was a little like entering a transplanted bit of India. She watched the proportion of Indians increase among the pedestrians, and saw shops purveying saris and Indian sweet-meats appear among the English department stores and supermarkets. Doe-eyed girls smiled down from cinema marquees and the film titles were proclaimed in Hindi script as well as Roman. The cab paused at a crossing to let two women, with bright fabrics showing beneath the hems of their winter coats, cross the road. "Pretty," the taxi driver remarked. "But not what you'd call right for this climate. Glad I'm not an old inhabitant of Southall," he added thoughtfully.

"Oh?" said Melanie.

"Well, it must be a bit funny, seeing the place you were brought up in just disappear all round you and turn into something else. If you were born here fifty years ago, you're living in India now, even if you've never left home. I'm not prejudiced, don't you think that. But changes this big take a bit of swallowing, in one person's lifetime."

Conceivably, he had a point. Ambersford had seen many changes in its long history; had she been miraculously wafted back to the days of Gavin, they would seem as un-familiar, as remote from her own world as India. But in Ambersford, the change from Gavin's world to Melanie's had taken about two hundred years, and therefore gone largely unnoticed.

But it had been a one-way change. Here in Southall, whether the new inhabitants knew it or not, it would be two-way. The Indians who had come to England blithely supposing that they could continue to live there exactly as they had at home, unmodified, had been wrong. They would alter, a little in each generation, just as she herself had been altered in a few years, by living in their country.

Gran had always admired the ability to change. If only he had been able to stand back and look at her and at Avtar calmly. If only, she thought, Avtar could manage the same thing now. In the back of the taxi, she braced herself. God willing, he would. God willing, she and Avtar would succeed where Gran had failed. God willing, they would sing the song for which Gran had only written the music.

She was longing for Avtar now with astonishing intensity. His voice on the telephone, this time without the curious psychological gulf which great distances created, had brought his face before her with such clarity that she had half raised a hand to touch it. Her children might inherit that amazing perfection of feature: the flawless placing of the highlights on the smooth bronze cheekbones, the width between the temples, the setting of the almond eyes. One day she would record those planes and highlights in paint. If only, today, she could reach the mind behind the features.

She sat making monosyllabic replies to the taxi driver, who was now away on the subject of income tax, and rehearsed the words with which she must transmit a vision.

A vision of their child or children, grown. Of people who would be East and West simultaneously, belonging to both and free of either. To whom the men who built the Iron Age fort above Ambersford and those who constructed the Taj would be equally akin.

They should have freedom which no one could have who

was completely one or the other. They would be free to court and marry as she and Avtar had done, free also to take advantage of the efficient introduction of India, with a series of Saranjits or Arwinders.

For her child and Avtar's, there should be equally the protective lattice of the Indian clan, and the opportunity of the unwatched wanderings which had done so much towards the shaping of Melanie: the lonely moorland treks on horseback; the solitary road from London to Gavin's Cliff; breakfast in a Basingstoke cafe, between two worlds, at dawn.

Indeed, because this child would be hers and Avtar's, no one else's, his or her inheritance would be even more specific than that. This child would be the inheritor, specifically, of Avtar's family traditions, and Melanie's. Would be a part, equally, of the family in Chandigarh and the community of the Heverton coast, in its way as close and interlocked as any Indian clan, making its own demands upon its members according to their place in it. The tradition of Gavin's Cliff, standing guard above the Fangs, with its cupboards stuffed with blankets, should, by some means or other, go on.

The burden might prove heavy. Maybe her privileged offspring would find the task of forming a human bridge between two hemispheres too onerous, would in sheer self-defence opt out of both and flee to the Communist party or a Buddhist monastery for shelter. Never mind. The attempt would have been made. If it failed, some other family like their own might one day take up where they left off, and succeed.

In practical terms it would be hard, not to say costly. She would have to contribute. Her briefcase, plump with notes about possible markets other than Hallowens, the re-

sult of a visit on Monday to the Design Centre, lay on her
knee. In her work, she hoped to find the necessary means.

Other practicalities might interfere. Constant travel
between India and England might be interrupted—by soaring air fares and restrictive legislation, by wars and tumults
and all the great horde movements which throughout history
had thwarted the endeavours of individuals to shape their
lives according to their dreams.

But she would try. She could do nothing else, and
nothing less.

∾

Avtar, his body tired from the long flight but his brain alert,
waited by the fire in Rehal's small house for his wife to come.
He was impatient to see her, impatient to present her with
the news of Balwant's marriage, as though it were a gift in
honour of, or in exchange for, the double gift that she was
bringing him. The exorcism of Professor Purvis, and the
child. He knew that he would not have wanted to come
empty-handed to such a tryst. Despite the price. For when
he had told Balwant to put aside fear and guilt, he had taken
them upon himself, and he would carry them now until
he died.

The house was cold from having been shut up unused
for weeks in winter. He put on the other bar of the electric
fire. He sat watching it grow red, and thought of the last
time he had seen Aunt Asha, just before he left Chandigarh.

Her maidservant had called him. "She sits all day in
her room praying, doctor, and she has gone on fast. But such
a fast! She sips a little water and nibbles a few lentils and
speaks to no one. If it goes on, she will die."

Most probably, she would. He remembered her, sitting

cross-legged on the small mat, her body already shrunken beyond recognition, the bones of wrist and forearm, the outline of the skull, already skeletal. He had warned Rehal, by telephone, that Balwant must on no account be allowed to see her. Balwant was in Delhi now with Rehal. He would come back to England soon and she would follow him. The sooner the better.

Asha had been furious when Balwant fled, but the rage burnt itself out in a few days. She had gone from household to household round the family but received no satisfaction. Some had agreed with her and some had not, but no one actually proposed to take any steps to get Balwant back. They enjoyed the gossip, some of them enjoyed being shocked, and that was all. So she had given up, and collapsed in on herself.

Asha had lived all her life in the assumption that there were things she could not do, taboos she must not break. Now Balwant had risen up and broken them and nothing had happened. The family was surviving the trauma and the skies had failed to fall. All she had left to hold on to was the belief that the heavens might yet blast them all unless she herself, in prayer and fasting, averted the anger of God.

He had said to Rehal: *Have you thought what this will do to Asha?* Now they knew.

A taxi was drawing up at the gate. He came quickly to his feet. Its door was opening. Melanie was getting out. He wondered what her first words to him would be, whether her visit to her home had changed her, what the years ahead would be like. They would not be dull. Melanie was never that.

He had been drawn to her, after all, by a quality of unexpectedness in her. A quite good-looking man had been waving at her to come and have a drink and she had been too entranced by a row of small Indian paintings to notice him. When her attention was drawn to the man, she had preferred to stay where she was and talk to him, Avtar. Whatever lay before them now would not be a monotonous jog towards old age. And who wanted one?

He went to the front door and opened it, calling her name.

For more information
visit: www.speakingvolumes.us